The Wolves of Mirr

The Wolves of Mirr

Paul S. Piper

Book View Café

THE WOLVES OF MIRR
Copyright © 2021 by Paul S. Piper

All Rights Reserved, including the right to reproduce this book or portions thereof in any form.

Published by Book View Café
ISBN: 978-1-63632-004-5

Background image by Angela Harburn, DepositPhotos.com
Wolf image by Reinekke, DepositPhotos.com
Cover Design by Maya Bohnhoff
Beta reader: Sherwood Smith
Copyeditor/proofreader: Sara Stamey

This book is a work of fiction, with all that it entails.

Book View Café
304 S. Jones Blvd, Suite 2906
Las Vegas, Nevada 89107

www.bookviewcafe.com

Make of the howling wilderness a fruitful field.
                                     -Cotton Mather

A wolf is a beast of waste and desolation.
                                     -Theodore Roosevelt

Bring in a Wolf Pelt, Get a Free Pizza
                          -Billboard outside a restaurant
                                        near Stanley, Idaho

The Bella Coola Indians once believed that God tried to transform all animals into humans, but succeeded only in turning human the eyes of the wolf.

Part One

Prologue

CALLAHAN HEARD THE SOUND of vacuuming inside and rang again. The vacuum cut, and a moment later he heard footsteps approach the front door. To his left, a lilac bulged with pale lavender clumps.

"Mike."

"Dan."

The man who stood on the other side of the screen door was stoop-backed, his thinning gray hair parted neatly to the side.

"Thanks for coming so fast. This way." He swung the door open, and Mike Callahan entered.

As he followed the man into the house, Callahan could see that Dan Sunder's limp had worsened.

An orange cat disappeared ahead of them into an unknown room. The country rambler was tidy, though plants and Hummels crowded the two windowsills. Dan's wife stood in the living room holding a vacuum over the couch.

"Carla." Callahan tipped his hat slightly.

The woman said nothing, staring at the rifle in Callahan's hand.

Dan led Mike through the kitchen, which smelled faintly of bacon, and out the back door. They crossed a large parking area. A tractor and two Chevy pickups, one with its hood up, were angled next to the barn.

They passed through a closed gate and into a gently sloping pasture. A quarter mile up, forest slashed dark and oblique across it. Above that, sheer grayish-white mountains rose into the morning sky.

"Over there." Dan pointed.

The wolf was lying on its side, but rose as Callahan approached, backed to the end of the chain that held the claw trap, and growled softly. It was a large male, with black-tipped guard hairs down its spine that stood on end. Callahan walked closer.

The wolf tried to back farther, but couldn't. It opened its mouth, pink tongue hanging slack, saliva dripping. Callahan could hear the sound of its breathing—nervous, ragged. The wolf's amber eyes appraised him as he raised the ought-six, sighted, and fired.

It took two shots to sever the leg, and even then the wolf surged and tore the remaining tendon. It limped sloppily away. Falling, righting itself, falling again, in a crooked line uphill toward the forest.

"Hasn't got the hang of being three-legged yet," Callahan yelled back at Dan. "He ain't going to, either."

Callahan spat, raised the rifle again, and put the beast out of its misery.

One

THE FEMALE WOLF STEPPED deftly onto the white granite crag and lifted her nose, catching the clean scent of resin, musty duff, a hint of smoke. Closer, somewhere up-canyon, carrion.

Hearing something, she cocked her ears forward and down. The sound came again, almost like the shriek of a hawk far below, from a small oval of limpid water. It was a wild laugh.

Gazing down, she caught motion. Two female human bodies playing and splashing two hundred yards below. The pool was shaped like a large eye, braced by a short cliff on one side, surrounded by forest on the two sides adjacent to the cliff. Directly across the pool from the cliff was a beach of coarse blond sand, shaped like a pale human hand stretching its fingers into the meadow grass behind it. Mica on the pool's bottom amplified the water's clarity and gave it an electrical charge. The center of the pool was dark and deep. On the beach lay a third woman on her back, sunning.

A feeling of deep kinship and recognition flickered in the wolf. Confused, she knew these creatures were to be feared. Still, there was wildness in these women that resonated across her genetic history, ancient and powerful.

The female wolf, beautiful by some standards, hideous by others, weighed ninety-six pounds. Her silver fur was tipped black, her eyes burned gold. She stood three feet at the shoulder, and just a hair less than five feet from the tip of her tail to the end of her snout. Four years old, she was in her prime.

The wolf had little knowledge of how humans conceived her and her kind. A form the devil chose as his earthly manifestation; a slaughterer of livestock; a symbol of wildness; one of the most intelligent and social mammals; an endangered species.

After leaving her perch she would return to her mate, the alpha male, and their small, loose pack where they lounged in a high meadow full of house-sized boulders. The pack currently consisted of the alpha pair, two sons, and an unrelated female that remained on the periphery. For the past three weeks they had traveled from Lemhi Pass, crisscrossing from Idaho to Montana and back, with no awareness of the geographical boundaries deemed so important by humans. They had traveled this far looking for a home.

Two

LEVI CAUGHT A RIDE with Art and Taki. A storm had broken an hour earlier and the rain fell steadily, as if not wanting to give up its grip on the valley. The windshield wipers kept a steady back-beat to the rain and muted conversation in the cab. Levi was filling Taki in on his current project. Art had already signed on as wheel man.

"I'm heading up Goat Creek the day after tomorrow to check out a lead that a small pack dropped in from Idaho. A pilot friend of mine saw four wolves just below the Idaho divide. Nobody knows anything about them. None of them are collared."

"You might not agree, but the concept of a radio-collared wolf is just wrong," Art interjected.

"Mostly I agree, but collars have their place."

"How do you plan to get through Leeson's land?" Taki asked.

"Climb around it."

"I told him that's impossible," Art said to Taki.

"Sounds fun," said Taki, laughing. "I'm almost inclined to invite myself along."

"No way." Art grabbed her hand and squeezed it. "You're staying right here with me, not running off with some wolf freak." Art's laugh was strained, and Taki squeezed his hand for reassurance.

Art slowed to pull into the parking lot, but a black Escalade cut sharply in front of him, bumper sticker reading in all caps "KILL A WOLF FOR CHRIST."

"One of your fans, no doubt," quipped Art.

"This will be a nightmare," Levi retorted.

At six-one, Levi no longer considered himself tall. These days, most of the young college guys were at least his height, usually taller. A climber and former runner, Levi had a lithe, muscular body, forged by years backpacking and pursuing wolves in mountainous terrain. His face was angular, skin weathered, eyes hazel. He was considered good-looking by many, feral by others. His teeth were stained from drinking tea. His black hair and beard migrated through various lengths and styles depending on his social and political obligations. Tonight he was shaved, shorn, and neatly combed for his upcoming role.

Levi was a panelist at tonight's town hall meeting, held in the Darby High School gymnasium, and the meeting was running late due to the rain. The topic was displayed in large black letters on a white sign at the parking lot entrance. "Wolves in the Valley: Is There a Problem?"

Two days earlier it had read "The Wolf Problem," but Steve McCandless called the council executive's office and threatened to pull out unless the title was neutralized. This was the best he could get. Steve McCandless was a biologist in the Department of Forestry at the University of Montana in Missoula. His field of expertise was wolf ecology. He and Levi often teamed up on projects, along with Mike Danner of the Forest Service, who couldn't make it due to a bad cold. Levi and Steve would represent the pro-wolf side, along with Bill Crow from SHARE, a three-state organization of ranchers who believed in sharing their land with wildlife, including predators. They considered the loss of some livestock as a kind of tithing they were comfortable paying. They believed in balanced ecosystems. Mike Callahan, Tom Bennett, and Mary Kay Reardon represented various aspects of anti-wolf sentiment in the Bitterroot Valley. Or, as Art liked to state succinctly, "The enemy."

The parking lot was jammed, cars jockeying for parking, groups of young men standing around smoking. Levi knew Mike Callahan would bring a contingent of rude, disruptive disciples with him. Mike had moved to the Darby area thirty years ago from California, and made it his mission to eradicate every threat to his cattle he could.

Wolves had been at the top of his list since his arrival.

Tom Bennett was the "reasonable" voice. He'd provide charts and graphs depicting the economic toll of wolves on Valley livestock, which according to Callahan and his group *Cows First!* was devastating. Levi knew this was bullshit. Typically coyotes, wild dogs, and cougars were the primary predators, with wolves the convenient scapegoat. Levi had documented only nine cases of authentic wolf-predated livestock kills in his twenty-three years in the Valley.

Mary Kay Reardon would cap it. Levi considered her a nut-job. She'd argue that wolves were a grave threat to the children of the Valley. Highly dramatic, she told tear-wrenching stories of wolves snatching kids off playgrounds and from school bus stops. She was particularly fond of the yarn that a sheriff had to shoot four wolves dead after they'd surrounded three school kids walking home near Darby. Never mind that the sheriff, Ed "Juicy" Jones, had publicly stated the culprits were three German Shepherds, not wolves.

A large number of the men heading into the gym wore openly displayed handguns. Some dual pistols, one on each hip like gunfighters.

"Looks like the militia is out in force," said Art, as they got out of the truck and walked toward the gym.

Levi glanced around as they entered. It was packed. At least 200 people had crowded into the folding chairs in front. More stood in back. On stage stood a battered oak podium with microphone, and a rectangular table with five chairs facing the audience. Each had a wood block with a name and a mic. Levi represented his own nonprofit, WolfRecovery.org. At least he wouldn't be sitting next to Mike Callahan, who'd once gotten so angry at Levi he'd punched him in the face. Glancing around at the crowd, Levi saw very few allies. This will be swell, he thought. A friendly chat with his Bitterroot neighbors.

"Wish me survival, guys," Levi said as he left Art and Taki with a couple of organic farmers from Victor, who'd saved them seats.

"You'll be fine," said Taki. "Just stay calm. Don't take any bait. It might have strychnine in it." She blew him a kiss.

"Smack'em, dude," said Art. "Total smackdown."

Levi was suddenly nervous. The room reminded him of a tank of sharks, waiting impatiently for someone to throw in handfuls of shredded meat.

As he walked toward the harshly lit stage, he saw Steve McCandless standing on the stairs talking with Bill Crow and another SHARE member, Angus Fiedly. He nodded to Levi and flashed him a weak smile. Steve had great energy, and was usually upbeat, but tonight he seemed sober. In addition to being a wolf-lover, Steve lived in Missoula, and was considered an "outsider" who couldn't possibly understand the Valley or its issues.

The county executive, Ted Byrd, was fiddling with the podium mic, tapping it, saying "test, test," and twisting knobs. He nodded to Levi, who walked by him to sit at the table.

"We'll go left to right," Ted told him. "That means Steve's first, then Mike, then Bill, then Tom, then you. We'll let Mary Kay make her appeal last." He winked at Levi. It was sometimes difficult to know where Ted stood on things. Often he just seemed bemused by it all.

Tom gave Levi a curt nod, while Mike ignored him, and Mary Kay flashed him a perfect smile. She was looking every bit the wolf expert in her thigh-high skirt, low-cut blouse, and cowboy boots.

Ted was repeating instructions to everyone.

"You'll have five minutes max to give your opening remarks, then we'll go to questions. I'll moderate and keep things civil. I know this is an important and emotional issue, but we are going to keep it civil. You all understand?"

A few panelists nodded.

"OK, let's roll'em." Ted stepped up to the podium, tapped the mic a few times, and bent close.

"Can everybody hear me?"

There were nods and shouts of assent.

"OK, I'm going to moderate. We have five wolf experts at this table who are going to make statements representing their beliefs and research. These will last around five minutes each. Then we'll open it up for questions. We've got mics set up in the two aisles. All questions will need to be asked at those mics. Understood?" He gazed across the audience. "And we're going to keep this civil. I know it's an emotional issue and many of you have deep-held opinions."

"They ain't opinions," someone yelled out from the back.

"Deep-held opinions," Ted repeated, "but that doesn't mean you will interrupt or disrespect any of the participants. Is that understood?" A group of men in the back started laughing. Levi saw the sheriff and his deputy, Taylor, standing in back. They both looked wary.

"OK, let's get started. I'm going to introduce our panelists, and then I want you to give them a hand. Then we'll start with the statements. We'll move left-to-right across the table." He paused and looked out over the audience again. "Right next to me is Steve McCandless, Department of Forestry at the University of Montana. Next to him is Mike Callahan, a prominent rancher and wolf expert." Levi cringed. "Next to him is economist Tom Bennett, then comes Levi Brunner of the non-profit WolfRecovery, and last but not least, Mary Kay Reardon, protector of the Valley's children. Steve, would you begin?"

Steve McCandless pulled the mic from its stand. "Everyone hear me OK?"

Steve, a university professor and someone who taught large lecture classes, was comfortable with a mic in his hand and had an easy-going, folksy voice.

He began by talking about wolf societies, how wolves cooperate and communicate, how many ethologists, or animal behaviorists, considered them as intelligent as primates, dolphins, whales and other "intelligent" animals. He described their social hierarchy, then began to concentrate on his main topic, their hunting behavior. Yes, wolves hunted in packs. Yes, they occasionally attacked and ate livestock, but their primary food was not livestock, and these attacks were actually quite rare. This drew enough catcalls and boos that Ted interceded.

"Quiet. Give the man a listen. You don't want people yelling at you."

Steve continued. Yes, wolves sometimes killed more than they ate. This was called surplus killing, and was true of many predators who didn't know where their next meal would come from. They were opportunists. And finally, yes, wolves had been known to kill humans, but this was only true before the age of rifles. There had not been a legitimately documented attack on humans by wolves in over a hundred years. This was also met with catcalls from the crowd.

Ted thanked Steve and turned to Mike Callahan.

"Mike?"

Mike was the polar opposite of Steve McCandless. He was incendiary, taunting and hateful. He called wolves the scourge of the earth, and stated that they should have been exterminated years ago. To let them live was a crime against humanity. To reintroduce them into areas where they didn't live anymore, as was being done in the Rockies and elsewhere, was insanity. Organizations that supported wolf reintroduction, governmental or otherwise, should be shut down and their members jailed.

"They're living off our tax dollars and our damn livestock!" he spat into the mic.

The crowd erupted.

Finally, Mike testified that he'd personally lost over a hundred sheep and calves to wolves. "So don't tell me that they don't kill livestock in this Valley!"

This was met with cheers, and cries of "Tell it like it is," and "The government lies."

Ted cautioned the crowd again, and when the noise died down, Bill Crow stepped to the mic.

"I'm seventy-six years old, and I've lived in this Valley all my life. Never wanted to be anywhere else. I'm a rancher, and my dad was a rancher. I love this land and what lives on it. And that includes wolves. They are beautiful, wild and intelligent animals. And I, and other members of SHARE, believe they have a place here. We also believe that losing a few livestock every year is a small price to pay for their existence.

"Every animal has a place in the food chain. If wolves didn't kill as many deer as they do, there would be more feeding on our alfalfa. What we need is a balance. The same balance God created when he created the heavens and earth. In addition to being a rancher, I'm a Christian, and I don't believe God makes mistakes. He created wolves, and put two of them on the Ark. I interpret this to mean that He wants them to live. And I do as well."

There was a buzz from the audience, then Tom Bennett took the mic.

After some minor technical glitches, he managed to address a power point of charts and graphs "documenting" the dramatically rising wolf population in the Valley, as well as the correlative increase in livestock deaths due to wolves. Last year alone, ranchers in the Valley had lost over $24,000 due to wolf kills.

Levi shook his head. This was total bullshit, he thought. Where do they get these figures? And then he was on.

"Hi. I'm glad you all could make it here tonight for this important discussion. My name is Levi Brunner, and I represent a small nonprofit called WolfRecovery. I think that as we talk it's important not to let our emotions run away with us, and to focus on the facts."

Someone in the audience yelled, "Fake news!"

Levi ignored them.

"WolfRecovery is dedicated to studying this remarkable animal, the wolf, in the field, and documenting its social structure, habits, behaviors, and communication, as well as its interaction with people and livestock."

Levi went on to detail how the populations of wolves, bison, and Native Americans had violently declined since the year of contact, and how westward expansion, or Manifest Destiny, was to blame. He talked about how wolves had been unfairly branded as "evil" by early Christians, and how they were eradicated in the early twentieth centuries by professional government hunters. Large bounties were put on wolf's heads, bounties that cost far more than the actual damage they did to livestock. And finally, he detailed the massive early twentieth-century strychnine campaigns that succeeded in killing thousands of wolves, along with foxes, coyotes, dogs, bobcats, cougars, birds of all types, prairie dogs, ferrets, and even some cattle and sheep that ate strychnine-tainted grass.

"Bring Strychnine back!" someone yelled. There was boisterous applause.

When the room calmed, Levi spoke again.

"Wolves represent what is wild, and wilderness is necessary. We live in an ever more civilized and technological world. Wilderness is being destroyed at alarming rates. We are, quite literally, cutting out our soul. When you put a cow, a product of human domestication, next to a wolf, there is literally no comparison. The wolf is noble, the cow a drooling, fly-ridden tumor. One was a divine creation, the other a pathetic slave."

Jeers erupted.

Ted again interceded, then turned it over to Mary Kay. Her shrill, petulant voice became shriller and more petulant as she spoke.

"I'd like to begin by saying that wolves represent a very real and violent threat to our kids! Every year there are hundreds of children killed by wolves in this great country of ours."

Levi couldn't hold back.

"Bullshit!" he yelled. "This is absolute bullshit!"

Tom Bennett grabbed a mic and yelled, "Stop that Levi!"

Mary Kay looked furious, then suddenly broke down in tears. Boos, cheering, catcalls and laughter erupted from the crowd.

And it went downhill from there.

When Mary Kay recovered enough to finish her rambling fictional anecdotes about children, near and far, who'd been mauled, killed, and eaten by wolves, it was followed by a huge outcry from the audience.

A chant of "Save the children, kill the wolves," started up, and it took Ted several minutes to quiet the crowd. When it did, Ted opened it up for questions.

The early questions focused largely on wolf biology and culture.

"How big do wolves get?" "How many wolves in a pack?" "Why do wolves howl?" but quickly shifted to questions about human and livestock fatalities. Levi and Steve attempted to create a voice of reason, and both spoke calmly and quoted scientific data, but the room belonged to Callahan. He acted as if his cattle were his own children, and wolves were savagely ripping them apart in the front yard next to the American flag flying from the apple tree.

When Steve McCandless asked directly how many calves Mike had lost to wolves last year, he replied, "Thirty-seven."

"Then why didn't you report them to Fish and Wildlife and ask for compensation?" Steve asked. "There's no record of you doing that. There's no record of anyone down here doing that. There's no official record of anyone in this valley ever losing cattle or sheep to wolves. No record what-so-ever."

Speaking with controlled fury, Callahan responded. "For the same reason I don't call 911. I deal with my problems myself. I don't want anything to do with the fucking government."

And the room erupted again.

Levi knew that Montana historian Edward Curnow had written that during the wolf eradication in the late 1800s and early 1900s, cattlemen achieved a "pathological hatred" of wolves. Levi could see that hatred livid and alive in the room, and it included a hatred of wilderness, Indians, and Montana Fish and Wildlife. It also included the BLM and the Forest Service, both of which allowed ranchers to overgraze and erode public lands for barely a thin nickel.

But the crowning question was one asked by a young woman named Hallie Jackson, the daughter of a prominent anti-wolf rancher.

"Why are wolves even necessary? All they do is kill and eat innocent animals and children. Shouldn't we just exterminate them all?"

The crowd again erupted.

Levi thought how hopeless this was, like trying to argue why spotted owls, marbled murrelets, wolverines, or any of the hundreds of endangered species were important. He wished he had something so pithy and obvious that the audience would go, "D'oh! I didn't think of that." But these were by and large people who believed a God who looked like their grandfather created the earth in six days, and gave his human spawn permission to grab anything they wanted. "Dominion over my creation," Levi remembered hearing.

Steve took a stab at how predators help control prey populations, Levi spoke of the mythological significance of wolves and wilderness, but Mary Kay was far less verbose.

"Wolves are absolutely NOT necessary. We should kill them all."

The crowd went ballistic.

Walking out with Steve, Levi joked that they'd hit it out of the park.

"Glad you have a sense of humor about it. To my mind this is a sad state of affairs."

"Humor and work are all I have, Steve. And I have to live here. These are my neighbors."

"Better watch yourself, or they'll string you up." He punched Levi lightly in the shoulder. "I gotta drive back. My granddaughter has an early soccer game. Otherwise I'd suggest we go meet Mr. Johnny Walker."

"I'll take a rain check on that very fine idea."

"Keep in touch."

"Likewise."

A group of young men in their early twenties passed by, and Levi heard the word "asshole," followed by laughter. The rain had ceased, and it was a beautiful night, the sky full of stars and the indifference of the heavens. Levi waited by the car until Art and Taki walked up.

"Let's get the flock out of here," Art jibed.

"What a depressing segment of society," Taki said. "It makes me sad."

"Me, too," said Levi. "Me, too."

As if to punctuate the mood, the angry growl of a Hemi diesel broke the quiet, a Dodge Ram fishtailing across the lot, spitting gravel into the night.

Three

ART PULLED HIS BLUE Tacoma pickup over to the side of the road just outside a giant log entryway with the name Leeson cut out of blue-black steel. The logs were mammoth Douglas fir hauled over from the Olympic Peninsula by three separate log trucks, one log on each. They'd been barked and lathered in shellac until they shone in the nascent sun like amber.

Leeson had brought a crane from Spokane to lift the beam atop its two matching poles. It was a spectacle, and quite a crowd had gathered, including reporters from *The Ravalli Republic*, *The Hamiltonian*, and *The Stevensville News*. The sheet of metal, into which the name *Leeson* had been cut with an oxy-fuel torch, weighed around two tons and was five feet high, just under ten feet wide. It hung on polished skidder chain. An eight-foot, locked, gridded steel gate completed the entryway. Shiny barbed wire stretched taut in both directions and caught the flash of sun cresting the Sapphire Range across the valley.

Art called Leeson a "fuck-head billionaire narcissistic land thief," and Levi couldn't help but agree. These out-of-state investors were so wealthy they could buy anything they wanted, and the flavor of the past ten years was ranching. They chopped up the valley, denied anyone but their rich out-of-state friends access, and were usually jet-setting around the world, leaving the ranching to foremen and hired hands, whom they secretly loathed and envied. To put it mildly, they played at ranching.

Just in case he was judging Leeson wrongly, however, Levi had reached out to him, talking on the phone with his wife, Brittany, explaining his request. Her husband was in Singapore, Brittany told him, but they both hated wolves, and would not cry a tear if every last one of them was removed from the planet. So no, Levi could not obtain access to cross their land and enter the canyon to look for wolves, unless he was going to hunt them down, kill them, and bring her the pelts.

Levi hefted his pack out of the pickup bed. "Thirty-three degrees," he said, blowing white clouds out of his mouth. "Up to the early eighties by afternoon. March browns will be hatching by then. Damn, I love Indian summer."

"It's a time to be alive, that's for sure." Art toed the dusty gravel. "Hey, Levi, I know you're a damn good free climber and all, utterly fearless and all that shit, but be careful, OK? I don't know anyone who's ever climbed these things." He pointed to the imposing gray granite cliffs, interrupted here and there by avalanche chutes, ledges, and scree, that rose a good three hundred feet above the valley floor. "Those wolves aren't worth losing my best friend."

Levi laughed.

"That's where you're wrong, Art. They are worth it. They're worth everything I can give them." He gave Art a quick hug. "I'll be back in ten days or so. Don't worry about picking me up. I'll hitch a ride. Maybe Leeson's foreman will give me one. What's his name? Jacob Blackburn?"

"Never met him. I hear he's not much of a socialite."

Levi flashed Art a grin and began climbing, using tiny crevices and pockets. After scrambling the first hundred feet or so, he paused to watch Art's truck heading back down Goat Creek Road, trailing a lazy cloud of dust. Art, a river guide, would meet his clients shortly for a quick breakfast before a day on the river. It would be another hot, clear day, possibly capped by a late afternoon storm. He could already smell smoke drifting in from the Skalkaho fire. He thought of how Taki smelled last evening, joining them for dinner fresh from a shower, her black hair cut short and casual, her eyes like rich honey. He momentarily regretted giving her up, but Art was good for her and there for her. Something Levi had never quite mastered.

The dream still haunted him.

He'd dreamt of a giant black wolf with blazing golden eyes, running through a dusky forest. Initially, there was little to the dream, just the wolf running, and Levi watching from a small clearing. He sensed that as the wolf ran through the forest, it also ran through time, from an ancient place to the present. And while dreaming this, Levi realized the wolf was searching for him. Just as sudden as that insight, the wolf stopped and turned its massive head, capturing Levi with its eyes. And then, without warning, the wolf charged Levi, its mouth open, its savage teeth slick and glittering. It leapt and was on him, yet there was no collision, no battle. The wolf simply merged with Levi's body. The wolf had entered him.

Levi could feel, in retrospect, the treacherous depths the dream contained. Certainly, black wolves had metaphoric significance, often that of evil, but this was more complex. This was personal.

Four

LEVI ANGLED ACROSS A rocky slope and tucked into a steep ravine. He could see the short headwall, thirty feet high, then broken cliffs above that. He was already scouting his route.

Climbing was one of Levi's favorite pastimes, and one he did exceptionally well. He'd come to it early. His father Florian Brunner, a geology professor at the university in Missoula, was from Austria. He had grown up climbing, taught by his father and his friends. By the time Florian settled in Missoula, he'd earned a sound reputation as a world-class climber, largely in the Alps, Nepal, and the peaks of Patagonia and Argentina. And of course, he taught all three of his children to climb, practically before they could walk.

Long before there were climbing walls, Florian built several in his back yard out of plywood, junkyard scraps, and rock. They weren't much to look at, but were functional, and taught the kids the basics, such as using equipment—ropes, belays, carabiners—and moves like edges, smears, jams, flagging, and so forth. Most importantly, he taught the kids the art of balance and technique. Climbing is never powering up a wall, but embodies strategy, tactics, careful planning, and patience.

Florian started the kids climbing the Bitterroot canyon walls as soon as they graduated from the walls, and long before it was popular. They'd often be out for a full day and encounter no one. Nowadays the parking lot at a major canyon like Basswood would be jammed full of cars, vans, trucks, and SUVs by 8:30 or 9:00, most of them belonging to climbers, largely college kids.

His brother Tyler quit climbing entirely when he was around twelve, but their dad, Levi, and their sister Wendy became more ardent.

Florian and Wendy liked peaks. They climbed everything Montana had to offer while Wendy was in high school, then started climbing in South America with a small group that aggregated around Florian in Missoula. And Florian began taking Wendy to the peaks he'd matured on in the Alps. Florian and his daughter shared climbing and traveling, and the social elements of climbing, but Levi was more of a loner.

Levi adopted a different approach to climbing than his father or his sister, taking to free-climbing. No ropes, pitons, crampons, belays, or safety gear. Just Levi and a cliff or mountain, and before Taki, almost always solo. And he never needed the peak ascent. He'd often stop short of the top just to short-circuit his ego.

While Levi's father fixated on climbing, and was obsessive about converting his kids, Levi's mother was another story. A former classical pianist, she was subject to a range of nervous "episodes," and was often rehabilitating in a hospital or rest home. The children were taught not to challenge her, or even, at times, to interact with her, due to her "delicate" condition. He often wondered if his relationship with his mother had robbed him of an essential intimacy, causing him to be incapable of intimacy with the women he met, causing him to fear commitment.

The family owned several Alaskan malamutes while Levi was growing up, and these became his constant companions. He became aware early on of their independent spirit, their high intelligence, and their ability to communicate using prolific vocal sounds, ear positions, and body postures. One of their dogs, Kola, recognized over forty unique words.

When he entered the University of Montana, there was no doubt his path would be biology, and no doubt his fascination with wild canids would narrow that path.

Now the canyon closed in fast on Levi with a V of lichen-covered rock, an easy ascent up the center scree. Fifty feet up, however, the V ended in a sheer wall of granite that rose nearly vertical for another fifty to sixty feet. From his current angle, Levi could not see beyond that. The wall wasn't high but it was unforgiving. Levi had projected a route up the left side, but he could see now that a shelf of rock jutted out, creating a horizontal overhang. The center and right looked easier, especially with a pack. He studied the course, and chose the center, shifting to the left near the top. He took his time, stretching his hands and feet as needed. Jams—wedging a hand, fist, arm, foot, and even leg into crevices—were constant. Levi's and Taki's hands were so callused from jamming and climbing that they joked their hands were rock caressing rock.

Near the top the slope mellowed from seventy degrees to around forty, and Levi began working his way horizontally up the canyon, using the numerous ledges and handholds. Soon the terrain opened even more into scree, clotted rock, and stands of ponderosa pine, Douglas fir, and some larch already turning. Larch were one of Levi's favorite trees, a deciduous tree that painted the higher slopes gold in autumn, then lost their needles, turning the forest floor the same golden color until it was buried in snow. Walking on larch needles in autumn was soundless.

Levi rested, drank some water, and gazed out over the valley.

The Bitterroot Valley, named for the Bitterroot flower, stretched nearly ninety miles from Missoula to south of Sula. Home to Salish peoples, it was first visited by Caucasians when Lewis and Clark's expedition came through in 1805. They bought more horses from a band of Flathead Indians, but leaving the Valley and crossing the mountains into Idaho tested the expedition's endurance. It took eleven days, and the men and horses were near starvation.

The Valley was also home to the oldest Montana community, St. Mary's, founded in 1841 in the present-day location of Stevensville. But the Valley was changing dramatically.

Since Levi had begun working with the Bitterroot wolves twenty-some years ago, the population had doubled, and the two-lane highway was now four from Missoula to Hamilton. The influx of retirees, outdoor enthusiasts, get-back-to-the-landers was monumental. As Art joked, "Every other person I meet is a real estate agent." But even as a fourth-generation Montanan, he added, "Every one of us came from somewhere else, even the Indians."

Directly below him Levi could see Leeson's land, brilliant green from irrigating creek water, pocked with sheep. It spread from the choked neck of the canyon and widened as it ascended, Goat Creek serpentine through the midst of it. Levi snapped a few photos with his ultralight Canon.

The sun was arcing higher above the Sapphire Mountains across the valley, and he began moving again. His only goal today was to penetrate the canyon at least three miles above Leeson's place, which would put him on National Forest land. Once there, he'd set up camp for the night, and hopefully establish a permanent camp the following day.

Levi felt, rather than saw, the blur of white above him, but when he looked, there was nothing there. Only a space in the sky where something had stood seconds before, followed by the sound of scattered rock falling. A mountain goat, he reasoned. He climbed up toward it and discovered fresh scat. Levi had been challenged by male goats a few times in the fall when they were nearing rut, but had never actually been charged. It happened, though. A biologist had been gored several years ago near Glacier Park, and a tourist in the Olympic Mountains had been killed. If one had to run from a goat in their terrain, the odds went quite rapidly to the goat.

By high noon Levi was descending through the forest, making use of the numerous game trails. Another half-hour, and he'd broken through the fringe of brush to Goat Creek. He shed his pack on the rocks, bent down, and splashed himself with icy water. A gray jay chattered in a cottonwood tree across the stream, and sunlight created abstract, ever-shifting color fields across the currents.

He sat next to his pack and broke out a bag of trail mix. It was as near a perfect spot as he'd ever been. A small trout, a native west slope cutthroat, broke the surface membrane in a seam of water below two boulders, and sucked in a small mayfly. The circle of the rise it created was instantly erased.

Levi ate several handfuls of his homemade trail mix, then tucked the bag back into his pack. He ate very little in the backcountry, and always lost weight. But his passion kept him strong, and he never seemed to lose energy or focus. The wilderness sharpened him.

Levi had studied Google Earth the past few days, and knew a series of small meadows, connected by Goat Creek, were a mile or so above where he sat. He'd camp there tonight. The canyon extended sixteen miles before it rose in cliffs to the divide that separated Montana and Idaho. A second larger meadow lay approximately four miles beyond the first meadows. That would place him over halfway up the canyon. A perfect base camp. And if wolves where in the area, there would be sign in the meadows. With any luck they would find him first, or he'd hear them conversing late evening. Packs often splintered in the summer, then reunited in the fall. They located each other primarily by howling.

Levi was an experienced howler, or put in different terms, he spoke wolf. He'd many times called wolves into view by howling or answering their howls. Levi knew wolves had evolved complex communication systems that paralleled their intricate social structure. They hunted in packs, which required elaborate, advanced, and often creative communication. Wolves had been known to use decoys, subterfuge, ambush, and numerous other hunting techniques. These required fine-tuned communication skills. Levi had heard a biologist describe a fascinating example, demonstrating the creativity and communication of wolves while hunting, as well as their communication on-the-fly.

As five wolves approached the shore of a stunted bay in northern BC, the flock of mergansers they were hunting swam quickly into deeper water and bunched. The wolves retreated back into the willows. A few minutes later a single male wolf ambled down to the shore and began barking, rolling on its back, kicking his legs, writhing, yipping and squeaking, and altogether acting "crazy." The ducks became curious and swam closer, while the wolf continued his "crazy" behavior. The ducks drifted closer. Suddenly from the willows shot his pack, rushing into the water and grabbing ducks before they could escape. Carrying their catch back to shore, they shared the harvest with the decoy wolf, and all feasted on the "uncatchable" mergansers.

While many of a wolf's social communication behaviors were postural, tactile, or scent-based, the majority were vocal. And howling wasn't even predominant. Vocal communication also included growls, barks, whines, squeaks, and numerous hybridizations.

Levi submerged his water bottle into the creek. He could feel the chill of the water bite into his hand. As he let the bottle fill, he turned and gazed into the azure blue sky. The sun was warm on his face, the air crisp and fresh. He loved this experience. It gave him a wildness he felt nowhere else. He could feel, and not in an abstract way, the cellular depth, the ancestral roots of his DNA stretching back to the times when his ancestors ran the savannahs, themselves bands of hunters armed with nothing more than primitive weapons, bursts of speed, and the rudiments of intelligence and language. Not much different from the wolves he loved. This was what he lived for, enduring town and city life, and the hassles of running a struggling nonprofit with all its attendant fund-raising, meetings, and paperwork. As hunted, endangered, loathed, and falsely mythologized wolves were, Levi envied them. Quite simply, he would have traded his life in a second for that of a wolf.

Wading the creek turned to be the easiest and coolest way of hiking to the meadows. Along the way, Levi stopped to watch the various dippers and warblers that inhabited the riparian zone. The warblers were brilliant flashes of yellow against the deep green of foliage—light incarnate—but dippers fascinated Levi the most. They were called dippers because of their bobbing or dipping behavior while standing, though their most remarkable behavior was their ability to, quite literally, walk underwater.

Levi sat on a log and watched the dipper as it gripped the rocks tightly, then took the plunge. Due to the water's clarity, Levi could watch it poke its beak into crevices filled with insect larva and small fish. He admired the way animals foraged for food as they moved through their days. The only human equivalents Levi could think of were the homeless people he'd see on the streets of Missoula, who would constantly forage from garbage cans, sidewalks, and gutters.

Beyond the dipper a large, deep pool formed, where years ago an enormous boulder had crashed into the creek from the crags above. Over numerous years, water had scoured a hole at its base and downstream from it. Even during low, late-summer flows, the pool was between five and six feet deep, and Levi could see several large cutthroat trout finning, rising every now and then to slurp an insect from the surface. Below them, hugging the bottom, was a school of silver-gray mountain whitefish.

While Levi enjoyed watching fish, he didn't fish, and had a difficult time understanding Art's passion. Loving fish, and then catching them, even though everyone these days practiced "catch and release," was analogous to Levi loving wolves, trapping them, then letting them go. Levi caught fish occasionally to eat, but catch and release made little sense to him. Art and Levi had both built their passions into livelihoods, neither very lucrative, but Levi was satisfied locating and watching wolves. He didn't need to catch them.

The meadow opened after a mile or so of creek walking. Narrow at first, and thick with elk scat and aspen groves, it widened after a hundred yards, and eventually stretched a half-mile across the canyon floor, hemmed in by scree slopes, and a series of step-like cliffs on the north wall. Levi watched a small group of mountain goats wander a labyrinthine network of trails several hundred yards above him. No billies, just two females and several kids. But the billies were close. Mating time was near.

Levi chose a camp spot on a level bench, below a clump of larch that divided the terminus of an avalanche shoot. By some fate or chance, these trees had been spared. He positioned his tent so the front looked out over the upper meadow, and when he'd set his tent, and selected a bear tree to hang his food, he lay down for a nap. Getting older had its small pleasures. Besides, he was a night owl and would remain up past midnight.

Before drifting into midday sleep, he thought, despite everything, how very lucky he was to be living a life he absolutely loved. A gray jay, also known as a camp robber, alighted on a low branch just outside the tent door and began chuckling. Then it hopped to the ground and began inspecting Levi's pack. Levi smiled and closed his eyes. It did not take long for sleep to seize him.

Levi carried two empty pans down to the creek to fill with water. In less than an hour the sun would sink below the canyon wall and put the meadow into shade. Levi found a small pool with a cobble beach and filled the pans. The sun caught the water so it flashed from bits of mica he'd stirred up getting water. A dipper sang across the creek, and Levi had the sudden awareness that there was an infinity right here, in this pool. The geology, the physics, hydrology, and chemistry of the water, the study of light and reflection on water, the aesthetics in practice and theory. Not to mention the aquatic life—algae, diatoms, aquatic plants, insects, crustaceans, reptiles, fish, birds. All of these complex life cycles, interacting with other life cycles in an ecosystem far more than the sum of these complexities. With enough attention and perspective, one could possibly approach knowing something of this, but never all.

And there was far more: the effect of climate and accident; the effect of human interaction, observation, and intrusion. Impossible to adequately map the overall sum of these known quantities, and to factor in the many unknowns: How does the presence of Venus at dawn affect this pool? Or a bull elk or moose walking into it, bending to drink? The questions were infinite.

Levi began looking at the rocks in the pool, quieting his mind, giving them all his attention without filter. There were reds, blues, and purples of every hue. Some had bands of quartz running through them. Some of the bands were straight lines, or thin and slightly curved. Others were like wispy clouds. The water heightened their colors. Some of the rocks were round, egg-like, or shaped like cucumbers. Others were irregular. Levi surmised these were newer, and hadn't experienced thousands of years being caressed by water, or tumbling against other rocks in the floodwaters of spring snowmelt.

We seldom give things our full attention, he thought. This was one of the purposes of art, to give us reason or permission to intensely focus on something and open to it. This opening had something to do with letting go of filters. Levi could understand this in flashes, but could not adequately articulate it.

If these rocks were placed in a gallery, and if they were assigned artist's names, we would approach them differently. We would approach them as a made thing. Yet they *were* made things. In a gallery or museum, we would consider the color, its name and hue, the contrasts, textures, shapes. We'd walk around them and examine them from all angles. Given there were thousands of rocks in this pool, this could take a long time. It could take all the time in the world. It was as Blake said, "To see a World in a Grain of Sand, And a Heaven in a Wild Flower, Hold Infinity in the palm of your hand, And Eternity in an hour." If we could just open ourselves to this. It was something Levi longed for and treasured, those momentary flashes of sudden insight that yielded something divine.

He walked back to his campsite in the late sun carrying the pans of water. Once there, he lit his featherweight MSR stove and placed one of the pans on it. He untied his food sack and found the baggie with tea. Bubbles were beginning to form in the pan. He waited a bit longer, watching a hawk drift across the meadow looking for mice or ground squirrels, then filled his cup with boiling water and watched the tea leach out into the water as he swirled it gently. He set it on a log. The sun disappeared suddenly behind the canyon wall, and he was in shadow. He felt a chill, picked up the cup, and sipped, blowing on it to cool it.

Five

LEVI WOKE ONCE DURING the night and got up to piss. The stillness was startling, the sky awash with stars. The Milky Way arced over the canyon, amazing him with its breadth and depth. His breath came out in clouds. The peaks above him were bare rock, but would too soon be covered with snow. Summers in the northern Rockies were brief.

He lay in his sleeping bag until sun broke over the Sapphire Range and flooded the tent. He let it warm him, enjoying the delicious embryonic feeling of his cocoon. When he rose, he boiled water for tea. Walking up into the larch, Levi found a patch of huckleberries. They were mostly gone or dried, but he picked a couple of handfuls and ate them. They were tart and wild, not at all like commercial blueberries, which Levi thought pulpy and tasteless.

He sat on a rock and sipped his tea.

The pikas in the scree above him were conversing loudly. He could see them darting from rock to rock, stopping suddenly, quickly gazing around. Like many rodents, they were nervous animals. When the shadow of a raven drifted across the scree, they squeaked in alarm and disappeared instantly under rocks. Better nervous than dead, as the raven could have easily been a hunting hawk.

The day had bloomed perfectly, but already cumulus clouds drifted in from the southwest, and wind lifted the edges of his tent as Levi broke it down. His tent was custom-built by ultralight tent expert Alex Kramer out of Boulder, Colorado. Freestanding, single-walled cuben fiber with boron poles, the tent weighed only one pound three ounces. It wasn't cheap, but Levi didn't skimp on equipment.

Lifting the pack onto his shoulders Levi set out upstream across the meadow, spooking three cow elk out of the fir at the far end. He figured it was another two or three miles of bushwacking to the upper meadow where he'd set up his base camp. The sky was now choked with clouds, and the wind had kicked up. The temperature crept into the low 40s but no higher.

It was rough going in the woods, the forest floor largely broken granite. Spitting rain made the rock slick, and he almost took one bad fall, but managed to snag a tree on the way down. He heard his dad's voice in his head. "No reason to hurry and be careless."

As suddenly as they had drifted in, the clouds drifted out, and sun blazed through the forest sending steam into the warming golden air.

"Delicious," said Levi out loud. "Just delicious." Then he laughed at the sound of his own voice. It sounded so out-of-place here.

He sat on a rock and ate his lunch, his second-day splurge, the only fresh food he'd brought—a McIntosh apple, a wedge of sharp white cheddar cheese, and a landjaeger.

"Delicious," he said again, startling a ground squirrel. He laughed. It was so good to be out here, and so good to laugh.

Levi gained the higher meadow by mid-afternoon. He set his pack against a boulder, stretched, and took his time surveying the area. The meadow was serpentine, and stretching over half a mile, varying in width. After walking the circumference and crisscrossing it several times, Levi chose a flat grassy bench bisected by a freshet fringed with late-blooming buttercups. It appeared to be one of the sunniest places, had immediate access to fresh water, and gave Levi a view of the meadow. Three large boulders gave him a shelter and protection from the wind. Levi set up his stove and boiled water for tea.

He sat on top of the rearmost boulder, a difficult sloping climb holding a cup of tea, but he enjoyed these little challenges. Sitting in the warm sun drinking tea, he had to remind himself that he was here to work. Thus far he'd not seen nor heard any sign of wolves. He'd found coyote scat, and that of a black bear in the lower meadow, but nothing more. If they were here, he'd hear them tonight or the next night. They loved to howl. Hell, who didn't? He threw his head back and let out a long howl. What happened next caused him to drop his tea.

"Hey! What are you howling about?" The woman's voice came from behind him.

"Christ! You startled the hell out of me." Levi turned to see a woman walking toward him with a compound bow. She wore a camo flannel shirt and pants, and her wavy black hair in two braids. She was as tall as he was, perhaps taller, and wide at the shoulders.

"I wasn't expecting company." Her voice was thick, rich, and bore an accent.

"Well, I didn't expect anyone, either." He gestured at the dropped cup. "Not an easy place to get into. You a friend of the Leesons?"

"Hardly. Never met the man and don't want to."

"Mind if I ask how you got in?"

The woman gave a throaty laugh. "I have my ways." Sun glinted off her hair. Her face was wide and strong. Levi thought her strikingly beautiful.

"Climbed?"

"Persistent, aren't you?" Still laughing. "What's your name?"

"Levi. What's yours?"

"Althea."

"I've never met an Althea before."

She laughed. Her tongue glistened behind perfect teeth.

Levi shook his head. "Damn."

"Damn what?" Her smile was bemused.

"Nothing. I'm just surprised, that's all. Pleasantly, though."

"What are you doing, besides sitting on a rock howling and spilling tea?"

"I'm back here looking for a renegade wolf pack. Have you encountered any? Heard them perhaps?"

"Are you a scientist?"

"A biologist."

"A student of nature."

Levi had heard that before. Maybe in school. Something he'd read.

"I heard wolves the night before last. I've been here a few days, but only heard them that one night. Quite a sound, eh? Wild." She laughed again. "Your howl was quite good. What were you saying?"

Levi slipped off the rock and stood facing her. He was six one but she beat him by an inch. She stepped forward and they were only a yard apart.

"Just messing around. Letting loose."

"Hmmm."

"Wolf howls often contain a statement and a question."

"What do you mean?" she asked.

"A howl says 'I am here.' That's the statement. And then asks, 'Is there anyone else here?' Something like that. It's a complex expression. Statement and question. But that doubling is quite common with wolves. Their language is very economic."

"How did you learn it?"

"I've studied wolves since I was eighteen. I'm forty-six, so twenty-eight years researching them, living amongst them."

"You love wolves." Her eyes were black, like onyx flecked with gold. Suddenly Levi felt himself pulled into them, into her, a vertigo. He looked away quickly, up into the scree and cliffs, the sky. The dizziness evaporated. He faced her again. Her eyes had changed, become opaque. A smile toyed with her lips.

"I do love them. I feel a kinship. Maybe I was one in a former life. If you believe that sort of thing."

"Oh, I believe a lot of things."

"Anyway, it's a strong connection. And I feel it's my vocation to protect them. They were almost wiped out here, and they're still endangered, but they're survivors." He stopped talking, suddenly embarrassed. "Sorry, I'm babbling, which I do when I tell beautiful women about wolves."

She chuckled. "Don't be embarrassed. I'm interested."

"Humans can fuck up almost anything, but we can make things better as well."

"That I agree with. Maybe there is a howl that voices those conflicting impulses. Both destruction and creation. There are many beings over history that possess both those qualities."

"Really? I don't know much about history." He wondered why she hadn't said possessed.

"Hmm."

"Are you a historian, then?"

"I know time," she said, smiling.

Levi didn't know how to respond, so he asked, "Where are you camped?"

"Up a ways. Near the top of the meadow."

"You hunting deer?"

"No, elk. I haven't found the one I want yet."

"You have a horse with you?"

"No, why?" Her lips had tightened.

"How do you plan to pack it out?"

"You are persistent." She frowned.

"Sorry. I'm probably coming off all wrong. It's just that I don't meet many women who hunt, and those who do usually go out with their boyfriend or husband. I've never met a woman who hunts elk and packs out her own meat, especially out of a canyon that's only passable through Leeson's ranch, or a tangle of cliffs."

Her gaze caught him again, and again knocked him off balance. It felt like she could capture him at will. Again, he broke away, but it took strength.

Her voice was direct, forceful. "I don't have a boyfriend or husband. I prefer to hunt alone. I don't need a man to help me."

She turned quickly and started to walk off, then looked back over her shoulder and flashed him a quick smile. "Don't scare the elk. And if you howl tonight, maybe I'll howl back."

Six

AFTER THE SUN SLIPPED behind the canyon wall, Levi built a fire at the base of one of the three boulders, where it reflected its heat and light back at him. Dinner had been a few pieces of jerky, some raisins, and a couple of handfuls of trail-mix. He hadn't eaten enough to quell the burn of hunger. It would be his constant companion for the next eight days. He leaned back against a log, stretched his long legs out on the ground, and stared at the dancing fire.

The woman, Althea, who'd snuck up on him earlier, had left him off-balance. First off, he thought, it was not that easy to sneak up on him. He was a creature of the woods, and became hyper-sensitive to his surroundings after being out a day or two. And he remembered distinctly glancing around before he climbed the boulder. Second, he'd worked and played in the mountains for over forty years, and he'd never met a solo woman hunter. The fact that she was after bull elk was also strange. Assuming she killed one, she'd be packing out three or four hundred pounds of meat without a horse. But maybe he was being sexist. She looked strong enough.

And he couldn't figure out how she'd gotten up here unless she knew the Leesons, and they'd let her pass through their land, which was heavily fenced and protected. She'd denied she knew Leeson. And he believed her.

But stranger still was her persona. Althea possessed a timelessness of sorts, but that wasn't it exactly. It was as if her real age and her biological age, around thirty he guessed, were in conflict. He shook his head. He couldn't explain it. And there were her eyes. He'd never been pulled into someone so forcefully, or played with such power. Althea seemed to be able to turn it on and off, raise or lower the volume, at will.

Once, when he'd tried to quit smoking, he'd gone to a therapist who'd used hypnosis. Ultimately it hadn't stopped his smoking, and he went cold turkey several years later, but the hypnosis had worked several times. He'd experienced a similar sense of surrender of control. However, he'd allowed that to happen. Althea could take his control away at will. That scared him. And Levi did not scare easily.

A full hour later he heard it, the long, plaintive wail of a wolf. It was across and up-canyon maybe a mile. He felt the hairs on the back of his neck rise as the sound died away, and experienced the thrill he always felt. The howl's absence intensified the silence it left behind.

Levi stood. He could picture the animal—it sounded like a young male—lifting its head and howling with an utter lack of self-consciousness. That had been the most difficult part of learning to howl, letting go of self-consciousness, an awareness humans were uniquely shackled to. He tilted his head back and answered. The subtle inflections and modulations he used communicated that he was also a young male open to meeting.

Almost immediately there was an answering call, on his side of the creek, above him on the side-wall. It was a female, dominant, older. It addressed both the young males. "I am here. Come to me if you wish." A few minutes later, the young male Levi had answered called from the creek bottom, still above him. Levi could picture him loping through the forest and stopping near the creek.

"I am coming," he told the female. And then suddenly, two more wolves called in quick succession. One was deeper, the alpha male. His call simply identified who and where he was, up-canyon and close to the female. The other call was another female, younger, more tentative. She was perhaps telling the others she was unsure of her status within the group, but she desired to belong. She would also come to the dominant female.

Four wolves in all. Levi guessed there were one or two others who remained silent. That could work to their advantage, since every howl revealed location. This time of year, the pack's structure and hierarchy was fluid, determined by scuffles and threats. Levi knew that in addition to howling, wolves used posture and body language extensively, particularly to display hierarchical dominance and inferiority. But with a pack like this, status would quickly solidify, and by first snowfall the animals would hunt together as a single organism, a hyper-efficient and ruthless killing machine.

Then to Levi's surprise, another howl came from relatively close upstream. It was a beautiful call, another mature female. Levi shivered. He'd never heard a howl that possessed such depth, such wisdom, if he dared use that word. This was surely a remarkable wolf. A second alpha female.

The moon was waxing and over half full, but Levi would be in the trees, so he attached his headlamp. He crossed the meadow at an angle that took him in her direction. Stopping once to howl, he skirted the creek bottom, and worked his way through small aspen and cottonwood. He heard the young male and the older female howl again. They were above him about a half mile, and close to each other.

Levi could imagine them approaching each other, tails wagging, circling each other, sniffing noses. The alpha female would chase the younger male, and they'd play for a while. The alpha male might join them. And possibly others. After greetings, and a skirmish or two, they would bed down for the night, one of them keeping guard.

Despite the fact that wolves are wickedly quick, have razor sharp teeth and a crushing pressure of 1500 pounds per square inch, double that of a German Shepherd, and skirmish continuously as they sort out hierarchy, they rarely seriously wound each other. There are exceptions, of course, particularly with territory or food, but they are rare. Wolves have evolved highly sophisticated and systematized methods of communicating dominance and submission. A submissive gesture, such as exposing the belly or the throat during battle, instantly stops an aggressor. The purpose of fighting among wolves is rarely to wound or kill, but to secure hierarchical position. Levi had never heard of wolves exhibiting "bullying" behavior, so common in humans. Levi would consider such a wolf deranged.

In another ten minutes Levi had neared the location of the mysterious female's call. He howled again, but received no answer. Breaking through a clump of fir into a small clearing, Levi expected to see the female wolf, but saw only the archer's tent, a green dome glowing in moonlight.

Seven

The morning dawned clear and cold. Frost lay heavy on the meadow grass outside his tent. Venus was a white eye in the eastern sky. Levi guessed it was in the mid-twenties, though temperatures would reach into the eighties by mid-afternoon. Dressed in a microfiber down coat, Levi heated water for tea, and sipped it while eating a few mouthfuls of granola.

The sun had not yet broken the canyon crest when he set off with his camera, notepad, and collecting bag. Walking quickly, largely for warmth, he headed toward where the gathering of the older and younger wolves had taken place. When he got within reasonable distance, he began zig-zagging through thin clumps of fir, meadow, and scattered rock, eyes to the ground. His persistence paid off. At the edge of a small J-shaped meadow, there were five circular frost-free imprints in the grass. Five wolves had slept here, and quite possibly he'd spooked them out. If so, they were most likely watching him from above.

He scanned the rugged slopes above him for several minutes, looking for movement, then spotting a motionless wolf staring down at him from a blunt promontory. It was relaxed yet alert. Curious, perhaps. It watched Levi carefully as he raised the camera.

The wolf flinched at the sound of the shutter, but Levi captured a burst of photos before it turned and ran into a small gully. It was a large male, over a hundred pounds, black with a white scar on his right shoulder. The alpha male. Levi had never seen him before, but would not forget him.

Following the alpha male but below him, two more wolves loped across the promontory. One of them, the alpha female he guessed, stopped momentarily and glanced down at him. Just as the sun crested the canyon rim, her amber eyes erupted with light. She was gone as he clicked the shutter. He missed the photo, but continued to hold the camera up. He knew there were at least two more. Sure enough, another wolf crossed quickly on the same path, now illumined by the morning sun. Levi pressed the shutter and captured another burst. This wolf was large, but smaller than both alpha animals. He guessed it was another young male. The fifth wolf never showed.

Walking around the small meadow, Levi found a kill, the remains of a hoary marmot. A quarter-sized chunk of meat, with distinctive silver-tipped fur, clung to a nearly intact femur. Scattered nearby were several broken bones, including the crushed skull. One of the wolves had killed the marmot in the scree field above, and carried it down to share with the others. It was one of the things that endeared wolves to Levi, their level of cooperation and sharing. There were many examples, some he'd seen, of them bringing food to sick or wounded pack members.

The wolves had left distinct tracks in the meadow frost as they traveled up-slope. Levi took several photographs, then followed them. A few minutes later, he came out onto the same promontory where he'd spotted the alpha male. Trailing its probable path into the gully, he found several paw prints in mud next to a rivulet. Placing a six-inch ruler next to each, he photographed them. There were at least two sets, one a few millimeters smaller.

He climbed further, and was making steady progress up the canyon, when he saw them again. All five of them were clustered below him next to a clump of subalpine fir. Two of the wolves, the alpha female and the younger male, had their noses to the breeze that blew down-canyon. They'd caught scent of something farther up.

Wolves were so expressive, and had such refined olfactory and auditory perception, that in the field they often acted as a sensory enhancement for Levi's own feebler senses. He remembered watching, from above, a wolf near Glacier Park walk a trail. The wolf stopped suddenly and abruptly, snapped its ears forward, and froze.

Levi could see nothing ahead, but the wolf leapt off the trail and melted into the forest. Levi waited. Half a minute later, a mother grizzly ambled down the trail with a two-month cub frisking behind. If Levi had descended to the trail behind the wolf as he'd planned, he could be dead. Mother grizzlies react with frenzied violence when they think their cubs are threatened.

He snapped a few bursts of photographs, capturing the small pack together. Hearing the shutter clicks, the alpha female turned and locked eyes with him. They held contact for nearly twenty seconds. Then she broke off and trotted away. The others followed. Levi knew this extended staring often occurred between a wolf and its ungulate prey. Wolf biologists sometimes called it the "communication of death." But he did not feel he was considered prey, rather another animal to be known. And that was the female wolf's invitation, to know her as another being. If true, it was a stunning insight. Levi knew from experience that the pack would probably acclimate to his presence within a couple days. They would remain wary, but would accept him at a distance. But he didn't follow them now.

Levi thought the alpha female a remarkable wolf, as light as the alpha male was black, a ghost wolf with white fur, tipped with silver and rust. She was only slightly smaller than the alpha male, and looked quicker. On the way back to camp he deliberately passed the site of the bowhunter's tent. It was gone, leaving only an oval of crushed vegetation.

Eight

LEVI SECURED HIS TENT, hung the food in a nearby fir, and headed up the canyon. His goal was to hike to where the canyon floor ended, and the peaks rose into the divide between Montana and Idaho. There were several trails over the divide in other drainages, but the only way to get into Idaho from Goat Creek Canyon was to climb. Levi estimated the distance to the headwall at four to six miles.

He chose the left side of the canyon, climbed up a hundred feet or so, and began paralleling the canyon floor, following the route the wolves had taken. It was another perfect Indian summer day. He'd stripped down to shorts and wore no shirt. His torso was tanned and muscular, his black beard and hair wild. Above him the larches were turning to gold. He felt an enormous sense of freedom, an unfettered wildness. The thought of staying up here for the remainder of his life, regardless how impractical, was so strong it was almost spellbinding. The canyon tightened as he wandered farther up, and he caught glimpses of the bright silver snake of the creek through the trees.

Levi made little noise as he walked, and his feet found their way like a blind man reading Braille. This freed him to study the landscape and snap photos as he walked. He took some shots of a hoary marmot community—at their watch stations like tubby little soldiers, whistling to alert the others of potential danger. Other marmots, the women and kids, he imagined, sat munching bear-grass tubers, or puttering about the entrance of a den. By this time of the year, after feeding all summer, many of the marmots weighed between fifteen and twenty pounds, and their meat was rich in fat. The wolves had definitely marked this colony for later hunting.

After a couple of hours walking, during which he saw three mountain goats, a bull elk, and the rump of a moose ducking into cover, the valley floor again widened. After paralleling this rocky meadow for a quarter mile or so, Levi saw water flickering between the trees. A hundred yards ahead, he left the trees, and had a clear view down to a large oval pool with a sandy beach on the far side.

Levi was staring at the pool when he experienced an abrupt, intense experience. The sunlight became more crystalline, the colors around him hyper-real. And he lost all sense of self. The pool below appeared a liquid eye that saw all, and it saw him as a pulse or wave in the infinite. For some moments he had no idea who or where he was. Nothing looked familiar. His boundaries became permeable, then dissolved, and he felt he was expanding at the speed of light into eternity. Wind washed through him, and he was surrounded by voices in languages he didn't understand. He began laughing uncontrollably.

Then it was over. He returned to his body, the canyon, the call of a crow, and soft wind. "Wow," he said to himself. "Wow."

Below him a woman walked out of the trees, crossed the sand, dropped her towel, and stood momentarily at the pool's edge. She was naked, and sun irradiated her blond hair. Her breasts and stomach were taut. She rose to the balls of her feet and stretched her arms above her. Then she stared directly at him. Levi felt everything freeze, and he felt profound emptiness. It was impossible for him to tell if he was experiencing absolute silence, or if every cell in the world was screaming. Then it broke, and she dove into the pool, her languorous breaststroke taking her out into the pool's depths, where it darkened to black.

Levi looked away, then back. She was still there, but had flipped and was now floating on her back. Levi saw how her left leg bent down slightly, how her breasts slid slightly to the side, and the blond furze of her crotch. The black water suspended her.

Levi, vertiginous, began picking his way down through the rocks, using clumps of trees as shields. When he was seventy feet or so above the pool, just to the left of the cliff, he crouched. The woman had returned to shore, and lay stretched out on her stomach, her head cradled in her arms.

Levi felt ferocious thirst, and lifted his water bottle to his lips. As water poured into his mouth, he was acutely aware that water is life. He knew this not as a thought, but as an experience. And then the water was gone, the bottle empty.

Below him a school of tiny silver fish flickered as they approached the surface. Below them the golden substrate angled downward, turning the water cobalt, then indigo, then black. The water was startlingly clear. Levi could see at least twenty feet down, but toward the center the depth was far greater than that. Levi felt a wave of vertigo staring at it, and although kneeling, grabbed a small sapling for balance. He felt he was staring at an ancient black sky devoid of constellations. Voices rose like waves, swelled, and crashed into a distant shore.

Levi didn't know how long he'd left himself. Minutes, seconds? Two women now floated in the pool. They both had black hair, though one wore it shaved to within an inch of her skull, a tattoo on her shoulder. Levi focused the telephoto on her, grazing over her nude body, then studying the tattoo. It was a symbol Levi had seen before—a labyrinth. The other woman's hair spread across the water like black vegetation. Levi felt suddenly embarrassed, like a pervert at a peep show. Still unbalanced, he shook his head forcefully, trying to clear it. He couldn't remember the women entering the water. It was as if they'd materialized from the black depths.

Nine

WITHOUT REVEALING HIMSELF, LEVI side-hilled downstream, back toward camp. The sun was intense, the air so dry it rasped his throat as he gulped it. Dust rose with every step like miniature storms coating his shoes and pants. He ached for water. He closed his eyes and an image came to him. He saw himself diving into the depths of the spring pool, followed by the three women. Their faces were white, and oddly serene, almost mask-like. They were pushing him deeper into the pool's dark depths. Fear spidered him.

Again, Levi woke to himself. He realized his eyes were closed, that he was gripping a small sapling. Levi took a deep breath, exhaled slowly, then forced his eyes open. Light ricocheted off the white granite cliffs. His thirst evaporated, and there was only a faint breeze, the side cliffs, and a brilliant blue sky. Levi felt joy lift him out of his body into the vast light and air. And then that left him, and he was standing on the earth again.

He wondered what was happening. Had he inadvertently eaten something toxic or psychedelic? He could think of nothing. He had eaten no mushrooms or strange berries. Was he getting ill? But no. He felt excellent. Vibrant and energetic as hell.

Were these strange women he'd encountered somehow responsible? He wondered who they were, how they'd entered the canyon. The most likely answer was that they worked for the Forest Service or BLM, and had entered through Leeson's property. He'd find out tomorrow. He'd climb to the pool and meet them.

Levi crossed the stream a mile or so downstream from the pool. He stopped and drank heartily, then poured a bottle-full over his head, letting water slosh down the sides of his face. Feeling its cool wetness baptize him, he gave silent thanks. Then he left the creek-bottom and climbed several hundred feet up the north side. The north side was steeper, more rugged and irregular than the south. Levi felt incredibly alive, his movements a predestined choreography, every step nuanced, balanced, perfect. Yet once, when his attention wavered, he slid, and watched as a small avalanche of rock slid over a cliff and dropped soundlessly below.

Ahead and slightly below him, in a tangle of willows, dogwood, and grass, a mixed flock of ravens and crows had assembled, a number of them circling, others in trees or on the ground. Scoping the area with his camera, Levi saw the carcass of a moose, its hindquarters torn away. Then he spotted a wolf, the alpha female. She lay in close proximity to both of the young males, and the young female lay fifteen feet or so to the left. In all there were five, lounging or sleeping near the carcass. The alpha male lay closest to the kill.

Occasionally ravens landed on the carcass, walked across the hairy terrain, tore off chunks of flesh before winging off to perch and eat. The wolves had gorged themselves and were resting. Levi knew they ate as much as twenty pounds of meat from a large kill such as this, and they slept up to twenty-four hours following. Their lives were literally feast or famine.

Levi took a number of photos, then sat and opened his notebook. He drew two maps, the same as he'd done for the other wolf contacts. One detailed the identity and position of each wolf with relation to the prey, and a larger scale map located the kill with regard to his camp and other landmarks in the canyon.

With a kill of this size, the pack would not move for at least a few days. Levi decided to try something. He tipped his head back and gave a short howl. Two of the wolves picked up their heads and one gave a feeble reply. The other three were so far into sleep they didn't wake. Even the two who responded looked like they could barely keep their heads up, and within moments were drifting back into sleep.

Ten

BACK AT CAMP, LEVI boiled water for tea and ate a few bites of trail mix. The gray jay had called in its friends, and several of them were hopping around his pack chattering, trying to worry it open. He tossed them a handful of trail mix, which he'd probably regret when he ran out, but they amused him with their antics. One had so many nuts stuffed in its mouth it couldn't swallow.

Sipping tea, Levi stared across the meadow, and thought about what had happened over the past few days. He'd had several experiences that caused him quite literally to lose his sense of self, to dissolve into a much larger being. Aside from a small number of college explorations with LSD and "shrooms," and smoking a little pot now and then, Levi was rational—oriented in, and by, science. Distortions of time and space, and experiences of infinity, were foreign to him.

There was the remote possibility these experiences were caused by lack of food, but it had never happened before. There was also the remote possibility he was fighting some weird virus, but other than these experiences he felt healthy and strong. And the vertigo had left him. Tomorrow he would visit the women at the spring, and learn more about them, and possibly about himself.

Levi spent the remainder of the day writing in his journal about the wolves he'd seen. For convenience sake, he named wolves using a code he'd devised that identified sex, age, and status in the pack. The first of the five wolves he'd seen was the black alpha male with the white facial scar. He named this wolf AM4, the A standing for Alpha, M for male, and 4 as an approximate age. AF4 was the female alpha. Levi decided the two younger males were siblings, most likely offspring of the alpha wolves, and he named them SBM21 and SBM22. The younger female he named SF3. The S stood for subordinate, the B for brother, the 2 for two years of age. He then sketched a relational hierarchy of the five wolves.

As he sat studying his work, the wind quickened and began to sound like water in the trees. The water in the trees contained myriad voices, some of them wolves. And then in a totally inexplicable move, he scratched out his coded names and renamed the wolves. Where AM4 had been scratched out, Levi wrote Sala, then Mirr for AF4, Anar and Rill for the two brothers, and LLow for the three-year old female. He stared at the page, stunned. He had no idea where these names came from.

That night no wolves howled, and Levi envisioned them asleep after gorging themselves on meat.

Eleven

THE NEXT MORNING DAWNED clear, with almost hallucinatory striations of pre-dawn color across the cliffs at the canyon mouth.

Levi gobbled some trail mix, packed his small fanny pack, adding his headlamp, and headed out. As he walked, he thought about the second dominant female wolf he'd heard howling. Although it happened two nights ago, he thought of it often. He'd originally thought it was the bowhunter he'd met, but no human could howl like that. After thinking it through, he decided that there was another she wolf, a unique and dominant animal that was not in a pack and was a loner. This was rare among wolves, but did happen. He could still feel the visceral thrill upon hearing the power and depth of her howl.

Passing the meadow where the wolves had killed the moose, he saw three still at the kill. Mirr, Llow and Anar. Sala and Rill were gone. The moose hindquarter was torn asunder from the spinal column and largely devoured. The belly had been ripped out, and the entrails eaten. Scraps of meat lay scattered as if by some frenzy, and crows still hopped from piece to piece, enjoying their sudden bounty. Levi found a secure and partially hidden perch, where he sat watching them for nearly an hour, taking notes and snapping photos.

Careful observation told him that the young wolf Anar had an injured left front paw and alternated between walking with a limp and using just three legs. It seemed to depend on how fast he was traveling. A run would put him onto three legs, while in a slower walk, he'd limp. Mirr possessed a poise and self-confidence that was palpable, and Levi wrote wisdom, knowing he was flirting with anthropomorphism. And Llow was now feeling comfortable as a member of the pack.

Although there were over a hundred pounds of moose meat left on the carcass, Levi guessed that Sala and Rill were out scouting more prey. If they found another moose, or an elk or goat they thought susceptible, they would bury the remainder of the moose carcass and move on. Wolves did not remain in the same place for long, moving continuously around their loose territory. This pack was what Levi called a "vagrant" pack. It had not identified and claimed territory yet. Perhaps it would settle here.

Sala and Rill did not return. A band of showers passed over, soaking Levi as he huddled under a clump of mountain ash, then was replaced by blazing sun, and Levi watched steam burn off the rock. He was pretty sure the wolves knew he was there. With all three sleeping, he got up, stretched, and set off.

A half-mile or so below the spring, Levi crossed the stream and came up the north side. The woods thinned here, a mixture of lodgepole, larch, and subalpine fir. Looking up through the tops of the trees, h watched a few puffy cumulous clouds tag the peaks above. He was pretty sure the peak directly upstream was called Paintbrush. It was the peak behind the spring.

There was a narrow mantle of mixed meadow and aspen groves along the stream now, interrupted by large boulders. The forest thinned further, and Levi spotted the women's camp ahead. There were three dome tents, one orange, two green. They were arranged in a rough semi-circle, across from a blue tarp that had been stretched between four trees. Glassing it with the camera, Levi could see a cook stove and kitchen area. There were also three canvas coolers, and a few folding cloth camp chairs. Additionally, several logs had been positioned as seats.

Between the tarp and the tents was a fire pit built up with rock and surrounded by stumps. One of the women, the one with the tattoo and short black hair he'd seen in the pool yesterday, was dressed in a light Gortex windbreaker. She stirred the ashes of a fire that appeared dead. Looking more carefully, Levi could see a pan of water sending steam into the air under the tarp. The woman quit the fire and ducked under the tarp, where she began pouring hot water into a porcelain cup. Levi was suddenly very thirsty for tea.

He began strolling downhill into the clearing, and when he was thirty feet away, he said, "Hello," loudly.

The woman looked up sharply, then smiled.

"Well, if it isn't our voyeur."

Levi closed the distance between them. "Yeah, sorry about that. I didn't want to disturb you yesterday."

"And now you do?" Her smile danced, mischievous, teasing.

Levi smiled as well. "Now I do."

The woman's skin was as white as porcelain. He thought of Mirr momentarily, her white guard hair tipped in black. The woman's black hair flamed as she stepped into the sun, and he could see the labyrinth tattoo finely etched onto her shoulder.

"Would you like some tea?" she asked.

"I'd love some. I usually have a cup in the morning, but forgot it."

"Anxious to come see us, no doubt." She poured water a second time. "Here." She handed him a red clay mug. "It's a home blend. You'll like it."

He took the cup, which was quite hot, blew across it, then took a sip. It burned, but the little he swallowed had a thick resinous flavor.

"What's in it?"

"It's a secret." The woman winked. "Good though, right?" She nodded at the tents with her head. "The girls are still sleeping. Wild night, dancing around the fire, sacrificing goats. All that." She sipped her tea, then asked, "What are you doing out here? Besides spying."

Levi felt his ears turn red. "Hey, I'm sorry about that. I didn't think you saw me, and I…"

"I know, didn't want to disturb us. Yesterday." She laughed. "Yet here you are without an answer to my question."

"I'm a wolf researcher. A small pack dropped into the canyon over a week ago, and I'm studying them. The pack composition, behavior, that sort of thing."

The woman sipped again and made a wry face. "You don't kill them, do you?"

"Hell, no. I run a small nonprofit dedicated to protecting wolves. They need all the help they can get."

The woman was shorter than him, but wiry and strong. She held her cup, and herself, with casual grace. When she spoke, there was both power and verity in what she said. "They do need all the help they can get. There's a full-fledged war against nature going on in the world. There always has been. Humans against everything else."

"The forces of ignorance at work," Levi replied.

"Humans have better weapons nowadays."

"I try to remain optimistic."

"That's foolish." The woman shook her head. "We only fight to the death when our backs are against the wall."

Levi looked at the woman to see if she was joking, but her face was hard.

"I can certainly understand how you feel that way." Levi traced a circle in the dust with his foot. "My name is Levi, by the way."

The woman didn't answer immediately, rather walked to the edge of the tarp, looked up, then came back. "I'm Arianna."

Levi started to ask why the women were here, when a second woman backed out of her tent. She was wearing a pair of tight shorts and a fleece top.

"Tea, I need tea." She paused, taking Levi in. "And we have a visitor. A very handsome man." She stuck out her hand. "I'm Cali." She was the blond woman Levi had initially seen.

Levi took her hand and gave it a light shake. "Levi."

"Like the jeans you're not wearing," Cali said, laughing.

"Yeah, these are definitely not Levis." Levi felt suddenly stupid. Both women were staring at him and his torn nylon shorts with teasing eyes.

The moment was interrupted by a loud "Fuck!!" coming from the third tent, which was now shaking perilously. The shaking stopped suddenly, and the third woman emerged. Levi could see now that she was tall, and her hair was black and full of unbroken waves. She had a rudimentary resemblance to the bow-hunter, but was thinner. Her eyes were such a bright and penetrating emerald, he could see them cleanly from twenty feet.

"We have a guest!" she exclaimed. "Our first!"

Levi stretched his hand toward her as she walked over. "I'm Levi."

"Kayla," the woman said, taking his hand, not shaking it, but holding it as she studied his face. "Glad to meet you. I saw you yesterday. From the water. Arianna and I were swimming. You remember?"

"How could I forget?"

"He didn't want to disturb us," said Arianna teasingly.

"Because we were naked?" asked Kayla.

"Partly. I'm not sure what the protocol is for approaching naked women in the woods."

"He's cute, isn't he?" asked Cali. Levi noticed the fan of freckles across her nose and lower face.

"He's a wolf researcher," said Arianna.

"Interesting," said Kayla. "Interesting." She poured the remainder of the hot water into a cup and added a teaspoon of raw tea, stirring it carefully. "And have you found any wolves to research?"

Levi noticed the women all had an accent, the same as Althea. He remembered that a climbing friend of his father's who was visiting from Turkey or Greece had a similar accent.

"As I was telling Arianna, a small pack, five or possibly six wolves, dropped into the canyon a few weeks ago. They're not a known pack."

"Is that common? That a pack is known?" asked Cali.

"These days, given the state of wolf reintroduction, and their inclusion on the endangered species list, wolves are heavily managed. Almost every pack in the country, those in Minnesota, Michigan, Montana, Idaho, and Washington, the states where most wolves live, have at least one radio-collared animal so fish and wildlife can track them."

"Doesn't it seem contradictory to 'manage' something as wild as a wolf?" asked Kayla.

"It seems a violation," said Arianna.

"I've felt that many times," said Levi, "but I've come to realize it's for their own good. Wolves are still shot, poisoned, and hunted illegally. Tracking them helps catch the bastards who do that. It also gives us important population data and pack movement. I wish there were a better, less intrusive way to do it."

"I think the central issue here is wildness. Can an animal still be wild if it wears a radio-collar? If it can be tracked?" Kayla wore a bemused look, anger crouched behind it.

Levi said nothing, staring into his empty cup. Then he looked up suddenly. "I don't like it, either, but it's the hand we're dealt. We can't go back in time."

All three women stared at each other in astonishment, then broke down laughing. When their laughing died enough for Levi to get a word in, he asked, "So, are you women on a camping trip?"

The women exchanged glances and continued laughing. After a few minutes they became more serious, and had a rapid exchange in a language Levi couldn't even begin to fathom. Then they suddenly stopped, and Levi heard the silence echoing off the rock walls above them, and then the wind.

"We're camping, as you can see," said Kayla, waving her arm at the tents.

"Where are you from?"

"Far away."

"I met a woman hunter yesterday. An archer. Her accent sounded like yours. Do you know her?"

"Yes," answered Cali. "She is a friend."

"Who wants food?" Kayla interceded. "I can make some eggs. We have fresh squeezed orange juice!"

"You have eggs out here? Oranges?" Levi was thinking now they must have been dropped in by copter. They were field biologists of some kind. Patience would tell him what he wanted to know. Levi felt his stomach gnawing itself with hunger.

"I'll have eggs and orange juice and bacon, and whatever else you have. I'm starving."

"All right, a hungry man. Our first up here."

There was melon in addition to the eggs, potatoes smothered in oregano, a spicy sausage, goat they told him, and toast. The melon was golden orange, and melted instantly from solid to liquid in Levi's mouth. He had never tasted anything like it. In fact, everything was incredible. Then Kayla said, "Yogurt," and a chorus of "yes" ensued. It was unflavored, and so tart it cleansed Levi's mouth.

After their meal, they moved to the pool, where they sat on rocks and sand, talking as the sun journeyed across the canyon. Levi learned they were from Greece, but not how they arrived at their camp. There were allusions to horses that had come and gone, to a copter, to hiking in over the divide from Idaho. Whenever Levi tried to pin them down, they were evasive.

Later in the afternoon, Cali announced she was going swimming, then stood up and calmly shed her clothes. She turned to Levi before entering the water.

"I hope this doesn't embarrass you," she said laughing.

"Not at all. I grew up skinny-dipping."

The women all laughed. They'd never heard the phrase before.

Before the afternoon was over, they'd all stripped and swam, lounging on the small crescent beach, talking more, feeling comfortable, leisurely. Levi could feel himself drawn toward Cali, and found himself talking with her more, and more intently. Cali told him that she'd grown up in Athens, had led a rather typical boring life, and at some point, needed to get out of Greece and travel. It was a vague and unsurprising story.

At some point Kayla announced that she was making dinner, and extended an invitation to stay, which Levi accepted immediately. He was feeling very relaxed in the company of these women.

Kayla pulled two packages of lamb chops from one of the coolers, along with asparagus, red pepper, onions and mushrooms. Soon the two cook stoves were jammed with pots and pans, and the kitchen area under the tarp was a flourish of motion and intoxicating scents.

Several bottles of red wine materialized. Glasses were filled, and toasts were given, the women's all in Greek.

"Na pethani o charos," said Arianna. "Death to death. Eternal life."

It seemed to Levi the women were smiling secretly, as if sharing a mystery.

They ate dinner under the emerging stars, and night chill moved in as they ate, but the liquors they now drank, one tasting of anise, one of resin, and one like the inside of a shoe mixed with honey, was keeping them warm and more.

At some point Kayla disappeared, then Arianna lay back on the ground and began snoring softly. Cali moved closer to Levi, then closer still. She kissed him.

"Do you want to go swimming again?" Her voice was a whisper and brushed him like a breeze.

"It's pretty cold," Levi said, pulling Cali to him. "Why don't we go into your tent instead?"

She kissed him again and brushed her hand lightly against his bare thigh. "Let's go swimming. I'll keep you warm."

Twelve

THEY SWAM OUT TO the center of the pool. Levi admired Cali's pale skin, accentuated by the blackness of the water, the night. The sky above them was brilliant with a million stars. Holding each other, Cali made Levi promise to follow her.

"We're going to dive into that hole."

"Why?"

"I want to show you something."

"It's pitch-black. How am I going to see anything?"

"You have to have faith, Levi. You have to trust me." She looked anything but innocent, but Levi was high enough from beverages consumed to go along with it.

They held hands and dove, kicking and digging with their free hands. Cali was a remarkable swimmer, pulling ahead, and pulling Levi with her, deeper. Pressure built in his lungs, intensifying, becoming intolerable, yet still Cali dove deeper, and Levi was powerless against her strength. He felt fear invade him, and his headlamp, which somehow had slid around his neck, felt like it was choking him. This woman was trying to drown him.

He tried desperately to pull away, but his strength dissipated. Cali continued to pull him down. The pressure was now extreme. Lightning flashed in his brain, and there was a sustained roar that intensified. Then he heard her calming voice in his head cut through everything. "Let go, Levi. Trust me. Let go." What choice did he have?

The roar was different now, the sound of waves on a beach, crashing and receding. He was lying curled to Cali on coarse sand, the wave-foam brilliant white, the musk of salt air in his lungs. A large white moon lay a path on the water, stretching into the distance, disappearing into a sky exploding with stars. Darker areas revealed islands far offshore. It was warm, and a mild breeze stirred the scents of exotic flowers and citrus into the salt air. The roar and exhalation of waves was the only sound. Cali's fingers brushed his face, and he felt as if he were witnessing the stasis before the beginning of time. One careless action from him would ignite it into motion.

He woke again and heard a waterfall. He was farther up the beach, lying next to a spring pool. The dark was dissipating and dawn was near. The pool was rimmed on three sides by rock draped with impatiens, their orange, red, and pink creating a pointillist tapestry. Below him breakers were feathering the sand with foam, then withdrawing their fragile fingers. Levi lay against a rock. His head felt clear, and he tried to stand, but his limbs, and the muscles within them, failed to obey.

Then he saw the women. Cali, Arianna, and Kayla. They were holding hands and pulling each other through the breakers. He heard scraps of laughter. It seemed to come from a great distance, as if there were a hollowness to everything. He looked around. To his left, white marble stairs, built into the hillside, ascended to what Levi guessed was a temple overlooking the sea. Light danced within from what could only be a fire. There was a large bas-relief over the pronaos that faced the sea. The letters "Λυκάων" were carved into the white marble, and shadow in the cuts made them readable.

Out of the breaking dawn, wolves begin howling. They were far above him, above the temple, and seemed to be running as they howled.

When he woke again, it was to birds he didn't immediately recognize. He reached out to touch Cali, but she was gone. Then he remembered the women dancing, and he looked down the beach to where they'd been. Gulls were wheeling over open water, and the cobalt sea was like nothing he'd ever seen. There were several islands not far offshore. He saw no one. Looking behind him, he witnessed sparsely forested cliffs stagger into a crystal blue sky, the white temple like a ghost ship hanging from the hillside. He vaguely remembered hearing wolves, but the effort to remember was too much, his head like stone.

Levi woke in his tent, not remembering at all how he got there. His hair was damp. The sun was strong, and the familiar embryonic feeling overpowered him. He closed his eyes again, giving in to the dreamy state.

When he woke again it must have been mid-afternoon. He wondered again how he'd gotten back to his tent, but could only remember dreaming he was on a beach. And that was fuzzy. He looked around for his headlamp, but couldn't find it. He must have walked two miles back to his tent, bombed out of his mind, with only moonlight as his guide.

Levi pushed himself up, fighting through the fire in his head, made some tea, then set about cleaning the tent. It was an hour before he could stomach anything. The trail mix caught in his throat, and he drank a ton of water. He was hung over and fatigued. He did a thorough inventory of his pockets to make sure he hadn't lost anything else. Memories of last night were fragmentary. He remembered the chill of the water, the burning heat when Cali embraced him. He vaguely remembered eating dinner with the women camped at the spring, and drinking an ungodly amount of alcohol. But that was it. The rest was gone.

He turned in early, hearing wolves howl shortly before he drifted off. They were above him, near the women and the spring. But the spring he saw in his mind was surrounded by impatiens, and he heard the roar of breakers before drifting into slumber.

The next morning Levi walked back to the spring. The women were gone. There was no sign they, or anyone, had camped there.

Thirteen

OVER THE NEXT FEW days Levi again located the wolf pack. They'd traveled upstream to the plateau above the pool where the women had camped, if the women had in fact existed. His memories of them seemed more and more vaporous.

The wolves had killed another cow moose and were fanned out, sleeping around the carcass. There was an additional wolf that seemed to have joined them, although he was the farthest from the kill. An older male past his prime. When Levi had seen him walk earlier, it was with a slight limp in his left hind leg, and the wolf had a touch of mange over his back that left part of his hind hairless. This would be his last winter, but the pack would care for him as they would a pup, and the wolf's transition into the next world would be far easier than if he were alone.

Levi stayed with the wolves for two days, taking numerous photos and notes. The next day it began raining heavily, and he decided it was time to leave the canyon. It was getting colder and would snow soon. The cliffs would be impassable then.

As he walked back to camp, a fog moved in, and Levi spotted three cow elk moving slowly through the trees like ghosts. Even as he walked, felt his feet hit the solid ground, and breathed the chill air, Levi felt as if reality had become diaphanous. The entire canyon experience had turned into a dream.

Fourteen

Levi doubted that beer, or the burger he'd just bitten into, oozing blood and the sweet jalapeno sauce the pub was known for, had ever tasted so good. Deprivation and excessive trail-mix did that to a man.

He sat on a hard wooden bench on the deck of the Bitterroot Public House, shortly after 1:30 in the afternoon, taking large bites of his hamburger and nursing a homegrown IPA, while watching the small-time hustle of Hamilton.

There were more people with money than ever, and he could see it reflected in the fashionable clothing, new Audi and BMW SUVs, and the shiny, work-free trucks. People seemed to walk more quickly. No one ambled, except the occasional senior citizen. And there was the proliferation of cell phones. Everyone walking and talking. Hamilton was starting to think itself important.

Levi always had difficulty with his first taste of civilization after a stint in the mountains. While things like a burger and brew brought ecstasy, the spoiled, self-indulgent materialism and increased speed brought bile. He watched the people on Main Street hurry by, leisurely ate his burger, and licked the last foam from his beer off his lips. His next taste of civilization would be a shower. Then he needed to immerse himself in the world of mail, email, texts, and tweets. Home was where technology lay waiting to ambush him.

Levi let the near-scalding shower hammer his shoulders, head, and upper back. He stood there for a long time. While still in the shower he shaved, then stepped out, toweled, and put on clean clothes for the first time in days. Then he fired up his laptop.

He lived in a two-story colonial set back from Ninth Street in Hamilton. Across the street was a strip of second-growth forest that stretched west a quarter mile to the Bitterroot River. Levi's house was also headquarters to WolfRecovery.org, his nonprofit. Although he hired people on a sporadic basis, largely to fulfill time deadlines required by grants, he handled most of the business solo. He liked it that way. He called the shots and answered to no one but himself.

WolfRecovery occupied two rooms. The first room, just off the living room to the right, had floor-to-ceiling bookcases, a solid oak desk, a set of black metal file cabinets, several lamps, a couch, five chairs including than the one behind the desk, a couple of end and coffee tables. A desktop computer sat front and center. Piles of books, papers, magazines, and newspapers crowded every flat surface. The one exposed wall was faded robin's egg blue and contained several photographs. In one of them, Levi stood with a Nunamiut hunter who held a large wolf carcass and grinned widely. Another showed three wolves crossing a gravel bar next to a river. A third was a head-shot of a timber wolf facing the camera, its eyes golden and hypnotic.

Off this room was a conference room with a large, rectangular oak table that weighed a ton. It had taken Levi, Taylor, Art, and Justin nearly four hours to move it in, and they nearly said "fuck it" until Justin got his Stihl saw from his truck and cut the thing in half on the front lawn. A woodworker friend had restored the rip. Eight chairs surrounded it, and there was room for several more. Numerous photographs and paintings, largely of wolves, adorned the walls. There was also a red circle drawn around a jagged hole where a .45 bullet had entered the wall. The bullet was the gift of Kevin Henderson, a rancher from Stevensville, who'd reacted violently during a meeting with Fish and Wildlife. Other than deafening everyone momentarily, no real damage was done, and Mr. Henderson let himself out, never to return.

Levi spent a good part of the afternoon dealing with various communiqués. Taking a break for some phone calls, and a read-over of a Canadian grant he was applying for, he began typing his notes.

Around five-thirty he drove down to the Red Barn, where he was meeting Art and Taki for dinner. The Red Barn was built adjacent to the Bitterroot River. The weather had cleared, and sun streamed through the windows. The Beatles' "Yellow Submarine" filled the room as Levi walked through, waving to the barmaid on the way. Out on the deck he chose a seat overlooking the river. It was the table Art always chose. Art needed to be as close to water as possible.

Levi ordered a beer, which the barmaid brought immediately.

"You looked like a man in need of a beer," she said, handing him the froth-topped glass and a menu.

"I bet you say that to all the guys."

"I do. You want to order yet?"

"No, I'm waiting for a couple people. I am ravenous, however, so forgive me if I drool while reading through this."

"Ravenous is my favorite word in the English language." She laughed.

"Why?"

"Because it contains raven, and they're my favorite bird."

"I just saw a bunch of them at a wolf kill. A pack took down a moose, and the ravens were camped out, feasting on scraps."

"Oh! You're that wolf researcher." She looked suddenly interested. "I saw you at the meeting the other night."

He'd thought he recognized her from somewhere. "That was pretty dreadful, wasn't it?"

"Sometimes I can't believe people like that exist."

"And that they're our neighbors."

"Time to move farther out." She winked. "Let me know if you need anything else."

He saw Art and Taki walking across the parking lot. They were holding hands, swinging them in unison. They both looked happy, and he felt a tinge of jealousy.

"Will do," he said, waving at them.

"Hey, stranger," Art said as Levi stood and gave him a hug. Taki did the same, adding a peck on the cheek. Then they all sat.

"You made it out alive," Art stated solemnly, then punched Levi in the shoulder.

"Almost didn't want to come out."

"How was that climb around Leeson's?" Taki asked.

"It was OK." Levi knew it was probably the only part of the trip she was interested in.

"OK? Don't give me that shit," she said in mock anger. "I would love to climb that."

"Come with me next time."

She threw a glance at Art.

"Probably not a good idea right now," she said to Levi.

Art nodded slowly. "We're working this out step-by-step, Levi."

"Sorry," said Levi. "I didn't mean anything by it."

The barmaid returned. "Hi. I'm Shayla, and I'll be your waitress. Do you want to hear about the dinner specials?"

"Sure," said Art. "And make it a pitcher of whatever he's drinking." He looked at Taki. "Is that OK?"

Art asking permission from Taki? This must be getting serious. Or weird.

"I'll just have lemonade," Taki told Shayla, "and yes, I'll drive." She flashed Art a funny face.

"Yes, Ma'am," he said, giving her a mock salute.

"Dinner specials?" Shayla asked again.

"You bet," said Levi, and Shayla rattled off a short list. Everything sounded infinitely better than trail mix.

Levi filled them in on the trip, leaving out the woman bowhunter and the three women camped at the spring, concentrating on the wolf pack. He didn't feel comfortable sharing the "supernatural" details yet. He wasn't entirely sure why.

"That is so cool," Art said excitedly. "The Valley's first resident wolf pack."

"Well, technically there have been a few packs up by the Big Hole that range into the Valley, but yeah, it's tres cool."

"Will they stay in the canyon?"

"It's possible, but not likely. They usually range over a much larger territory."

"Well, I hope they stay," said Taki, "and don't get shot by Leeson or some other asshole." She was twisting a straw in her teeth. Levi felt himself becoming slightly aroused, felt the three beers blurring boundaries. He didn't know if he was ready for this. Or if Art or Taki were either. It was still recent and raw.

But dinner flowed like a river with a few small rapids, and the hugs afterwards were hard and genuine.

Driving home, Levi realized he'd been dishonest by omission with the two people he cared for the most. He should have told them everything. About the women, the spring, the bow-hunter whose eyes contained infinity. He wondered again why he hadn't, and it nagged at him. It all still seemed dream-like. Maybe he was having a difficult time admitting it had actually happened.

Later that night Levi did some research. He couldn't get the memory of the dream, where he'd sat by the ocean and heard wolves howl, out of his head. It haunted him with its timeless sounds, the crash of waves, the howl of wolves running behind the temple above him. On a whim he looked up the natural history of wolves in Greece. Only 200-300 remained, but they were being "managed," and the population was listed as stable. Historically there had been substantial populations in Greece, particularly in a region called Arcadia. Levi read that in the arts of the European Renaissance, Arcadia was celebrated as an unspoiled, harmonious wilderness, home of the god Pan.

Wolves were also considered the companions of Artemis, who seemed to have an affinity with many wild animals. Artemis always carried a bow and arrow. Levi shook his head as he studied depictions of her, both sculptures and images. She reminded him of the bow-hunter, and seemed more than capable of carrying an elk out of the Bitterroot wilderness.

The next day a mammoth blizzard struck the Valley, shuttering Highway 93, the main north-south artery between Idaho and Missoula. Most secondary roads were also shut down along with schools, stores, and much else. Winter had come early and with a vengeance.

Levi tucked in, staying home and working up a report, including photos, on what he was calling the Goat Creek Pack. He emailed a copy to Steve McCandless at the University, Mike Danner at the Forest Service, and his counterpart Tom Baines at Montana Fish and Wildlife in Helena. Along with Levi, they were the only scientists in the state who gave much of a damn whether wolves lived or died.

On a whim he emailed Jakob Kristoff, a professor of Greek and Hebrew languages at the University of Montana. Levi sent him the word, or combination of letters, he'd seen at the temple. Λυκάων. He described the setting, telling Jakob he'd dreamt the scene, and asked for any assistance identifying the word, structure, or location. It was beyond a long shot.

Then he added that he had heard wolves howling in his dream. He read it over, almost deleted it, but his finger was quicker than his brain.

Three days later, the weather cleared, and there was the constant thump of snow melting off the pines onto the roof. Levi received an email telling him that his two NSF grants were stalled and would probably be denied, as the new administration took control of the EPA and put their particular spin on things. It was not a spin that was sympathetic to wilderness or wild things. Above his desk was a framed cover of *Where the Wild Things Are* his mother had given him for his twenty-first birthday. She'd inscribed it "To my son Levi who will always be where the wild things are." Levi looked around the room and was suddenly struck with loneliness. Without intending it, he had chosen a solitary life, and the irony struck him. This was not a lifestyle a wolf would have chosen.

The following day he received an email response from Professor Kristoff. It read:

> *Dear Levi,*
> *Please forgive the delay in answering. I've been home sick with the flu and have not had the energy to do much. However, I read your*

note with much interest.

Who knows where dreams come from? Some say from the unconscious, others from the spirit realm. Perhaps they are the same thing. In your case, I'm guessing this is something you saw in a book, magazine or film and it came back to you in the form of a dream. But forgive me. You don't need to read the hypothesis of an old academic.

The word you sent, Λυκάων, is Greek for Lycaon, a king whom Zeus turned into a wolf. The story is quite fascinating, so let me know if you want more of it and I'll send you all the details. Lycaon was king of Arcadia, so the temple, if it was a temple, and it sounds like it was, exists, or existed in or near Arcadia, which is on Peloponnesian Peninsula of Greece. It is a rather large area, and I have no idea where that particular temple might be, but I am sending you the names and contact information of two gentlemen who may be able to help you further. Mr. Nikos Papas works at the Archeological Museum in Sparta, a city on the Peninsula, and Mr. Gregorios Sikelianos works at the National Archaeological Museum in Athens. They could possibly provide you with further leads as to the location of this temple.

One interesting bit of information is that there was a cult that arose dedicated to worshipping Lycaon. I'm guessing that's the reason for the temple. The worshippers believed in the supernatural powers of wolves, worshipped wolves, and worshipped Lycaon as a leader of wolves. They also worshipped Pan and Artemis. It is said they were some of the earliest protectors of wilderness in the world. Needless to say, they were labeled pagan and anti-Christian in later days. They seem to have died out. But perhaps the men I told you to contact will know more.

I wish you luck with your search, and if I can be of more help don't hesitate to contact me.

My best.

Jakob Kristoff
Professor of Greek and Hebrew Studies
University of Montana

Levi was due to present at an International Wolf Center conference in Paris in late November, then a meeting in Lyon, and another conference, this one presented by the IUCN, in Rome directly following. He would be among friends and colleagues who would make him feel less lonely, less crazy. It was reifying to know there were others around the world who valued wolves as much as he did. It struck him suddenly that he could visit Greece after the Rome conference. Jakob had mentioned Sparta. Levi hit Google and did some browsing. He found what looked to be a decent hotel, the Menelaion, and made reservations for four nights. Then he booked a flight on Aegean Air from Rome to Sparta leaving immediately after the conference ended. He left the return to Rome open-ended, and for a reasonable price, changed his return to Montana from Rome to "Flexible." He had no idea what he'd find in Greece, if anything, but didn't want to hem himself in. Then he reserved a rental car. He checked his international license to make sure it was still valid. It was.

Over the next few hours Levi sent an email to the two men that Jakob recommended he contact. He told them pretty much the same story, but with additional information, added that he'd love to locate and visit the temple if it still existed, and learn anything he could about the "wolf cult" followers of Lycaon that Jakob had mentioned. If nothing else, it would expand his historical and mythical understanding of human-wolf relationships, a subject of which he had only minimal knowledge.

By the end of the week, snow had melted in the Valley. Art called, inviting him to float the river and fish for a day.

"River should be down and clear by Monday. Weather is supposed to hold. They'll be some good hatches. Late season cutties, humongous spawning browns."

Levi wasn't much of a fisherman, but a day with Art would be justified. Since Taki had left Levi for Art, there'd been tension between them. Levi had sensed it at dinner the other night. It was a complex situation. Taki and Levi didn't work as a couple any more. Taki took up with Levi's best friend, with Levi's muted blessing. Taki and Levi remained sexually attracted to each other. Art was jealous. Levi didn't want to be jealous but was. It would be good to float, fish, drink beer, and talk some of this out.

Early Monday morning Levi pulled into Art's driveway. Taki answered the door in PJs decorated with crazy clowns. She looked sleepy and softer than usual.

"It's nice you're going out with Art," she said. "He's been excited about it. He's been worried you two are drifting apart. Because of me."

"Nonsense," Levi said, a bit too brusquely. "I've just been really busy, and am about to get busier."

Levi was telling Taki about his upcoming trip when Art slid behind her, kissed her neck, and handed Levi a cup of coffee. Levi thought of a male wolf inserting itself into an encounter between its mate and another male.

"Glad you could make this, dude. It's going to be epic," Art said.

"I'm into epic." Levi laughed.

"Being late October, we've got time for a leisurely breakfast before the water warms enough to make trout hungry."

Levi glanced around. It had been a while since he'd been in Art's house. He noticed Taki's subtle touches taking hold. A watercolor here, a photograph there. Although she'd spent most of the summer in the field studying mountain goat populations, she was definitely going to winter here. It looked like whatever they had was beginning to work. Levi secretly wished them luck. He was no expert with relationships, but he knew that luck didn't hurt.

An hour-and-a-half later, Art and Levi loaded up the drift boat and drove to a put-in above Hamilton, dropping a bike at Tucker's Crossing on the way. After the float, Art would ride the bike back to the truck and trailer, then come pick up Levi and the boat.

The day was perfect, and a few late season warblers fed on the odd caddis and mayflies that seemed startled to be alive. They talked in depth about what had happened, caught some trout, and enjoyed lunch on a slough so clear they watched caddis wandering around the substrate, and giant uncatchable brown trout pick them off the rocks. Levi thought suddenly of the Goat Canyon spring, and the three women, particularly Cali, but again he didn't mention it to Art. He doubted he'd ever see them again.

.

Fifteen

A FEW DAYS AFTER the fishing trip Levi heard back from Nikos Papas, an archeologist with the museum in Sparta.

> *Dear Levi Brunner. Thank you for your inquiry. Unfortunately, I do not know of the temple you mention, nor much about the wolf cult that followed Lycaon, but I know several people who might. You mentioned that you may be visiting the Peloponnese. I suggest you come to Sparta for a few days so we can meet. I find your interest in this research intriguing. Greece is a beguiling country and culture, and I am confident you will find what you are looking for, or something equally valuable.*
>
> *I do hope you can come and visit. I look forward to meeting you.*
>
> *Nikos Papas*
> *Professor of Archaeological Studies*
> *Archaeological Museum of Sparta*

Part Two

Sixteen

Levi read about Sparta on the plane over from Rome. Located on the Peloponnese, the southernmost peninsula of Greece, Sparta had originally been a powerful city-state known specifically for its military training, which was incorporated into education and the general social fabric. In a nutshell, they bred soldiers. It was also regarded as the Greek state that gave women the highest status and the most rights, including the right to soldier.

Contemporary Sparta was in the same location as the Sparta of antiquity, in a valley surrounded by towering mountains. The Sparta of antiquity had been destroyed by war and conquest over thousands of years, and the new Sparta was a modern town that one guide book called "rather boring." It was a hub of olive and citrus production and processing. He'd checked the weather before he'd left and was ready for rain and temperatures in the low sixties. Warmer than what he'd encountered in France and Rome, and downright tropical compared to the weather in Hamilton, Montana, which was hovering around ten below.

As the plane circled for landing, Levi glanced out the window over the woman sitting next to him. The landscape glowed green in pale haze, and numerous buildings with red tile roofs stared skyward. Clouds clogged the valley and restricted views of Mount Taygetus, and to east, Mount Parnon. He saw what looked like a large stone amphitheater as the plane banked, and then they were braking and bumping to a stop.

Levi was surprised that the young man at the Avis rental car desk spoke English. Quite well. The book of tourist Greek words and phrases remained unopened. Rain fell steadily as Levi walked across the parking lot to his rented Toyota. It cost him an additional thirteen Euros a day for a GPS, but he felt it was worth it.

The Menelaion Hotel occupied a four-story neoclassical building on the corner of two streets with names, unpronounceable to Levi, near the city's center. There was parking on Vrasidou Street, and Levi locked the car and walked half a block to the hotel to check in. The streets were broad and clean and open. The main street, Palaiologou, on which the hotel was located, was divided by a thin garden hosting palms and other tropical plants. It was raining lightly now, and the air felt dense and fresh. The streets were bustling with multicolored umbrellas, and Levi noticed numerous restaurants and shops. As he walked, the scent of grilling meat triggered fierce hunger. After he checked in, quelling it would be his first priority.

The hotel lobby was spacious, with a terrazzo floor featuring circular tile designs and a collection of potted palms in huge terra cotta pots. The handsome middle-aged man at the check-in desk was extremely accommodating. He spoke excellent English and gave Levi a map of the city and a guide to local activities.

Levi's room was white accented with a rich, almost fruity brown, and spacious. Windows looked out over Palaiologou, where umbrellas wove through the rain. He studied a bas-relief of an ancient Greek hunting scene above his bed. A woman with a long bow aimed at a giant stag, while a pack of dogs surrounded it. He'd been doing some research and thought the woman to be Artemis.

After a wonderful meal in a comfortable taverna—grilled lamb, saffron rice and salad—Levi walked back to the hotel. The rain came in fits and starts, but the evening was mild, and by the time he approached the hotel it had turned to mist, giving the street lamps yellow coronas. Levi suddenly felt very far from home. He passed a man and woman walking together arm in arm to the sound of easy laughter, and he felt the sting of loneliness. But he thought then not of Taki, which still happened now and then, but of Cali.

A different man, much younger, was staffing the desk, and he called out to Levi as he crossed the lobby.

"Mr. Brunner?"

Levi stopped and turned. "Yes, that's me."

"You have a message." He handed Levi a folded piece of paper, which Levi read standing at the desk.

I'm glad you've arrived safely. Come by the Museum around 8:30 tomorrow morning, and I'll give you a tour. Then we'll meet a friend who may be able to assist you with your search.

It was signed Nikos Papas.

"How far is the Archeological Museum?" he asked the desk clerk.

"Not far. Maybe two blocks. It's on Lykourgou. That way." He pointed.

"Thanks. Good night."

"Kali nychta."

Levi turned on the TV when he got to his room and lay down to watch, waking hours later to a soccer match. He was on top of the bed, still dressed, and couldn't even remember his head hitting the pillow. The conferences, meetings, and travel had suddenly caught up to him. In addition, he'd been fighting a cold that was finally fading. He stripped and slid under the sheet and cobalt duvet. Within seconds he was deep asleep.

He woke early, and lay in bed rehashing the past week. Two days in Paris, one in Lyon, and two more in Rome. He'd met some old friends and some new soldiers in the trenches, but because of the cold, he'd ducked most of the social events.

Wilderness advocacy, which was a critical component of wolf reintroduction, was the major theme of the Paris conference, and several representatives from the Wilderness Society and Wilderness Watch discussed what the U.S. had achieved, and what they were losing. A French wolf biologist talked about a recovery plan they were attempting to get through parliament, to supplement the forty plus or minus wolves that called that country home.

Several of the top wolf researchers, including Levi, had been invited to Lyon for meetings with French legislators. The meetings went well, and the politicians seemed sympathetic. French people generally had positive opinions of wolves, as long as they remained in the mountains and stayed away from agriculture.

From Lyon, Levi had traveled to Rome, where the conference was dominated by researchers from Italy, Mongolia, China, Canada, and the U.S. The keynote speaker was Luigi Boitani, an Italian biologist and co-author, with L. David Mech, of the book *Wolves: Behavior, Ecology and Conservation*. An excellent speaker and global thinker, he truly expanded Levi's perspective, which was often Montana-centric, or U.S.-centric at best. Wolves were becoming, although somewhat haltingly, a global issue.

In addition to the papers on behavior, genetics, communication, and food and hunting, the theme of preservation was a major one. There were 400 to 500 wolves in Italy, and they largely had protected status, though regionally administered. Models from other nations were discussed. The problematic relationship between wolves and livestock was discussed in depth, with the most popular model being either eradication or relocation of problem wolves, and reimbursement to farmers and ranchers. Wolf biologists were not the same as many of the popular wolf lovers Levi had met. These people didn't approve of killing problem wolves, which to Levi demonstrated a lack of judgment. Problem wolves, like problem bears, needed to be removed or put down. Wolf preservation and reintroduction was a life-long project, and there was no easy fix or final solution. Anti-wolf and anti-wilderness sentiments were always beneath the surface, waiting for the right political milieu to rear their ugly, vindictive heads.

Levi showered, then caught breakfast at the restaurant, Zeys, attached to the hotel. After a heaping bowl of yoghurt, honey, and fruit, and some thick, bitter coffee with heavy cream, Levi was prepared to meet the day, and more importantly professor Nikos Papas.

The day had opened its envelope with bright sunlight, and had a crisp, damp, spring-like feel to it. The museum was a wide, one-story umber building with Corinthian columns. The walkway to the front door led through a garden, and headless statues, like surreal greeters, lined the path. A guard was just opening its doors when Levi arrived, and Levi asked him where he could find Nikos. It was obvious the only words he understood were Nikos Papas, but he smiled and pointed down a hallway that led off to the left. Levi thanked him.

"Efcharistó." He hoped that was correct, as he'd cracked the phrase book this morning, and hopefully remembered a few basics. The guard responded with something unintelligible and smiled, bobbing his head.

Levi glanced into galleries full of statues, columns, and display cases as he walked across the lobby and entered the high-ceilinged and ghostly quiet hallway. His footsteps echoed off the white walls. He passed several closed doors with small brass nameplates. The fourth office was open, and morning sun streamed through large windows. A man sat at a large desk covered with pamphlets, piles of paper, books, a computer, and two small ficus plants. The man was dapper, extremely well dressed, with a neatly-trimmed moustache and beard. He looked up as Levi entered and smiled widely. His English was heavily accented, but exact.

"Mr. Levi Brunner. I've been looking forward to this pleasure." He stood up and extended a hand. His grip was firm.

"Hello, Professor Papas. I hope I haven't caused you too much trouble."

"Not at all. You make my job more, how do you say it, interesting?"

Levi chuckled.

"Would you have time for a short tour of the museum? We are meeting Aristos Karnezis at 9:30, and it is not far. Aristos is an interesting man. An archeologist, a philosopher, a linguist, and a specialist in arcane Greek religions and beliefs. You will like him."

"Great! If we have time, I'd love a tour."

The museum was arranged around a central hall and featured seven rooms in all. Much of the architectural ruins, sculpture, tools, and weapons displayed were from the area, and were representative of the Neolithic to the Roman era. One hall was dedicated primarily to Artemis, which immediately piqued Levi's interest.

"What is the relationship of Artemis to wolves?" he asked Nikos.

"Artemis is often pictured with dogs or a wolf. She was the goddess of hunting, and so honors other great hunting animals, such as the wolf. It is said that her mother Leto could assume the shape of a wolf at will."

"Interesting. I have a relief above my bed at the hotel with a woman hunting a deer with a bow and arrow. Is that Artemis?"

"Yes. She is the goddess of the hunt."

"I'd like to learn more about her."

"She is an intriguing goddess. There are many good books. Unfortunately, many of them are in Greek, and I don't know if they are translated. I will find out. I will recommend a few."

After the tour they walked several blocks to a small taverna. The mountains were in full view this morning, and Nikos pointed out several peaks. Levi was surprised at their height and power. Living in Montana, he'd become somewhat of a snob regarding mountains, and he didn't associate craggy peaks with Greece.

"Did wolves once live here, on the Peloponnese?"

"Of course. Many did. Some still do."

The taverna Psara's was ripe with the scent of rich coffee, citrus, and honey pastries. A large man, swarthy, with an eruption of salt-and-pepper chest hair, was sitting at a table by the street-facing window reading a paper. He stood up and waved his cap as they entered.

"Ah! Aristos. I hope you haven't been waiting long," Nikos said loudly. The two men hugged.

"Not long, not long. And this must be your guest from America, Mister Brunner. It is an honor. I am Aristos Karnezis." He stretched out his hand, and they shook.

"And Nikos! It's been a while. I have something for you at the house, so you'll have to stop by. A find from Mani. And Niki is dying to try out her new moussaka recipe on a guest, so let me know what works for you." He talked with a laugh in his voice.

"I will. Thank you."

Levi and Nikos sat down at the small table, and within seconds a plump, pleasant-faced woman sporting a babushka came with coffee and cups and cream.

"Ah, Cybil. Thank you so much," Nikos said warmly. "You are lovelier every day. You will make some man a fine wife."

She laughed. "What makes you think I like men, Nikos?" She flounced away.

Aristos turned to Levi.

"So, you are interested in Lycaon?" His eyes twinkled as if he were amused, yet his voice was sober.

"Well, I'm interested in wolves, so possibly. I read that Lycaon was turned into a wolf by Zeus. And I have heard there was a cult that followed and worshipped him."

"One of Lycaon's sons, with Lycaon's blessing, tried to feed Zeus the meat of a child! Imagine! He's lucky Zeus didn't tear him into tiny pieces and feed him to the fishes." Aristos had a deep, rich laugh.

"I heard that Lycaon was killed by Zeus."

It depends on the version of the myth. And you know, too, that many of these mythological characters are immortal."

"Immortal?"

"Of course." Smiling widely. "It's Greece, land of magic and enchantment. But that's another matter. Do you know of *Eléftheros Erimia*? They are a nonprofit pro-wilderness group here in town. And also, they have an office in Athens."

The name rang a bell. Levi remembered a woman on a panel at the Italian conference discussing European wilderness preservation. She had maybe been from that group. "I'm not sure."

"We'll go there in bit and pick up a colleague and friend. But tell me how I can help you."

"I had a dream. I was on a beach, here in Greece. I'm sure of that now, because of the scent. The air smelled similar to what I smell here. Above the beach there was a temple built into the hillside. There must have been a fire inside, because the light was erratic, dancing and flickering as if caused by flames. There were white steps leading from the beach up to the temple. This was written on the stone piece on top of the columns. It was one of the things I remembered exactly, as if it were etched in my mind." He handed Aristos a sheet of paper with the word Λυκάων written on it.

"It was on the pediment," Nikos said as Aristos took the paper and studied it briefly.

"That was a remarkable dream you had, Mr. Brunner."

"I'm beginning to realize that," Levi said.

"This word, Λυκάων, is the name of Lycaon in Greek. What you saw in your dream was a temple dedicated to him."

"Do you know of it?"

"I don't, but the woman we are going to see, Sachi Karavia, told me she does. I will tell you, however, that it is probably destroyed by now. I don't know if Nikos told you, but we have suffered many, many wars here in the Peloponnese. This town for example, Sparta, was almost totally destroyed many times. What you see around you is largely less than 100 years old."

"Do you know if such a cult, one that worships Lycaon, is still extant?"

"Sachi might know. She has a, how do you say it, fascination with wolves." He shrugged. "For wolves? Her organization is critically involved in trying to protect wild areas in Greece. They are scientists, but Sachi is, how you say it, also a mystic. I'm not sure she would describe herself that way, but take it from me she is." Aristos took a large bite of an almond pastry, wiping crumbs from his lips.

"Lycaon did have a number of followers at one time, hence the temple that you dreamt of. There were other temples as well, but they are all destroyed. We are a country of conquest and destruction."

Cybil came by with a refill of coffee and more pastries, which Levi ate heartily, relishing the honey and walnut filling. The coffee was strong, and Levi was getting buzzed. Aristos seemed the chatty one, and he and Nikos talked briefly of local politics.

"Getting back to Lycaon, you know about Lycanthropy?" Aristos asked.

"Werewolves. I know a bit. I've never really explored the phenomenon."

"Lycaon was turned into a wolf by Zeus, and Zeus' lover Leto reputedly assumed the shape of a wolf when she wished. These were perhaps the earliest werewolves."

"Perhaps. The idea of shape-shifting is also prevalent with many native American tribes," Levi said.

"Shape-shifting? What is that?" Nikos interrupted.

"The ability of certain humans, often shamans, to turn themselves into animals."

"Shaman. Like a god?"

"More like someone who can communicate with gods. A priest or intermediary."

"Ahh, I see. Go on."

"In many ancient indigenous American cultures, shamans had the ability to change into animals at will. They often had a power animal, and wolves were one of them. A prevalent one."

"So perhaps the Greeks did not invent the werewolf." Aristos pursed his lips. "But also the god Pan and Artemis, the goddess of the hunt, were associated with wolves and wild places. And then there are the nymphs and naiads, which also have an affinity for wilderness. We are fortunate to live amongst the mountains, and we have a few wolves on the Peloponnese. I myself have heard them howling at night while on archeological digs. They create an eerie music."

"Yes, it is eerie and beautiful," Nikos said. "I have only heard recordings, but they are powerful."

"Yes, beautiful and powerful." Aristos drained his coffee. "Come, my new friend. It is time for us to go. I told Sachi we would drop by around 10:30."

They stood up, and Nikos and Aristos hugged, a long affectionate hug.

"I'll settle up the bill. You two get along. And Mr. Brunner, please let me know if I can be of any other help. I will send you some recommended book titles on Artemis."

"You've been so kind. Thank you."

They shook hands warmly. He was getting the impression that Greeks were friendly, passionate people. He felt very comfortable here.

After leaving Nikos and the restaurant behind, Aristos drove through the city to the outskirts, narrating as proficiently as a tour guide. They drove by several ruins, Aristos noting one that was under reconstruction.

"That's our ancient theater, built in year thirty before the Christ. It's very important historically, one of the oldest in Greece, and we haven't destroyed it totally." His laughter here took on a more sardonic tone. "There's money for reconstruction now, though not much, so the archeologists are busy. Let me tell you, Mr. Brunner, if you want to live in Greece, there are three careers you should consider – a bureaucrat, a waiter, or an archeologist."

The green grass and vegetation around the site, and the snow-capped peaks in the distance, made Levi think of the Bitterroot Valley in spring. Several turns brought them to a plateau overlooking the city.

Seventeen

Aristos pulled up next to a flat, one-story white building with a red tile roof. The parking lot was still damp.

"Here we are. *Eléftheros Erimia.*"

They entered the building with Aristos leading the charge, walking up to the receptionist's desk and charming the rotund woman with rapid-fire Greek, causing her to laugh heartily. Still laughing, she picked up the phone.

A few minutes later a tall woman with a narrow face, full lips, and intense expression walked into the lobby. Levi recognized her instantly as a woman from a conference panel in Rome who'd spoken passionately about the need for wilderness.

"Wilderness is a reservoir," she had said, "of what we were, and what we are, and what we can become. If we lose it, when we lose it, we lose ourselves."

Above all, Levi had remembered that sentence. He'd even written it verbatim in his notes. He had tried to meet her after the presentation, but the panelists were mobbed, and he ducked out with a friend from Spain to have a drink.

Sachi wore Asics, worn black jeans, and a gray rain parka. A jade Vuitton purse was slung haphazardly over her shoulder. She gave the impression of moving even while standing still, which it seemed she rarely did. When she broke into a smile, Levi realized how extremely lovely she was, though she wore no makeup or lipstick, and had gathered her wavy black hair into an erratic bun. She exchanged words in Greek with Aristos, then turned to Levi, greeting him.

"Chaírete." She extended a hand. "I am Sachi Karavia."

"Very pleased to meet you. I'm Levi Brunner."

She held his hand a bit longer than necessary, staring into his eyes. Then she broke contact. "We can talk on the way, in the car, as I have a busy day and it is two hours to where we are going. Near Methoni in the south. You are looking for a temple, no?"

"Yes. Aristos told you?"

"Neh. Yes. There is only one possibility." She said a few words to the receptionist, who nodded. "Pame. Let's go."

With Aristos driving, they left town, merging quickly onto a four-lane highway, which gently slalomed higher and higher into the mountains. Soon pines crowded the slopes, and yellow flowers covered the understory.

"Arnica," Sachi said, pointing. "The old women still come here to harvest it. They make medicine, for the stomach and salve for sore joints. It is very effective."

The day became bright, almost brilliant. Sachi spoke in a rushed manner, pausing dramatically, then rushing on. Levi was captivated with her energy.

"I don't know what Aristos has told you, so I'll probably repeat some of it. I work for *Eléftheros Erimia*. I was one of the founders. We are an organization dedicated to preserving as much wild land as possible here in Greece, and we work with many European counterparts. I am a biologist, an ecologist."

"I saw you at the conference in Rome. *Natura Selvaggia*. I attended your panel."

"Ah! *Natura Selvaggia*. You were there!?"

"Yes. I tried to talk with you after the panel, but there were too many people."

"It *is* a small world." She laughed like quick water. "So, we do this work and it is, it seems, sometimes hopeless. Maybe mostly hopeless. So many money against us. Development. Business and politics. You know much about Greek politics?"

Levi shook his head, and Aristos quipped, "It is not unlike all politics. It starts out idealistic, then falls to pragmatism, and then to the life-denying greed that crushes our spirit." He gave a cold laugh.

Sachi nodded, then continued, "Anyway, I am a scientist, but I am very interested in the primitive ways. You are interested in the wolves, no?"

"I work as a biologist in Montana, Alaska, some in Canada. I have my own nonprofit. WolfRecovery."

"You study their behavior?"

"Yes, and population, group dynamics, communication. I'm pretty broad-based. The bottom line is preservation of wolves and preservation of wildlands. We have much antagonism against wolves in the States. Much of it generated by agriculture. Ranching in particular. And there is a religious bias as well."

"I know of that as well, here. But I think here many people are willing to live with wolves, and let them live, if they don't get in the way. If they stay in the mountains."

"It's a very common reaction."

She turned and looked out the window at the rocky abrasions, the clots of pine. "They are out there. Right now. Not many, but they are there."

Aristos said something in Greek.

Sachi turned back to Levi, who was in back, facing him over the seat. "This temple you saw. You have heard of Lycaon? The followers of Lycaon? There is a temple you saw, in a dream, a vision? This is very powerful. This indicates a connection to ancient powers. I am a scientist, but I believe there is much more. Much we do not know."

Levi smiled. "As a friend told me, I probably saw a photograph in a book somewhere, and incorporated it into a dream."

"No! That is impossible. This temple was largely destroyed hundreds of years ago. There are no photographs. Not even any drawings that I am aware."

"I must have seen a drawing or painting somewhere. I couldn't have made it up from thin air."

"What book would this have come out of?"

"I don't know."

She stared at him intently, her mahogany eyes seeming to flash emerald in the sunlight. "There is no book like this. You did not see this in a book. You will understand when we get there. We are going near Methoni, as I said. You will see. You have been there before."

After an hour or so they exited the freeway. The highway was narrow and serpentine, but Aristos was an excellent driver. Levi enjoyed the sights as well as conversing with Sachi, who seemed to relax with the rhythms of the road, but never lost her edge.

Levi learned from Sachi that the cult of Lycaon had once numbered over a thousand. Followers believed they could become wolves. They howled to communicate with wolves, and there were claims that wolves would join in their meetings and rituals. During the rituals, participants, thinking they were now wolves, would rend apart small animals such as lambs and kid goats with their nails and teeth, and eat the flesh raw, often while the unfortunate animal was still alive.

"Wow, that's gruesome."

"But not when a wolf does it, right?"

"But we have a sense of morality that a wolf doesn't possess."

"Perhaps wolves possess a higher morality." She was smiling, and Levi couldn't tell if she was teasing him. "The morality of nature."

"It's possible," replied Levi. "I know people who hunt, but they use guns, or bows. And they don't always need the meat."

"Well that's a difference, isn't it? Wolves use the means they have, and they do need the meat."

They were silent for a few minutes, gazing at clusters of old houses made of stone surrounded by a stone wall covered in ivy.

"Does the cult still exist?" asked Levi. The atmosphere in the car had changed.

"It does," Sachi said, "although it is very secretive. How would you feel if your neighbors turned into wolves at night, and tore your little poodle apart?"

"That sounds just like my neighbors." Aristos laughed, breaking the tension. "The way they carry on."

"You've heard of Lycanthropy?" Sachi asked.

"Werewolves." Levi nodded. "I never paid much attention to it. Too much of a scientist, I guess."

"Me as well," said Sachi, "yet I like to leave the door open. Shape-shifting occurs in many indigenous cultures worldwide. It seems a common element of transcendence. Of visiting the spirit world."

"Animals were our first gods," said Aristos, "or rather amalgamations of animals. Deer with alligator heads. Dragons. That sort of thing."

Forty minutes later they topped a ridge, and the sea spread before them, a cobalt expanse jagged with silver. Levi shivered. He'd never seen anything so beautiful. And he felt a remembrance, like a déjà vu, but different. A familiarity. And then the feeling dissipated.

They descended the road along rock walls and scattered stone houses into the small town of Methoni, entering the narrow, crooked streets. Aristos pulled up in front of a small taverna, its white paint faded. An equally faded blue sign read Aleria.

"I haven't been here in years," he said, "but if the grilled octopus is anything like it used to be, it's to die for."

"So is the fassolatha."

"What's that?" asked Levi.

"It's a white bean soup. Equally to die for. And less endangered than octopus."

"Touché," said Aristos. "But my tastes have always run to endangered things."

Sachi shrugged. "Then we will eat heartily."

"Then it looks like we will all die happily here," said Levi, and they shared a laugh.

"Not until we see what we came here for," said Sachi. "Not until then."

After a marvelous lunch, they drove up out of town and paralleled the sea for another twenty minutes. At an overlook, Aristos pulled onto the gravel parking area. They got out of the car. The sea shimmered out beyond them to where it joined the sky, and the sky flowed back above them. Several islands hovered like dark mist floating above the cobalt sea.

"This way," said Sachi, pointing to the far end of the pull-off. A faint trail began at the barricade and descended to the beach a hundred feet below. They started down.

Along the trail grew small shrubs and patches of daisy-like flowers, as well as lemons, limes, small hard oranges, and occasional cactus.

"That is a fragosyka," Sachi said, pointing. "A cactus pear. Very good to eat."

They passed through untended groves of olive trees with lush grass understory, breaking into a short, rocky escarpment. And then they were on a beach composed of walnut-sized black cobble, waves feathering it with brilliant white foam.

"This way," said Sachi, who'd taken off her shoes and was walking along the breakers.

"The men follow," said Aristos, smiling at Levi. "It is as it should be."

They walked for fifteen minutes in silence. Just up ahead the beach curved around several stone buttresses.

"It's just ahead," said Sachi.

As Levi rounded the corner, he momentarily lost his balance. He was back there, vividly remembering the sound of surf, the scent of citrus and mint.

"God!" he exclaimed.

Fifty yards ahead, he saw white marble steps leading up the hillside to a small plateau. But these steps were in ruin, broken apart by the years and whatever forces they'd brought with them. Sachi ran and stood on a piece of the bottom step, spreading her arms.

"Is this it?"

"Yes. Amazing!"

Levi saw where he'd lain against the rocks, where the three women, Arianna, Cali, and Kayla, had frolicked in the surf, where to his right the temple steps led upwards. The sound of wolves had come from above, where the highway now ran. But there was no doubt this was the place he'd been a short three months before, and God knows how many years back. The feeling receded but didn't fade entirely.

Levi and Aristos joined Sachi.

"Does this seem familiar?"

"Yes! This is exactly where the dream took place. But the time of the dream was long ago. The temple was intact. I remember the islands," he pointed, "and the gulls crying at dawn, and these scents are vivid. It was an incredibly realistic dream."

"It was not a dream, I don't think."

She began climbing the broken steps, and Levi followed.

"I'll wait down here," said Aristos. "My knees are not what they used to be. And we still have to climb back up to the car. You two have fun." Levi watched him sit heavily on a rock.

The climb was largely over jagged rock, as most of the steps were broken and tipped. They gained the temple after five minutes, and Levi looked around. The top was even more broken. Nothing stood higher than eight feet. There was only a pile of rubble, a jumble of shattered columns, walls, cornice, and roof tiles, interrupted by gorse and thorny shrubbery clawing through cracks. A fairly substantial arbutus grew in the midst of it. Tiny blue and yellow daisies clotted the wreckage, and above them the slope ascended to the highway. Levi could hear the waves crashing and threading beach rock below.

They watched a yellow butterfly flit, and nearly land on a chunk of marble where a lizard bobbed and distended its rusty throat. High above, an accipiter rode the updraft.

"It seems odd to think that hundreds of years ago people were trying to turn into wolves here."

"I believe in cyclic time, like the peasants," said Sachi.

"I don't know what that is."

"A nonlinear time. Events can repeat or interrupt according to laws outside our ken. Look!"

Sachi pointed to a sliver of marble with the fragment of the name, υκ, engraved on it. Levi tried to budge it but it was wedged beneath another, much larger chunk of granite.

"I wish I could take this with me, but I'll have to settle for photos."

"It's illegal to remove ruins, anyway."

"Of course."

Levi pulled out his phone and took a number of photographs, documenting not only the letters, but the ruins, and the view out over the ocean. And somewhat surreptitiously, he managed to capture

Sachi in one of them.

"Look." It was Levi's turn to point. Spray-painted on a flat slab of marble toward the rear of the ruins was λύκος ζωές.

"Wolves live, or wolf lives," said Sachi.

The black paint was fairly fresh, barely faded, even though there was no shade.

"A believer."

"A werewolf," Sachi said, smiling. She caught Levi's eyes in a rare moment of stillness and held them, her eyes sparking in the sun.

"More like kids partying," Levi said, pointing to the empty beer cans nearby.

Eighteen

When Aristos dropped Sachi off at her office it was nearly 4:30. She gave Levi one of her cards and told him it had been good to meet him.

Aristos had not wanted Levi to be lonely, and offered him dinner at his home. Levi accepted.

"But I should shower first, and change clothes."

"Nonsense. We don't care. We are not like that."

Levi met Aristos' lovely wife Medora and their teenage son Belen. It was a pleasant and informative evening. Medora had nothing prepared for dinner, so they decided to order out for pizza. They spent the next two hours discussing politics, Greco-American relations, and China, but mostly Greece's economy and future, of which there was little optimism from his hosts.

"All the brightest kids are leaving," said Medora. "Belen is already targeting schools in Germany and Britain."

"And maybe America, too," said Belen.

While riding the elevator to his hotel room, Levi took Sachi's card out of his pocket. Under her name, Sachi Karavia, she'd written with a black pen. *Call me. Important,* and left a phone number different from the one on the card. The writing was small and neat.

It was late, after 11:30, but Levi decided to risk it.

She answered after the third ring, sounding sleepy. "Chaírete."

"Hi. Did I wake you?"

"Oh." There was a pause. "Maybe."

"I called too late."

"No. It's OK. I need to talk with you. But not tonight. How much longer are you here?"

"A day or two or three. My flight is open-ended."

"How about a drink and some food tomorrow evening? I'll pick you up. Say eight?"

"OK. I'll be in the lobby at eight."

"See you then. Kali nychta."

The next day dawned misty and cool. After a quick breakfast, Levi drove up to explore Mystras, which Aristos had told him was a fantastic and well-preserved ancient city. Mystras lay at the feet of the Taygetos Mountains, a rugged range, with deep gorges carved by the forces of nature and time. Separated into the Lower, Middle, and Upper city, as well as Villehardouin's Castle, a castle built by the Franks in 1249, Mystras later served as the center of Byzantine power in southern Greece until the mid 1400s. Then it was captured by the Turks, and later by the Venetians, each of whom added their architectural styles to the city.

Levi was not a world traveler, and seldom played the tourist anywhere, but he was in awe here. Rock walls divided the town, and groves of cypress grew everywhere, mirroring in dark green the numerous citadels. The ruggedness of the crags and rock reminded Levi of some of the drier areas of the Bitterroot Valley, particularly in the Sapphire range. More than the numerous churches and frescoes, the ruins, and the silence interrupted only by the few tourists, here was a vast sense of time. Something that brushed against magic and infinity. He could almost hear the words in the wind that rushed down from the mountains. Perhaps it was true about time being cyclic, coming back, as Sachi said.

The rain cleared, and Levi spent the good part of the day wandering the ancient city and reading the accompanying materials and pamphlets. In early afternoon he ducked down to a small commissary and had a salad for lunch. There were several other groups of tourists, one large Chinese group that came, followed group leaders with flags, and piled into a waiting bus. But otherwise, the site was largely deserted. Levi enjoyed the solitude and the resonance of the cultures that had called Mystras their home.

It was also heartening to Levi that among the ruins, native plants asserted themselves, that without active preservation, this town would continue to crumble and be swallowed up by the earth from which it arose. There was something very powerful, yet humbling, about this to Levi.

Back at the hotel, as the time for dinner with Sachi approached, Levi found himself exchanging one shirt for another, and fussing with his three pairs of pants. He finally had to admit this woman was making him anxious. Anxious and excited.

Sachi pulled over to the curb outside the lobby at eight sharp, and Levi, who'd been standing waiting for a few minutes, walked over to her car, an aged green Audi, and got in.

"Chaírete," she said warmly, bending toward him and kissing his cheek.

"Hello. Chaírete. I'm glad we could do this."

"Me, too."

Sachi, who had been talkative from the second Levi had met her, was quiet as she drove. She didn't break her silence until she pulled into a parking lot. She pointed across the street at a sign that read *Yiayia's Kitchen*.

"My favorite place for an evening meal," she said.

As they walked across the street, she took Levi's arm, and he didn't resist. Entering the restaurant, Levi was overwhelmed with warm air heavy with the aromas of food. The brick walls, wooden tables, and subdued lighting gave the restaurant a natural coziness, and the boisterous crowd gave it life.

Although the restaurant was crowded, they were welcomed immediately. On the way to their table, Sachi stopped to take an old woman's hands, and they greeted each other affectionately. She introduced the woman to Levi as Yakira, the owner. He took her hand and said, "Hello," but the woman shook her head. He deduced she spoke no English.

"She's eighty-seven," Sachi said as they were seated, "and still works every night." They each ordered a glass of a white wine,

Assyrtiko, that Sachi recommended.

Clinking glasses, Sachi said, "Na pethani o charos."

"I've heard that before," said Levi, then remembering that Arianna had said it at their dinner up Goat Creek Canyon. "But I've forgotten what it means."

"Death to death. Eternal life," said Sachi. "It means death is not death, not annihilation, but a transition to something different."

"Could be," Levi said, smiling, "but you'll need to convince me."

Sachi just smiled.

The wine was fresh, dry, and intense.

"I hope they have wine this good in heaven."

Sachi laughed.

"It is good, no? This grape is grown in an extremely dry climate on Santorini. The roots reach down over seventy feet to water, but the grapes are small, and the flavor is very intense. It is one of my favorites."

Levi wanted to say, "Intense, like you," but held back. He didn't know her well enough yet, and he wasn't naturally a teaser. Instead he said, "Well I guess it's one of my favorites now, too." He turned the ordering over to Sachi. "You can be my culinary guide."

"I will choose a selection. You will not be disappointed."

Over appetizers, more wine, and eventually the meal of pea soup, unleavened bread, salad, and fish, they relaxed and shared their personal histories. Sachi had been born in the north, near Veroia, and had attended the Aristotle University of Thessaloniki, majoring in biology. She initially intended to study medicine, but became fascinated with ecology, and eventually attended the University of California at Berkeley, earning a doctorate in Environmental Policy and Management.

"That's why you speak English so well," Levi said.

"Hah. Not so good I think," she said, laughing.

She'd returned to Greece, working for several governmental agencies, and eventually getting into the nonprofit sector, then starting her own with two biologist friends.

"It's all soft money. We have to write all our own grants, so our salaries are on our own shoulders."

"That sounds familiar," Levi said ruefully.

After a desert of custard pastry, Sachi ordered them both raki, then leaned across the small table, candlelight dancing on her face.

"So tell me about the dream you had. When did you have it? How did you come to that beach? Tell me all of it."

Levi hesitated. Until now, he'd kept this story to himself. But somehow this felt safe, even necessary. He began telling her about the wolf pack he discovered in Goat Canyon. He told her about the amazing alpha female wolf, Mirr, the woman bowhunter he'd met, and finally about the three women camped by the spring. He described the minor bacchanal, drinking too much, and then falling asleep. It was then he dreamt of being dragged by Cali into the dark depths of the spring.

"So, so interesting," Sachi said.

He described waking several times, in his dream, while sitting on the beach. He told her of seeing the temple lit from within, as if a fire blazed there. He told her he'd seen the three women, naked, playing in the surf. And finally, he told her of hearing wolves above.

"There were many wolves here in those mountains. A long time ago. There still are a few, but not like then."

"When do you think that was? The time-frame of the dream?"

"Quite possibly over a thousand years ago. Maybe longer."

"Wow! That's incredible."

Sachi was silent.

"Well, what do you think?" Levi finally asked.

"Did you go back and talk to the women about what had happened?"

"I intended to return to their camp the next day, but I was too hung over. I went the following morning, and they were gone. More than that, there was no sign of them."

"Don't you think this strange?"

"Very. But a number of strange things happened on that trip."

"So, let me tell you what I think. And I felt this was the truth from the beginning." She signaled the waitress for another drink. "I am a scientist, but I am also a Greek woman. We are an ancient and very magical culture. I do not discard or discount the ancient ways."

"Such as shape-shifting?" Levi smiled.

"Neh."

"So given your context, how would you explain this?"

"Have you ever heard of the Pegaiai?"

"The what?" Levi shook his head. "No. What are they?"

"They are water nymphs. There are several distinct nymphs, but these are the nymphs associated with the springs. But not just any springs. The ancient Greeks believed that certain underground springs and rivers connect the entire world. More than that, they not only connect places, but times as well. I think these Pegaiai came through the spring to your canyon from a long time ago. And they took you back there that night."

"That's ridiculous!" Levi laughed. "How do you explain their knowledge of English? The American food and equipment they had? They, one of them anyway, even told me she grew up in Athens."

"I don't know. While not goddesses, water nymphs are very powerful, and very magical. They have some powers over space and time. They like to play with mortals, especially men. Did Cali seduce you?"

"No… I'm not sure."

"So you say no." Sachi laughed.

"I can't remember. I was really drunk."

"It is likely that she did." Sachi thought for a moment. "She may be pregnant."

"That's crazy!"

"Pegaiai often use human men to give them children."

"Wait a minute…"

Sachi smiled quickly. "I'm teasing."

The waitress came bearing two additional glasses, some bread, and a small pitcher of clear liquid.

"Ouzo," she said.

Levi drained his raki, which he thought tasted like old socks, and poured a glass of ouzo. "Sorry, but I hope this stuff is better than the last."

"You'll like this. It's anise. Licorice."

Levi took a sip and wrinkled his nose. "Not bad."

"You look silly when you do that." She laughed.

"Do what?"

Sachi wrinkled her nose.

"OK, suppose I believe you about these Pegaiai, and the springs, and the connectedness and time and all that. What spring did I emerge from that night? There aren't any springs down on that beach."

"There had to have been at the time you emerged, as you put it. It may have dried up, or it may be farther down the beach, near the ruins. You should go back and look."

Nineteen

Levi woke with the memory of Sachi's kiss outside the hotel. A feather kiss, here, then gone. He knew he hadn't imagined or dreamed that.

He ate breakfast, booked a flight for the following day, checked out of his hotel, and drove back to Methoni. He stopped in town and secured a small vacation villa for the night, then had a quick lunch and drove back to the overlook. Like last time, there were no other cars parked on the gravel pull-off. He stood for a minute and gazed out over the rusted metal railing. The sky was gray and indistinct, and the Ionian Sea gray as well. Whitecaps were being driven by the quickening wind. He could hear their roar as they hit the beach. It felt like rain.

Levi descended the trail to the beach. The tide was in, the beach nearly swallowed by the waves and surge. Several gulls wheeled and shrieked, and Levi felt violence in the air. As he stood staring out over the changed sea, there was a sudden swirl as a small shark struck a large, whitish fish. Blood gushed into the water. Several other sharks rushed to join the frenzy, churning the water, their brownish dorsal fins slicing the surface just beyond the breaking waves. Then they were gone, and the blood was erased by the waves. It was all so quick that Levi wondered if he'd imagined it.

Levi walked to the temple steps and once again climbed them. This time the sense of déjà vu was missing, and it seemed just a ruin. Rain started to spit and hit the rocks with force, and he zipped up his parka.

Levi made a careful search of the temple, expanding his search beyond the walls to twenty feet, but found no spring. The litter of broken bottles, beer cans, and used condoms marked this as a party spot for local teens.

Back down on the beach, he turned right and began walking farther. The hillside choked the beach, and he saw ahead a series of small cliffs that eventually eclipsed it. Reaching the bulkhead, he was at a loss as to what to do. There was certainly no spring here. He stood for a long moment, thinking about the dream, trying to jar memory loose, trigger something. He closed his eyes and returned to where he'd sat.

And then he had it. When he'd visited before, he'd mistaken the location of the rocks where he'd been sitting. He remembered now there had been a partial arch of dark rock just to the left. If the tide had been out, it could have been this far down.

He began walking back toward the temple, focusing carefully where the hillside met the beach. Then he saw, fifteen yards or so ahead, the arch that had been to his left as he sat. But he was suddenly confused. He closed his eyes again. The temple had been to his right, so this couldn't be correct. Puzzled, he thought back again, struggling to remember. The rain intensified, rattling on his parka. He pulled the hood up and tied it. Wind gusted then slacked, a rhythm without symmetry. Then he understood. There were two places he'd sat. He'd moved between them at some point in the dream.

He began walking toward the arch, studying the rock face, and finally saw it. Water poured from a thin rock channel, hitting the beach and disappearing into the stones. He walked over and stuck his hand into the flow. The water was warm, maybe eighty degrees. He looked up. The top of the cliff was only twenty feet up. The rock was porous, a limestone, and there were plenty of holds. He started climbing.

As Levi eased himself over the lip, he saw a near-perfect circle filled with water. The spring was bordered by cliffs and vegetation, a hanging garden of impatiens, which he vaguely remembered. The light was indistinct, but as he walked over to the edge, and looked out over the spring, the water plunged into darkness. And then something light blue caught his eye. Off to his left. He carefully picked his way through the broken rock and vegetation, and bent to pick it up. As he turned it over in his hands he was stunned. It was his headlamp.

Part Three

Twenty

MONTANA WAS IMMERSED IN harsh winter when Levi returned, a drastic shift from the mild weather and damp green of the Peloponnese. Back to short days and extreme cold. Regardless, it felt good to be home.

Levi spent the first week catching up on correspondence and paperwork. Two of his grant applications had been turned down, perhaps reflecting the political shift in Washington and Helena, and one, from the NFS, had been partially funded. Another was pending decision by the state. With a bit more data, he was hoping to apply for money to study the Goat Canyon pack, if they were still there. He'd need to wait several months to climb back in.

He texted Sachi, then called, then she called him. They danced through the airwaves, feeling around each other, defining, clarifying. They both agreed that for now their work was priority. Even so, Levi was elated to hear the lilt of her voice, and felt empty when it was gone.

In a few days he was heading to Glacier National Park to study wolves with Steve McCandless. They were part of a coalition involving Montana, British Columbia, Idaho, and Washington studying wolf migration across the United States-Canadian border. In an attempt to create an intensive and comprehensive snapshot, they would use helicopters, snowmobiles, and snowshoes to record population and pack movement within the northern part of the Park, particularly along the North Fork of the Flathead, where meadows and deer were prevalent.

There were four or five wolf packs inhabiting the Park, but

movement with packs north of the border was fluid, and largely flowed southward. Both Washington and Idaho had experienced significant southward migration of wolves from British Columbia, and in twenty years, over thirty packs had established themselves.

Before he left, Levi shared a meal with Art and Taki, went skiing with an old skiing buddy, Conner, and attended a party. Here he ran into Taylor Dikestay, whom he hadn't spoken with in a long while. Their friendship went back to the second grade, and the T-ball game where they first met. They'd hung out as kids, but drifted apart as Levi went to the university in Missoula and Taylor went into the service, then to police academy in Spokane.

Life placed them on very different paths. Taylor was now a deputy sheriff under Ed "Juicy" Jones, and one of the people who kept Levi informed on wildlife legal issues. Catching up with Taylor at a party, Levi could tell he'd changed. His funny, ebullient nature had cooled, and he wore a cynicism and arrogance Levi hadn't noticed before. It had to be a tough life, being a cop, constantly immersed in the underbelly of humanity.

Aside from modest socializing, Levi felt reclusive. More than usual. He didn't feel comfortable telling anyone, except Sachi, what had happened in Greece and before. They'd think he'd gone off the deep end. Rather his descriptions of recent travel focused on the conferences and visiting some ruins in Greece with a colleague. He mentioned Sachi to them, but described his meeting at *Eléftheros Erimia* as strictly business.

Levi found that he suddenly had a secret life he shared with no one but Sachi. And she had her own spin on what had happened.

The wolf survey in Glacier went well. He and Steve had known each other for years, and Steve always invited Levi's input on his child-rearing, which Levi secretly chuckled about. He'd never even thought about having kids. But Steve needed a sympathetic ear. Steve had three children, two now out of the house, and one a senior at Sentinel High School. For some reason, Steve had always felt insecure as a father, yet Levi knew him as a concerned, loving man, who if anything was overly tolerant of his children's wild antics.

They drove through light snow to Bigfork, the white flakes disappearing into the dark water of Flathead Lake. Grabbing lunch in Bigfork, they drove on to West Glacier. It was snowing heavily by the time they reached their basecamp cabin.

Only once during the next week did Levi try to feel Steve out about his experience up Goat Creek and Greece, and that was a mild foray into shape-shifting by Native Americans. Steve was a scientist at heart, which made him a consummate skeptic concerning anything religious or mystical, and the conversation didn't go far. But the memories of his recent experiences floated through Levi's consciousness like scraps of cloud.

.

Twenty One

LEVI WALKED THE ELEVEN blocks to Mandy's Café Saturday morning. It was a clear, clean dawn, sun just cresting the Sapphire Range to the east. He pushed open the stubborn glass door, glancing around at the sparse, scattered diners. Strange. He was used to a bustling crowd. He grabbed a *Ravalli Republic* from the newspaper rack and walked into the interior. He passed Carol, Mandy's reigning waitress, as she was hurrying back to the kitchen.

"Sit wherever. I'll be right over." Levi noticed she was limping slightly.

He was reading the front page of the *Republic*, an article about a rash of car break-ins at hiking trailheads, when she walked over.

"Hey, Levi. How you doing?" Her voice sounded rusty, exhausted.

"I'm good, Carol. How are you?"

"Tired. Sylvie's sick, and I was up half the night with her."

"Sorry to hear. Kids at your mom's?"

"Yeah. Thank God for moms."

"How's business been? Looks slow."

"Slow? Sluggish is the word. That damned new pancake house up the way has pulled the entire breakfast crowd in."

"The Pancake Haus? I saw they were open. Parking lot was jammed when I drove by the other morning."

"They've got a different special every morning."

"You guys have specials."

"Not like theirs. Can't compete with a national chain. This morning it's two eggs, sausage, toast, and hashbrowns for a buck."

She smiled and winked. "I've got a spy over there who texts me."

"Well, hell, I'm heading over there." Levi, laughing, started to get up.

"Don't you dare, buster. I'll shoot you and stuff your head. Hang it on the wall over there." She pointed to the far wall, and Levi followed her point. The wall, known as the trophy wall, belonged to Mandy's husband's kills. A black and brown bear, a mountain lion, trophy deer, two Boone and Crockett bull elk. Levi noticed two men secluded in the corner booth by the window. One of them was Taylor Dikestay. His back was to Levi, but Levi recognized him by his milk-brown cowboy hat ringed with a snakeskin band. Taylor probably slept in that damned hat.

"Hard to compete with the chains," Carol said. "They buy bulk. Huge quantities. Get enormous price breaks. We just can't compete."

"You guys have a faithful following." Levi knew Carol was a single mom with two kids whose husband had skipped the state and hadn't sent her a dime. She needed the job, and the tips.

"Yeah, but some of the clan aren't too faithful. What can I get you, Levi?"

"A safe haven for some coffee, a Danish, warmed please, and this newspaper." He tipped the coffee cup up, and she filled it.

"Some more cream, too." He showed her the empty pitcher.

"Be right back with the goods."

He glanced at the far booth again. The man sitting across from Taylor was poking a finger across the table at Taylor's chest. The man was tall, maybe six-three, broad shouldered, wearing a cowboy plaid with the sleeves rolled up. His long, black hair was slicked back with pomade, his face chiseled by the elements. Even from across the room Levi could see that his eyes flamed, but the flame was cold. He looked like some of the hardened vets Levi had met. Those who had taken a life, not just once, and knew it well.

Carol brought the warm Danish and more cream.

"Here ya go, Levi. Not the healthiest breakfast in the world. Sure I can't get you some eggs?"

"Nah. Think I'll head over to The Pancake Haus. Catch that special."

Carol swatted him in the shoulder with the back of her hand. "Don't you dare."

Levi held up his hands in mock surrender. "Just kidding. Say, do you know who that guy in the corner with Taylor is?"

"No. They came in separately, but I've seen them in here before, sitting in that same booth. I don't like the guy. He's rude and doesn't tip."

"Taylor tips well, though, doesn't he?" Levi smiled.

"Not as well as you, Levi."

Levi returned to his paper. There was a page two article by Monica Sands about a new development, going on the east side of the Valley. It was on a shelf of land once owned by the University of Chicago. In the twenties, the university, in a hare-brained scheme, had purchased several hundred acres on the east side of the Valley and divided it into retirement plots for their faculty. A large ditch, appropriately called the "Big Ditch," brought Bitterroot River water to the semi-arid land, allowing for irrigation.

The University had planted thousands of young apple trees trucked over from Washington State. The plan was to offer retiring faculty a place to live in a picturesque montane valley, where they could supplement their pensions with the sales of McIntosh apples. Even the notable architect Frank Lloyd Wright became involved, designing some of the dwellings. The entire pipe-dream went up in smoke within ten years, when apple maggots decimated the trees.

The land was then purchased by two large ranches, The Double Bar and Tweed's. Charlie Flynn, who owned the Double Bar, was getting up in years, and his two kids had moved East. Apparently a developer had offered him the right amount for the land, and he was selling off. Levi couldn't blame these ranchers. Their kids were moving out more and more frequently, bailing on the ranching life for the glitz of a city. And land was worth a small fortune down here. Levi thought It was a shame to see rural land become suburban lots stuffed with mini-mansions, but that was the trend.

Levi's thoughts were interrupted by a shout, and he saw Taylor stand up. The man facing Taylor was eclipsed momentarily, but as Taylor turned to leave, he came into view. The man sat frozen, his face contorted into what Levi could only describe as a snarl, while Taylor stormed by Levi without seeing him.

As the days and weeks passed, and with the gradual and often erratic transition into spring, Levi's thoughts turned more and more to Goat Canyon. He wanted to get up there as early as possible. He wondered if the wolves were still there, or if they had wandered north, or west into Idaho. But his thoughts also returned to the spring, to Cali and her friends, and to the mysterious bowhunter. He still had not fully accepted the supposition that he had "traveled" through a watery portal to a beach in Greece, but the headlamp he'd found worked hard to disable his own skepticism. His rational self, the scientist within him, was being rudely challenged, and that created a state of unease. He found he could focus better when he didn't think about any of it. When the memories drifted in, he forced himself to think of other things. And he was missing Sachi something fierce, but she was traveling, largely out of contact.

Out of the blue, Taki called him, inviting him to cross-country ski in the Metcalf Wildlife Refuge. Incredibly athletic, Taki had taken to cross-country like a duckling to water. She had even briefly formed a racing group, until a pulled hamstring put that on hold. Levi and Taki had skied constantly while a couple, and she'd loved it when Levi pointed out tracks in the snow and told her about the animals that made them.

The Metcalf Refuge, a 2800-acre riparian area just north of Stevensville, housed an enormously diverse habitat. Meadow, mixed forest, thick woods, ponds, streams, sloughs, and the Bitterroot River all collaged. One of its claims to fame was a stable population of yellow-bellied marmots, typically a mountain-dwelling rodent.

Taki picked up Levi in her red Subaru Outback, Levi strapping his skis into the roof rack next to hers.

"Just like old times, eh?" she offered.

"Almost," Levi said, thinking of those lazy mornings when he and Taki woke slowly, exploring each other's bodies for new crevices and pleasures, then piled in the car for explorations of a different sort.

"Almost," he said again. "Where's the old man?"

"Busy. He doesn't ski, anyway." Taki seemed a bit dismissive.

"He doesn't mind?"

"Not a bit."

"We had a good thing, didn't we, camper?" Levi said suddenly.

"Yeah we did, but…"

"But what?"

"I saw this quote the other day, from Dr. Seuss of all people. It said, 'Don't regret the fact it's over, celebrate that it ever happened.'"

She placed her hand in Levi's.

The day was cold and clear, minimal wind, and the temperature hovering around ten degrees. There were few cars in the parking lot. A network of ski tracks and groomed trails left from there.

"Look," Levi said, pointing up as they unstrapped their skis. "A Northern Harrier. Bet it's looking for brunch."

"A nice plump rabbit," Taki said.

They skied for a couple hours, Levi being Levi, pointing out various tracks—moose, deer, elk, and badger, as well as beaver slides near a slough. The highlight was a group of elk huddled in a stand of Ponderosa, expelling clouds of steamy breath into the frigid air. The elk didn't seem particularly perturbed by the skiers, and Levi and Taki kept a respectful distance.

They stopped for lunch in a covered shelter with a wood stove and healthy supply of kindling. Levi lit a fire, and Taki unpacked the goodies: elk sausage, Valley hard bread, white cheddar cheese, last fall's Macintosh apples, and a bar of dark chocolate. Levi took a pot and began to heat water for tea.

They ate with small talk for a while, then Taki asked if she could talk to Levi about something "heavy."

"Of course." He poured hot water into two heavy plastic cups. Taki was silent while he watched steam rise from the tea.

"I'm going to leave Art." Her words were laced with sadness and finality.

"Whoa! You're kidding, right?"

"No, I'm not."

Levi stared at her, shaking his head side-to-side. "Have you told him?"

"Not yet. I'm planning to tell him soon. Kind of waiting for the right time."

"There might not be one."

"I know."

"Why?"

She didn't answer.

"Well. This is a surprise, Taki. I thought you'd finally found what you were looking for."

"I'm going to hate this, Levi, and hate myself for it. Art is the sweetest guy in the world. He loves me so much. He'd do almost anything for me."

"But..."

"But I don't love him." She looked off across the meadow. "I probably never did."

The sky was crystalline, and the mountains cut through it with serrated rock.

"After us, I was looking for something stable. I mean, Art's a fishing guide. Not exactly your nine-to-five office drone. But he's got a good gig. Steady clients. He sells a ton of flies. He's starting to build custom fly rods." Taki was starting to cry. "This is going to be so hard."

"Hey." Levi took her hand in his. "What will you do?"

"I'm moving back to Hawaii." She brushed at her tears. "I suppose that's running away, but there's another reason. My mom is sick. She was diagnosed with cancer last month. Colon cancer. She may not last long, and I want to be with her."

Levi had met Taki's mother on several occasions, an extremely warm and generous woman with a stately home up Manoa Valley. "I'm sorry to hear this. She's a terrific person. There's a lot of her in you."

Taki seemed lost in thought.

"Maybe you and Art could take a break. You could leave it open as to how your relationship will resolve itself."

"No. I've decided. I just need to tell him. And I know it's going to break his heart."

Levi hugged her hard, and she held onto him.

"Art's strong. He'll recover."

"I know." She broke away from Levi, and shook out her hair. "I hate this. I hate causing anyone pain."

They drank tea in silence for a while, then Taki asked, "How about you? How are you doing?"

"Wow. That's actually a big question, Taki." And he proceeded to tell her about Sachi.

"Are you lovers?"

"She kissed me once."

"But you love her, don't you? I can tell."

Levi hesitated. The crystal air seemed to vibrate.

"I think maybe I do."

"Oh, Levi, you are just a big romantic, aren't you? I'm so happy for you." And she hugged him hard.

Twenty Two

ONE DAY IN LATE February, Levi received a large manila envelope in the mail, plastered with Greek stamps. It was a collection of materials on Lycaon worship from Sachi. She enclosed a short note explaining that she had contacted several friends, and had been able to gather some materials together. She hoped they would help him expand his research. Unfortunately, she wrote, much of this was in Greek, and she didn't have time to translate it. Perhaps he could find someone who could. The note ended with a warning to be careful.

> *Don't get too close to this. I'd worry. I miss you.*
> *Se agapó, S.*

The envelope contained copies made from books, journals, magazines, newspapers, several blogs and Internet sites, and a number of drawings, paintings, and photographs. Several of the articles were in English. One in particular, from *The Journal of Ancient Culture and Antiquities,* was very insightful, and gave an overview of Lycaon and the cult that had arisen after his death. It described rituals where followers would work themselves into a frenzy while wearing masks and wolf skins, howl and dance erratically, then tear animals apart with their hands, teeth, and knives, feasting on the raw meat, often before the animal was dead. There were rumors of human sacrifices as well. The cult had a following in the 1200s of over 2,000 initiates, but had largely died out by the 1700s. There was no remnant of it today. However, one of the websites, even though it was in Greek, contained a photograph of a woman wearing a wolf skin eating a raw, recently killed lamb, blood staining her lips and mouth. This was one very weird world he had briefly entered.

But with other projects consuming much of his time, and thoughts of getting back up Goat Creek frequently occupying his mind, Levi now felt this werewolf stuff was a distraction. Every time he tried to process the women and his dream of the temple on the beach, he became tangled in self-doubt.

He wrote Sachi an email thanking her, placed the envelope and its contents on a shelf in his study, then returned to his real work, which at this time was co-authoring a report on wolf migration from British Columbia into the U.S., incorporating the data he and Steve had accumulated in Glacier.

Over a rare beer one night, Taylor Dikestay told him about a new anti-wolf group that had formed, bankrolled by Ted Leeson, and headed up by Mike Callahan. Juicy had tasked Taylor with keeping an eye on them. So far, they were meeting in the library basement, and Taylor thought the whole thing was a lot of hot air. Still, they were actively recruiting other ranchers, and Juicy saw it as potentially incendiary.

"Hey, do you know the Leesons?" Taylor asked out of the blue.

"We don't exactly travel in the same circles." Levi took a sip of amber.

"Too bad. I met his wife Brittany. She is *such* a fox. Tightest little butt you ever saw."

"Haven't seen her, but she's got you outclassed by a mile, dude."

"That's what she thinks," said Taylor. "We'll see."

Twenty three

IT WAS LATE APRIL before Levi returned to Goat Creek Canyon.

The entrance cliffs faced northwest, and a warmer than usual April had melted the snow off them. They were a bit wet and soft, but climbable. In a déjà vu moment, Art again dropped Levi off with his gear outside Leeson's fence, telling him to "be careful" and giving him a bear hug. He hung on too long, and Levi could feel his enormous sadness at Taki's departure.

Leeson's carved metal name caught the early morning sun, and Levi watched the dust stirred up by Art's truck. It invoked the poignant memory of climbing in last fall, and everything that had followed. Levi skirted the fence, climbing up the lower scree alone, the way he preferred it.

The cliffs were dotted with sedum, balsamroot, paintbrush, and lupine, and the rock warmed as he climbed. The air was fresh and sharp with the scent of thaw. Off to his right a red-tailed hawk rode the updraft, its razor-sharp eyes scanning the fields below for prey. Opening to this canyon, Levi began to leave the Valley and his doubts and hassles behind.

Levi felt more comfortable this time, using the same route in as he had before, and enjoying the act of climbing, emptying his mind of everything else. The chess moves of where to place hands and feet, how to balance and isolate, took over his consciousness, until there was nothing but the body and its dance with rock and sky. Until there was only climbing.

Ahead of him, a billy mountain goat materialized like a ghost on a rocky promontory. Almost the same location where he'd seen another male, or this one, the first time in. The canyon and creek had gotten their name from the large herds of goats that used to congregate there, gathering at several natural salt licks up-canyon.

Topping out, he walked to a plate-rock, sat, ate some mixed nuts, and studied the ranch below. Sheep dotted the lush green pasture. Many of them had newly born lambs sticking close. Golden eagles took advantage of this time of year with the bounty of calves and lambs, but Levi didn't spot any. He wondered if the wolves were still here, and thought they might be interested in the lambs as well, though he hoped not. Ranchers were not yet legally allowed to kill wolves, although there was legislation waiting to pass that would change this. Ranchers had to contact the state, which would send out a government hunter. But many ranchers took matters into their own hands. They hated the government as much or more than wolves.

The territorial aspect of the pack in Goat Creek, if they were still here, would make an interesting study since it was a relatively small canyon, and wolves typically established very large territories, often over a hundred miles across. However, there were also studies of packs occupying much smaller areas if the geography was restrictive and game plentiful. The Isle Royale work that Mech had done was groundbreaking in this respect. Levi loved the fieldwork and research, and the fact that he might add something meaningful to the growing body of knowledge.

He planned to spend between four and six days in the canyon. Anticipating snow, he had a pair of ultralight snowshoes strapped to his pack, and they quickly turned out to be necessary. Descending into the canyon above Leeson's property, Levi immediately encountered snow. Walking out on it, he broke through the crust and had to resort to snowshoes. They were so small and light it wasn't much different from walking. He remembered doing a winter wildlife study in the Swan Valley twenty-some years earlier, when snowshoes were large wooden teardrops, forcing one to walk bowlegged. He and two team members had put in an average of twelve miles a day in them. He remembered being so tired one night, he fell asleep at the dinner table with his face in a plate of spaghetti.

Levi camped near where he had the first time. He felt more alive than when he'd begun climbing, senses sharper, more feral, like he was a creature returning home. The meadow was snowed in, but there were several relatively flat spots above it where the snow had melted off. Levi chose one of these, setting up his tent to face the snowy meadow, gathering rocks for a fire ring and wood for a fire. It was late afternoon by the time he'd gotten everything settled. The air was chilled from the snow and would get colder. It was still light, and would remain so until after eight, the Montana days lengthening until by July it was light until 11:00.

He took a quick exploratory trip across the meadow to the creek, crossed it on a giant snowy cottonwood log, then traversed the north meadow to where the scree and cliffs cut it. He was looking for tracks, and there were many of them. One was a heavily traveled trail of elk tracks blazed earlier in the winter, but still active. The elk had compacted the snow like a snowmobile track. Several moose had wandered through recently, breaking the crust and bulling their way through. He also spotted snowshoe hare, bobcat, mountain lion, coyote, numerous mice, and the ermines that hunted them. But he saw no wolf tracks.

Levi planned to travel up-canyon as far as the spring. Hopefully the pack was holding out farther up. He wondered if there would be any sign of the women. The Pegaiai, as Sachi called them. And he laughed out loud. How crazy was all of that. Some vertigo, a dream, and a few words, that was all it was.

The still air carried a cluster of song from a flock of siskins across the meadow. Levi gazed up the wooded cliffs, tipping his head back until he was filled with sky. And suddenly he felt the infinite, as if anything were possible. Could this truly be a sacred, magical valley? Was it possible the wolves were here for a reason beyond his ken? He wondered if Leeson ever came up here, if he had any idea what this valley offered, what it was.

For dinner, Levi enjoyed a packet of freeze-dried beef stroganoff, his only apple, and a cup of Earl Grey tea. He lit a fire using dry grass and sticks gathered in a grove of aspen. The grass caught fast, and flames climbed the tinder.

He watched the fire dance as light bleached the sky white, then faded to gray. Several stars showed themselves. Levi realized he was anxious. He was waiting for the perfect time to howl. He was afraid nothing would answer him, and nervous they would. And then he could wait no longer. He tipped his head back and something let loose within him, a fear and loneliness so deep, he'd buried it to never see light. It felt like reaching across centuries and thousands of miles. He came back into himself in time to hear the long, plaintive howl echo across the canyon, reverberating off the frigid rock walls, dying out until there was only silence, the darkening canyon, and the vast, vast sky. And into that Levi had thrown whatever he had within him.

And then after the long silence, a wolf howled, answering him. It was a long wail that attenuated, and seemed to embody the silence that came after the echoes died. He was immediately thrilled, confident it was Mirr. The hairs on Levi's neck stood up, and enormous gratitude flooded him. Tears poured from his eyes. "Thank you," he said to the night, the wolf. "Thank you."

Twenty four

Over the next three days Levi traveled up-canyon and set up camp near where his second camp had been. Here the snow was pervasive, but even so there were bare rocky areas, and balsamroot and lupine bloomed in profusion just inches from snow banks. Levi opted for the meadow's edge and pitched his tent on snow, clearing some rocks for shelves, digging snow from a rock face for a fire. The weather was a mixture of clouds and sun, and the second afternoon there was a sudden snow squall that was extinguished by intense sun after fifteen minutes.

Everything was thawing, and the melting snow dripped sun-blazed diamonds from the trees. Juncos, chickadees, siskins, and a few warblers were active, harvesting seeds from dead thistle and lupine.

Levi found wolf tracks about a mile above his first camp. They were most prominent on the south side of the creek, the same side he was camped on. The side with the most sun. He stumbled upon several kills, including a recent moose calf. Blood was sprayed on the snow like a Pollock painting, smeared by a frenzy of footprints.

On the third day out, he found the den.

He was high above the valley floor, scoping the scree and rock faces with his camera telephoto, when he saw movement: a pup wrestling another pup on a bare rocky hillock. Studying the area more intently, he spotted a dark hole, the den mouth. And then an amazing sight, as if two wolf pups wrestling was not amazing enough. The alpha female Mirr emerged from the den carrying another pup in her mouth. This one she placed with the other two, who instantly began grappling clumsily. Mirr disappeared into the den and reemerged three more times, each with a pup. There were now six of them wandering and stumbling, little balls of fluff on the hillock, biting flowers and rocks and snow and their siblings with the same enthusiasm. Their eyes were not open far enough to qualify for sight, and Mirr constantly herded them to keep them somewhat contained.

Levi was ecstatic. He spent hours watching the wolves and cubs interact, snapping photos, and scribbling notes about their behavior. He counted a total of six adult wolves in addition to the six cubs. The interactions between cubs and adults were particularly interesting. All the adult wolves contributed to parenting. The model was much more of a kibbutz than a nuclear family. One of the researchers in Rome had spoken at depth about what he called the "open family" concept of wolf parenting. Rather than learn and be influenced by only one or two adults, the cubs benefited from the knowledge of the pack.

Levi was thrilled that the wolves had stayed in the canyon. Whether they would when the cubs were larger remained to be seen. They wouldn't leave for a few months anyway. He howled every night, and was answered intermittently by various pack members.

On the fourth day, Levi got an early start, and after his breakfast of trail mix and customary cup of tea, he headed out for the spring. This was the hottest day yet. Almost sixty when he left, and soon the crust warmed and began breaking under the snowshoes, making the going extremely tough. He finally opted for traversing the northern side-wall in favor of better snow. He made the spring a little after noon.

Tracks revealed the spring was used by a number of animals for water, but Levi saw no wolf tracks.

He walked down to the shore where the sandbar was buried in snow. The water was clear, and Levi watched some amphipods swimming with their peculiar galloping motion. Suddenly a young cutthroat trout flashed in and struck one, swallowed it, then disappeared into the deeper water. Levi followed the cutthroat with his eyes, and then beyond to where the water turned black. He was suddenly dizzy.

He tried to bring that night back to memory. He could faintly hear the women's voices, their laughter, and he again felt the pressure and terror of diving into the spring, but the memories had faded and were frayed. The dark center of the pool was only fifty feet from him, and to believe it was a portal to another space and time seemed ridiculous. There had to be another explanation. With the snow covering the land, there was only stillness here. Peace. The sun blazed, and clumps of snow fell from the fir to the ground. There was only this, only nature.

Levi turned to his right and cut up-canyon. That was when he saw the wolf tracks, recent and quite large. An alpha wolf, he guessed. He followed the tracks away from the spring, through a copse of trees and into a small clearing. They had come from down the canyon, the direction of the denning pack.

He turned back and followed the tracks past where he'd cut them. Several yards later, it was clear they were heading to the spring. They wound around several willows and approached the shore near the cliff face. Levi followed them to the water's edge and stopped dead. A few feet from the water, the wolf tracks turned into the imprints of human feet. These tracks led directly into the water and disappeared.

Then, in what Levi later decided was a hallucination, he saw the large wolf emerge from the woods, walk toward the water, and turn into a naked woman. It was the bowhunter. And then as he watched the gossamer scene, she walked into the water and swam for the center, diving and disappearing. He shook his head, hard, to clear it. Then he walked over to where she had walked. There were no tracks. He shook his head again, feeling disoriented. He crouched for a few minutes, pulling the crisp air into his lungs and releasing it slowly. After a few minutes he felt clearer. Then he stood, walked over to the wolf/human tracks, and took several photographs.

Twenty five

Levi had no logical explanation for what he'd seen by the spring. He sat back at his camp, scribbling into a blue notebook he'd started after his first foray into Goat Canyon—pages of observations and conjectures relating to the supernatural aspects of this particular wolf study. The body of evidence was growing, but Levi wasn't sure where it was leading, or if he wanted to follow it. If he did, he would lose his sense of self. He knew that now more than ever. Yet he had experienced things with his previously reliable senses that challenged his scientific worldview.

Levi wrapped up his study and climbed out of the canyon six days after entering. The weather had turned ragged, and he ended up bivouacking in a shallow cave. When a fleeting clearing arrived, he climbed out, emerging just as the rain started drumming again.

Once home, he lit a large fire in the woodstove, grabbed a beer, and took some elk steaks out of the freezer to thaw. Then he gathered his data together and wrote up his trip, adding it to the narrative he'd constructed entitled the "Goat Canyon Pack." Aside from Sachi, the only people he'd told about the pack were Steve McCandless, Art, and Taki. Existing in such a confined area had its obvious benefits, but it also meant the wolves were highly susceptible to being hunted.

He covered the two thawed steaks with olive oil, seasoned salt, and pepper, and threw them onto the grill, returning to the kitchen to whip up a salad out of wilted lettuce.

Sitting at the oak table, eating steaks and salad and sipping his second beer, Levi thought about the Goat Canyon pack and their relationship with the spring, the bow-hunter, and the women, the Pegaiai. The connections between the wolves, the canyon, Greece, and Lycaon continually connected and broke apart in his mind. He felt there was a major piece missing.

Levi had dinner the next evening with Dee Lopez and Bill Crow of SHARE. Dee and her husband Boll owned the Bar MB Ranch up Skalkaho Creek, and she hosted. There were three other SHARE ranchers present, including Todd Johnson from the Swan Valley. They were working on a module for third and fourth graders that painted wolves in a realistic light, and wanted Levi's input.

"If we can un-demonize wolves for these kids, maybe they'll grow up with different attitudes," Bill told Levi as they were walking up the flagstone path to the house.

Levi spent a couple hours analyzing and improving several modules about bears that the group was adapting to wolves. It was a challenge for Levi to get his head into a third grader's, but he was pleased with the result. The modules would feature, whenever possible, a visit from a real wolf. There were several around the state that were "humanized" and quite safe. Levi had been guest at an elementary school in Boise, Idaho, and a fellow had brought such a wolf into the classroom. The wolf, Toko, was an incredible hit.

He remembered one of the kids asking, "But don't they eat sheep?" to which the wolf's owner answered with the question, "Do you eat sheep?" The class had gotten a good laugh out of it, while the wolf looked around and yawned.

Dinner was on Dee and Boll's deck overlooking the Valley. The evening was a bit chilly, but clear and windless. It was a sumptuous meal of mutton, root veggies, and homemade huckleberry ice cream. They finished off with tumblers of scotch as the evening light purpled.

"Serve a meal like this to the kids, and you'll go a long ways at winning them over," Todd said, wiping some renegade ice cream from his cheek. "Minus the scotch, of course."

Twenty six

Levi awoke abruptly from a dream. In the dream he'd been lying on a strip of warm sand, his arm draped over a female wolf, embracing her. His cell phone was hammering out the intro to Beethoven's Ninth. He shook his head abruptly, glanced at the time, 6:10, and answered.

It was Taylor Dikestay.

"Levi. Hey, man, sorry to wake you. You should get down to the Bitterroot Brewery right away. Bring a camera."

"What's going on?"

"Just go, man! I'll meet you there."

Levi threw on some clothes and grabbed his camera. It wasn't like Taylor to be cryptic, and that put Levi on edge. Morning was creeping over the Sapphires, and the air was crisp. Levi jumped into his truck, roaring out onto Third Street, hitting a hard right at Main. He could see flashing lights a few blocks ahead. Three police cars spoked in front of the brewery, two with their lights flashing. The third had its door open, the interior light illuminating Taylor and another deputy, Danny Sullivan.

"Taylor, what's up?"

"Check this out."

He got out of the car, followed by Sullivan, and crossed the sidewalk over to the skinned lodgepole deck railings of the brewery. Three wolf carcasses were nailed to the top railing with six-inch spikes through their necks. A pup, and two others that Levi recognized immediately from the Goat Canyon pack. The young male sibling, Rill, and Mirr.

Levi had to brace himself on the rail. He'd seen all three of these wolves alive just weeks ago. He tried to catch his breath.

"You OK, man?" Taylor asked.

"Yeah. A bit of a shock."

"I know, right?" said Sullivan. "I mean, I hate wolves as much as the next guy, but this seems pretty radical."

Taylor ignored Sullivan's remark.

"You recognize them from any of your studies?"

Levi hesitated. It would be best to level with Taylor, but he held back. "No. No, I don't."

Sheriff "Juicy" Jones lumbered over. Juicy was a big man. Six-three and running between 280 and 300 pounds, depending on the season. His belly spilled over a large silver belt buckle of two elk locked in battle.

He nodded at Levi. "Wolfman," he said. Juicy spoke slowly, as if always weighing the effect of his words. "This is pretty cold-hearted, I'd say. Killing a cub, and nailing it and two other wolves to a railing in downtown Hamilton. Pretty harsh. What do you make of it?"

"Obviously a statement," answered Levi. He was aware his voice shook. "Has anyone reported livestock killings?"

"Haven't received any. But you know as well as I that most of these guys clean up their own shit. We haven't had a report of wolves killing livestock in over five years."

"And the pup." Sullivan spat into the dust. "No way that one killed anything, 'cept maybe a grasshopper." To Levi's mind, Sullivan was an outsider who tried too hard to be cool, to fit in. Levi hadn't dealt with him much, and hoped it stayed that way.

"If we knew where these wolves came from, maybe we'd have a lead on who killed them," Juicy said. "Sure you haven't seen them before, Levi?"

"Sorry. Wish I could help." He fought to contain his rage. The way Juicy was staring at him, he doubted he was doing that good a job of it.

"You are sure you've never seen these wolves, Levi? Think hard now. It's probably our only chance to figure out who did this."

"I told you no!" Levi barked. "But I'd like to find the bastards who did this."

"That's our game, Levi. You tell us what you know, and we'll do the dirty work."

Levi said nothing, just stared at the carcasses.

Juicy went on, "You know how folks view wolves down here. Most folks would like it just fine if they all disappeared." He scratched his nose. "I'll put some feelers out. These spikes could have been bought anywhere. They're as common as dirt. We'll dust the heads, though. Who knows?" He took out a handkerchief and pulled at the spike that held the cub. It didn't budge. Then he pulled some fur away from an obvious bullet wound.

"I'm guessing an ought-six or seven millimeter. Which are also as common as dirt." He turned the carcasses around, studying them. "Looks like the bullets all passed through, so there's no slugs."

"They've all been shot, not poisoned, so that tells us something," Sullivan said.

"Shooting seems more direct, more violent," said Levi. "Somebody ambushed a pack that was hanging out relaxing, playing with the cubs." Then he stopped. He was getting too close to admitting the truth. "They took out the adults first, maybe wounded another one or two. The cubs wouldn't know what was happening. Then they shot the cub." He coughed. "Maybe several cubs. We don't know how many they left behind."

"Damn! Wish we knew where they came from," Juicy said again.

"I bet Mike Callahan knows something about this," said Taylor.

"Hamilton's claim to fame. Dead wolves nailed to a downtown restaurant. This won't go quietly." Sullivan was shaking his head.

"It will if we get these down ASAP," Juicy said. "Work on getting these offa here, will you, Danny?" Then he turned to Levi. "You want the carcasses?"

"They'll be valuable for field analysis."

"Find out what they ate, and we might find out where they lived."

"Possible."

"Levi, you think of anything else, you let me know." It wasn't a question.

"Of course."

Juicy caught Levi by the arm. "Look, I know how much these animals mean to you, Levi, but keep this legal, you hear me? If you have leads, you come to me, understand." He squeezed Levi's arm for emphasis.

Levi flushed but said nothing.

"OK then, let's clean this up."

Headlights swept the corner, and a Toyota Prius pulled up sharply, door swinging open and a young woman with a camera bouncing out.

"Oh, shit," said Danny, "so much for keeping this under wraps."

"Monica." Juicy nodded at the woman who was raising a camera, snapping photos as if it were second nature, moving like a dancer to cover several angles. Monica Sands was the chief reporter for *The Ravalli Republic*. She'd moved out from New York six years ago for a "simpler life." Levi presumed she'd found what she was looking for, since she seemed content to stick around.

"Sheriff. What do we have here?"

"These are some dead wolves, Monica, but I'm sure you knew that."

She made a wry face. "Any idea who tacked them up?"

"Nope. Any idea who called you and told you they were here?" Juicy asked.

"Nope. Mind if I ask you a few questions?"

Juicy smiled. "My pleasure. Danny, get these down before the traffic starts."

"Yes, chief." He began working on the spikes with a crowbar.

Levi turned to Taylor, who looked haggard. "Want to get some coffee?"

"Fuck, yeah. I'll meet you at Mandy's in fifteen or so."

"Sheriff, I'll stop by and pick up these carcasses in a bit, OK?"

Juicy was talking to Monica, but cocked his head. "Don't make it long, Levi. We might get hungry and decide to fry 'em up."

Mandy's Café had just opened and was still fairly deserted. Levi sank into a corner table. He felt violated, as if someone had reached into his body and torn out his heart. He'd considered telling Juicy where the wolves came from, but he didn't want anyone up in that canyon. He didn't want anyone near what remained of that pack, or near the spring.

Taylor came in a few minutes later and sat down heavily. "Helluva start to Wednesday morning," he said, palming his face. His eyes were bloodshot, and he hadn't shaved in days.

"At least it's midway through the week."

"I guess."

Carol came by and poured coffee. "You boys want anything to eat?"

"Maybe in a bit," said Levi.

"Yeah, Carol. Bring me one of those Denver omelets, will you? And keep the coffee running."

"Certainly, Taylor, you look like you could use it. Coming right up."

"And some extra tomatoes, please."

"You got it." Carol headed off towards the kitchen, and Levi was glad to see she was no longer limping.

"So what do you make of this?" asked Taylor, picking up his coffee and blowing across it.

"It's obviously a message. Killing a cub. Nailing them up in a public place. I'd push Monica for who called her. That might be a lead."

"I thought of that." Taylor sipped his coffee. "But even if she knew, which she probably doesn't, she wouldn't say. Protection of sources, and all that journalism bullshit."

"Fuck," grunted Levi. His head and heart were roiling.

"Yeah, yeah."

"Wolf pelts are worth a hundred or two hundred dollars. That female is a prime specimen, probably worth closer to three hundred. Whoever put them there didn't care about the money. And I bet they tipped the *Republic* or Monica off to assure press coverage. Hell, everyone in the Valley will know about this by the end of the day. And there's not a lot of issues down here as polarizing."

"I know. Hang on." Taylor pulled out his cell and punched a number.

"Sheriff. Hey, it's me. Is Monica still there? Good. Ask her again who tipped her off. Press her on it." Taylor nodded at Levi, then waited, listening. After a minute or so he said, "OK, thanks."

"She said it was a man, probably older. Didn't recognize the voice, and he didn't give her a name." Taylor hesitated.

"What else?"

"He said to go down to the Bitterroot Brewery and take some photos, then put it in the paper. He said it would 'rile some people to action.'"

"Those are the words he used?"

"Yeah."

"It sounds like Mike Callahan."

"Shit, Levi, could be almost anyone down here. And furthermore, what they did, whoever they are, is at best a misdemeanor. If we go after Callahan on this, it will just make him a martyr." Taylor played with his fork. "I told you Callahan has a new group. They're meeting regularly. Leeson's involved, I know that. I heard he told Callahan he'd help out any way he could."

"Bastards. I'd like to nail their hides to a railing." Levi slammed his cup down, sloshing coffee onto the table.

"Don't do anything stupid now, Levi. This sucks, but it's only a misdemeanor, and only if the Pub wants to press charges. It ain't worth breaking any bones over."

"That's bullshit, Taylor. It's an incendiary act designed to incite violence. The violent act of violent people. There should be some law that covers that."

"I don't know. Unless it actually causes something violent to happen, it probably ain't covered by anything. But I'm no lawyer."

Levi finished his coffee and stood. "I'll swing by and pick up those carcasses."

"Look, Levi, I'm sorry this happened, but…"

"I don't know what I'll do, but it won't be stupid."

"Shit!" Taylor hissed, shaking his head as Levi walked out.

Levi had barely kept himself under control. He drove out of town, pushing his truck to over a hundred on the Eastside Highway. He felt his peripheral vision blurring, everything focusing into the tunnel he was barreling down. Killing the wolves was bad enough. Nailing them to a public place, especially one where Levi hung out, was punch in the face. But Mirr was not just any wolf. She was connected to the women at the spring, to the bowhunter. He knew it now with certainty. This was the beginning of something that was beyond any of their control. He braked suddenly, skidding the truck onto a gravel pull-off.

"Shit! Shit! Shit!" he screamed, hammering the steering wheel. Then he sat back, breathing hard. It had to be Leeson. And Callahan. They'd taken a snowmobile up, stalked the pack, and shot at least three of them with a rifle. Maybe there had been a lamb kill. Hard to know. And irrelevant to Levi. This was more than revenge, more than removing wolves that were harassing livestock. This was a statement of hatred. Of war. And it was personal.

He took several deep breaths. He needed to get back into the canyon as soon as possible and assess the situation. He looked up and saw red bleed across the sky. Anger coursed through him, but so did extreme fatigue. He'd fought so hard for wolves, but often it seemed utterly futile.

What was he going to do?

He had no idea.

That night he woke and ripped the covers off. He was sweating profusely. An image from a dream was vivid in his mind, and he felt its presence in the room.

He'd been running fast, head low to the ground. Moonlight sliced through the forest. There was no thought, just running. Fluid as water, he flowed around trees, leapt downfall, his breath white bursts in the frigid night air. He did not run alone. There were three wolves with him. One was a powerful female with the same eyes as the bowhunter, another an extraordinarily large male, pure black. This wolf seemed to disappear and reappear into the dark at will, a black ghost. The third wolf was Mirr. They ran with purpose.

And now sitting awake in the bed shivering as cold air hit him, he tried to recover that purpose, but couldn't. Something in the future, something momentous that was destined to occur. He guessed the enormous black wolf was Lycaon, eyes blazing icy-gold in the night. And Levi also knew he ran with them as a pack-mate, as a wolf. He had to tell himself over and over it was just a dream.

Twenty Seven

THE PAPER COPY OF *The Ravalli Republic* wasn't due out until Friday, but Monica's story hit their website by eleven a.m. And shortly after, the comments began storming in. Over seventy percent applauding the act in the "comments" section.

Levi drank bourbon for lunch, reading comment after comment, getting angrier and angrier. Callahan had posted a tirade that deemed it a "call to action," and stated the "person who did this is a hero." He called for an outright war on wolves. "Every last one of them dead and burned."

Levi wrote several responses, but deleted them all. He wasn't thinking clearly, and the bourbon wasn't helping. He finally crawled into bed with the bottle, and fell into a bitter sleep.

It was after six that evening when Levi awoke with a blistering headache. He swallowed a couple of Tylenol with a shot of bourbon, then turned on his computer and read the additional comments that had been added over the afternoon. There were a few voices of reason, a few urging for the extinction of livestock and a return of the land to native wildlife, but the majority were in favor of eradicating wolves. It left Levi as close to tears as he'd been since seeing Mirr's body nailed to the pub.

Closing the computer, he got up, walked into the kitchen, and retrieved a beer from the fridge, which he drank in two gulps. Then he cooked himself some egg-fried rice and kept the bourbon flowing. He couldn't sit still, however, pacing the house with a plate and glass. Suddenly, in the midst of his anxious wandering, his gaze fell on the manila envelope that Sachi had sent him. He walked over and retrieved it, bringing it into the kitchen and falling into a chair. He pulled the contents out and began sorting it.

He put everything that was in Greek in one pile. That left eleven pages, including the article in the *Journal of Ancient Culture and Antiquities*. He looked through the pages carefully. One of them caught his attention. It was a print-out of a website dedicated to Lycaon worship. The author called himself Dmitri, and lived in Athens. The site was bilingual, and Sachi had printed out the English for him.

He found the website, and without reading any further, clicked Dmitri's email link and sent him a brief message. When he thought about it later, he was both embarrassed and appalled. The message read:

Dear Dmitri, I am interested in learning how to turn into a wolf. Please contact me. Email or phone. 406-243-7216. Thanks,
Levi Brunner

Pouring himself another finger of whiskey, Levi turned on the TV. He wanted to see who else had picked the story up. Sure enough, the six o'clock news out of Missoula featured it as their top story. They rebroadcast the photos Monica took, and pulled liberally from her story. There was a short interview with her where she described the eerie early morning scene, and a few comments from Juicy, who basically said the incident was under investigation. When asked if anyone had filed a complaint against wolves lately, he replied "Not to me."

The anchor, Joan Armstrong, went on to discuss the reimbursements for killed livestock offered by Fish Wildlife and Parks, as well as by several pro-wolf organizations such as Defenders of Wildlife. She then spoke briefly with a Missoula County rancher, who said that most of the livestock kills went unreported because the paperwork for reimbursements was so odious. Another guest, Joseph Bull Ranger, a Native American wildlife agent, said that there were legal ways of dealing with problem wolves, and that this act was basically a hate crime.

By ten o'clock, MSNBC had waded into the water nationally,

with coverage of the Hamilton incident. The hosts spoke with several pro and anti-wolf people from Montana, Wyoming, and Idaho. The anchor, a woman named Eileen Chin, seemed genuinely shocked, and kept focusing in on the photo of the cub. "Who could do this?" was her last comment.

This looked to be just the tip of an emerging media iceberg.

Levi's cell rang, and the news editor from KECI in Missoula asked him if he'd agree to being interviewed for tomorrow's evening news. He agreed. They would send someone by his house in the morning. Immediately after he'd hung up, KPAX called with the same request. Again, he said yes.

The whiskey was wearing on him, and he was suddenly exhausted. There was nothing more to be done tonight. Tomorrow he'd do the interviews, then head up into Goat Canyon. He could hear wind snapping the tarp over the woodpile. It sounded angry as hell.

He tucked the bottle away and turned in. He had no idea how long he'd been asleep when his cell kicked in. He heard his own voice answer, hoarse and disembodied.

A man with a Greek accent said, "Hello." There was a pause and Levi heard some faint music. "You emailed me. Levi, right? You want to be a wolf?" There was only silence then. Neither the man nor Levi spoke. "What are you prepared to sacrifice for this power? Your humanity? Because that's what it would be." Again silence. "Think about it very carefully, and if you're still interested, call me at this number."

The phone went dead, and Levi listened intently to the silence. Dmitri's voice had sounded like autumn wind in a forest rasping through dead and dying leaves.

Twenty eight

A SMALL SLEET SQUALL blew in, and Levi had to postpone his trip into Goat Canyon for two days. During that time, he was interviewed by three TV stations and the NPR affiliate in Missoula. Levi emphasized the illegality of the wolf kill, and its divisiveness. He gave rational answers containing statistics with regard to livestock predation. He did not sugarcoat the fact that wolves did kill and eat livestock, but emphasized that there were legal approaches in place to pay restitution to anyone with legitimate claims. For the most part he kept his cool, but inside he was still seething. And his anger had no apparent outlet.

He talked with Sachi multiple times, once collapsing into trembling and tears. He could hear the concern in her voice.

"Stay strong," she told him. "You need to stay strong. For the wolves' sake." But there was one thing she said that he hung onto for dear life. "I need to come to you, Levi. Soon." His need for her now verged on desperation.

Callahan was on the move, orchestrating a town hall meeting in Hamilton, although this time he was not inviting any pro-wolf panelists. It was shaping up to be a pep rally for the anti-wolf forces. The local pizzeria, Bitterroot Pizza, was offering a $50 gift certificate to anyone who brought a wolf pelt to the meeting. Taylor told Levi that they'd be passing out bumper stickers that read, among other things, "Kill a Wolf, Save a Life," and "Kill a Wolf for Christ."

Levi thought a lot about the phone call from Dmitri, and re-examined his website. Dmitri claimed he was a follower of Lycaon. "There are over 500 of us in Greece alone," he stated.

To the question of "How does one become a werewolf?" Dmitri's website was cryptic. He did not deny the possibility of shape-shifting into a wolf, but emphasized the psychological experience. "People become wolves in their minds," he wrote. "They become werewolves, but are not always altered physically." And he described in graphic detail, including several photos, the killing of animals by werewolves, but he claimed it had religious, sacrificial intent. Dmitri also wrote about the war on wolves. He hinted that werewolves needed to "attack and destroy" the enemies of wolves.

That night Levi dreamt he was feeding on a yearling deer, tearing through its tough skin with his teeth, and feasting on the warm, succulent flesh underneath. The taste was remarkable, and Levi felt its life pulse through the meat of his own body as the animal shivered beneath him. Another wolf walked up, an alpha female. He recognized her eyes. The bowhunter. It felt like he'd known her over the course of many lifetimes, many centuries. He lifted his jaws from his feast and backed away. She moved to where he'd stood, biting into the deer's flesh, and as he watched her feed, he was filled with erotic tenderness.

Twenty nine

The trip up Goat Canyon substantiated Levi's suspicions. From the top of the cliffs, he spotted a snowmobile trail heading up canyon. He dropped down and joined it above Leeson's, following it back to a half mile below the den. He followed two sets of snowshoe tracks to a ridge overlooking the den site. It was apparent where two tripods had been set up, mounted with rifles, the hunters prone and cold-hearted, squeezing off deadly shots into the unwitting pack. There was no activity at the den site.

Levi side-hilled down and discovered mayhem. Snow riven by blood and tracks. At least one wolf had been wounded but escaped up-canyon dripping blood. The hunters made no attempt to follow it. There was no sign of the pups. Levi hypothesized that they'd escaped into the den, and were rescued later by the surviving wolves and relocated. There were numerous tracks in and out of the den that seemed to substantiate this.

Levi camped just above the den site. He howled that evening, but was answered only by one wolf, the alpha female he'd now associated with the bowhunter. He didn't seem to be able to control his hand as later, huddled in his tent with a headlamp, he wrote the name "Artemis" as the wolf's name in his field notebook.

Thirty

It had been almost a month since what Juicy was calling "Carcassgate" had occurred. Leeson and Callahan had pulled together their pep rally. Several ranchers had brought in wolf skins, which they'd piled outside the VFW Hall after the meeting and burned. Juicy had watched the whole thing but refused to get involved. The media storm had died down, and life in the Valley continued to open into summer. According to Taylor, Leeson and Callahan continued to meet with five or six other ranchers and plot the decimation of wolves, brown-skinned immigrants, and liberals. They were concentrating on several legislative bills aimed at giving ranchers permission to legally kill wolves harassing their livestock.

Levi's cell rang as he was scrambling four eggs in an iron skillet. The radio was tuned to KUFM in Missoula, and harpsichord music wove into morning sun. Levi had slept well the night before, for the first time in over a week. He was feeling optimistic.

"Hello?"

"Levi, Taylor. I need you to come and look at something."

"Not more wolf carcasses?"

"No. This is the most fucked-up thing I've ever seen."

"Shit. What is it?"

"Can you get out to Leeson's place in the next half hour?"

"Leeson's!? Yeah, sure. I'm just finishing up breakfast."

"You might want to skip breakfast," Taylor said and hung up.

Thirty minutes later Levi pulled up to Leeson's massive gate. The gate was open, and police and sheriff's cars, as well as TV and news vans, were parked haphazardly. Blinking red and blue lights from the cop cars scarred the morning.

Levi told a policeman securing the gate that he was expected by Taylor and Juicy. The cop barked into a walkie-talkie, fielded the static-laden reply, and waved Levi in. Levi wound down the driveway for a hundred yards and pulled into the roundabout in front of the copper-roofed house. Police lights reflected off the bark and rhodie landscaping, the stone walls. Cops stood in groups talking, car doors ajar. Yellow crime scene tape hung between two porch pillars, blocking the massive pine front door, which hung heavily open. Juicy spotted Levi.

"Wolfman," he said. There was no humor in his voice. "Put these on and follow me." Juicy handed Levi a pair of blue latex gloves and white booties.

"What the hell is going on, Juicy?"

"You'll see."

Levi followed Juicy through a vaulted hallway into the main living area. The room was in shambles. Couches were torn apart, lamps shattered, an iron coffee table tipped over. But it was the bodies that caused Levi to turn and his stomach almost revolt.

Leeson, and a woman Levi guessed was his wife Brittany, were literally torn apart. Their bodies and clothes were ripped into shreds. There was a gaping hole in the woman's abdomen, and her entrails had been dragged across the carpet. Her long chestnut hair was partially torn out and scattered in clumps. Arms and legs had been raked and near torn from bodies. There were bite marks on both faces, and much of Leeson's nose was missing. His wife was lying on the floor, and Leeson looked like he'd tried to run but had been pulled down over a lounge chair where he now sat, looking almost peaceful, his thinning sandy hair still neatly combed. Despite his absent nose, his glasses remained intact. His eyes looked like they were clogged with smoke, sightless.

"What happened here, Levi?"

"Jesus Christ, Juicy, you tell me!"

Taylor joined them. "Don't touch anything."

"They look like they were torn apart by animals," Levi said.

"Wolves," said Juicy. "They look like they were torn apart by wolves."

"Impossible," said Levi. "I've never heard nor seen anything like this done by wolves." But he was thinking of the wolf tracks that turned human and entered the spring. And he was thinking of what he'd been told about the Lycaon followers. He was thinking about war and revenge.

"What about these bites? Let's start there." Juicy bent over Leeson and pointed to a row of teeth marks on his arm. "Are these consistent with a wolf bite?"

"They're definitely a large canid. Too large for a coyote. And see," Levi pointed to a distinct bite on Leeson's forearm, "the bite is narrower than a Pit-bull or Rottweiler. I've seen photos of attacks by those breeds on children that somewhat resemble this. But if this were a dog, it would be a large shepherd, malamute, or wolf hybrid."

"Fuck that," Taylor said. "No way German Shepherds did this. This is fucking sick! I've got to get some air."

Juicy popped a piece of gum into his oversized mouth, and offered one to Levi, who declined.

"Get back in here when you're steady, Taylor. I need some ideas here."

Another cop, this one in a suit, joined Juicy and Levi. He stuck out his hand. "I hear you're the wolf expert. Norman Bleak, state police. Looks like these wolves have been killing more than sheep."

"This has to have been staged. A lot of these wounds could have been made by knives." Levi knew his words sounded false, hollow.

"What about this arm?" Norman pointed to Leeson's arm, dislocated from the shoulder socket and bent at a ridiculous angle. The flannel shirt he'd worn was in scraps. Flesh was flayed and raked from bones. The ulna was broken and protruded like a ragged white knife.

"This wasn't no knife. This took enormous force."

"Is there any evidence that wolves were here? Fur? Tracks?"

"There are some tracks."

"Let me see them," said Levi. He was suddenly enormously tired.

Juicy led him and Bleak to the hallway that led out to the rear deck. Caution tape sequestered off a rectangle of hallway.

"There," Juicy pointed at a bloody set of tracks. "Those wolves?"

"They sure look like it. They could be a wolf hybrid, but they're the right size and shape." Levi snapped a couple of photos. "Any others?"

"Just human. Tennis shoes. Leeson's, we think. They're about the right size, and nobody's got shoes on. We bagged them and will run them down to the lab." Levi stared at Leeson's mangled foot.

"And there's a couple boot prints, but no boots."

"Just in the room?"

"Yeah."

"So, what do we have here, Juicy?" Bleak asked. "Where are you going with this?"

Juicy turned to Levi. "So is it possible that wolves did this?"

Levi didn't answer immediately, then blurted, "It's highly unlikely, but possible. They would have had to be locked in the room. They could have been induced to attack out of fear." Levi swept the room, then gestured. "But there's no way to lock animals in this room. There are several egress points without doors."

Taylor re-entered the room. He was pale and looked more haggard than ever. Levi smelled cigarette smoke on him, and he knew Taylor had never smoked.

"It's possible," Levi said again, his shell breaking, his voice collapsing with the horror of it all. The image of the wolf track becoming a human track and entering the spring was haunting him. Was there a connection between a shape-shifting woman and Mirr? Was this revenge?

A man and woman in lab coats entered the room.

"Oh fucking God," the woman said, taking a deep breath. "I have never seen anything like this!"

"This is slaughter," the man, older by twenty years, said.

The woman began dusting for prints, while the man began examining the furniture.

Another deputy poked his head into the room and said, "No sign of forced entry, sheriff."

"Thanks," he said to the deputy. "Let's step outside," said Juicy, guiding Levi out of the room. He cut through the kitchen and out onto the back deck. Taylor and Bleak followed them.

Once they had all gathered on the rear deck, Juicy turned to Levi. "Here's the way this looks to me. We had three wolves killed by humans and hung on a railing in downtown Hamilton less than a month ago, and now we have two humans killed by wolves…"

"You don't know that for sure," Levi interrupted harshly.

"We also have two of the major anti-wolf people in the Valley as victims. I may be stretching here, but this seems like a possible case of revenge."

Levi made a sound somewhere between a cough and a sob. "I should have told you this before."

"What?"

"The wolves that were killed are part of a pack I am studying."

"Yeah, you should have fucking told me that before!" Juicy yelled. "Where were they from?"

Levi hesitated, then spoke, his voice wavering. "Here in this canyon. They came in last September from Idaho."

"Shit, Levi! Why the hell didn't you tell us? That would have…" Taylor didn't finish, just shook his head.

"I wanted to keep the presence of the pack secret."

"Secret, hell! Leeson and Callahan obviously knew about it," Taylor spat.

"Levi," Juicy said, "Levi. I've known you ever since you moved to the Valley, and although I've disagreed with some of your beliefs, I think you are a stand-up guy."

"And?"

"And this doesn't look good for you. You have motive here. It's likely that the victims killed three of your study pack. And there's never been any love lost between you and Leeson."

"That's ridiculous! How would I have done this? How would anyone do this? Just invite wolves into the room and let them commit carnage?"

"That's what we intend to find out. If I were you, Levi, I'd get myself a lawyer. I'm saying this for your own good, son."

When they re-entered the murder site, the man in the lab coat started in with their initial findings.

"The man, Mr. Leeson, had his throat ripped out along with his carotid artery. That's what killed him. The woman was disemboweled, and probably died of loss of blood and/or shock. We'll know more after an autopsy. All the other wounds, though some were intense, were superficial."

Juicy nodded thoughtfully, and Levi just shook his head.

"I want a count of bites, wounds that could have been made by teeth and claws, and anything else that could have been inflicted by a knife. We're not ruling anything out here. I also want all wolf or dog prints isolated and photographed. We need to get these positively identified." Juicy paused. "And I want to know everything else you find. Got it?"

"Done," said the man in the lab coat.

Thirty One

THE DOUBLE MURDER HIT the media by mid-afternoon, and the previous wolf carcass story re-emerged, forging a connection between the two events. Levi had to admit that it was too much of a coincidence. There was only one person he felt comfortable talking to about this: Sachi. He called her cell and left a message, one he hoped didn't sound too distorted. He felt entirely scrambled. He wasn't hungry, but heated some potatoes and carrots in the microwave. Sitting, reading news, he shoveled food he couldn't taste into his mouth.

Callahan was on a rampage, blaming pro-wolf "nutjob fanatics" for the murder of two of the Valley's most upstanding citizens. Every time Levi's phone rang, he leapt for it, but it was never Sachi, only requests for interviews, which he turned down. He was too freaked out to talk to the press. He had no confidence in what he'd say.

He tried to busy himself with paperwork, but his concentration continuously dissipated. He finally went outside, stripped down to his T-shirt, and chopped more wood than he'd burn over the next four months.

Levi was watching TV when the phone rang. This time it was Sachi. He couldn't believe how relieved and grateful he was to hear her voice.

He poured out the story in a torrent, and she wisely didn't interrupt. It felt like a confession, and by the time he finished, he was breathless.

"You're the only person I can talk to about this, Sachi. I feel like

I'm holding all these terrible secrets, and I'm not able to tell anyone."

"I'm so sorry, Levi. You need, how you say it, a confidant. There is no one else you can talk with?"

"Not really."

She didn't answer right away, and for a moment he was scared he'd frightened her.

"I will come."

"What!?"

"I have time off I never take. I will fly to Montana to be with you."

"No. You can't. You don't have to do that."

"If you want me to come, I will. Do you want me to?"

"I'm sorry. Of course I do! Jesus, yes."

Thirty Two

THERE WAS A LOUD pounding on the front door, and Levi was startled awake on the couch. Across the room, the TV was muted, and a blond woman at a news desk was talking silently.

"Coming," he yelled.

He got up slowly, yawned and walked over to the front door, pulling it open.

"Levi, I gotta talk with you." Taylor stood leaning unsteadily against the railing. He looked like a minor train-wreck.

"Taylor, you're soused. Come on in."

"Got anything to drink?"

Levi gave him an appraising glance. "Looks like you've had enough, man."

"Fuck man, I'm not asking for judgment, OK? Could I get some fucking whiskey?"

"Jesus, Taylor."

He shoved past Levi into the living room.

"Sit down. I'll bring you a glass." Levi retrieved a half-full bottle of Dickle and poured an inch. Then a little more. What the hell was going on? He walked back into the living room, where Taylor had collapsed on the couch, and handed him the glass. Taylor palmed it greedily and took a slug. Levi sat across from him.

"Why are you here, Taylor?"

Taylor was slurring his words, and Levi noticed his grip on the glass slipping. Just before it dropped, Taylor regained enough consciousness to lift it to his mouth and finish it. Then he let it drop, his head fell back onto the couch, and he began mumbling. Levi could only make out a word or two, but they made little sense. Then something about blood, and Taylor jerked upright, his eyes blazing.

"So much blood!" he screamed. "So much blood!"

"Taylor, what's going on? Why are you here?"

Taylor looked stunned, then began to get his bearings. A cruel smile grew on his face. "Why did you do it, Levi? Why did you kill them? Was it those dead wolves finally made you snap?"

"Taylor, you're talking nonsense."

The whiskey glass flew by Levi's head, narrowly missing it. Taylor stood unsteadily, looking like he was going to charge, then his will collapsed and he began sobbing.

Levi stood up. "You better go, Taylor. Now."

Taylor wiped his face with his cuff, then lurched towards the door.

"Shape-shifter, that's what you are. I read about those. Stay the fuck away from me!"

And then Taylor was gone, and Levi stood baffled as to what had just transpired.

Thirty three

THE NEXT MORNING LEVI walked over to the Hamilton Public Library to return some books he'd been hoarding. The sunlight dancing in the maple leaves, bright red and yellow flowers, and hostas neatly arranged in neighborhood gardens, all belied the fact that a dark force was at play. He was becoming more and more embroiled in it.

Levi dropped the books into the return slot, then studied the "New Arrivals" shelf, not seeing anything that interested him. He heard his name being called and turned.

Alice Gibbons, the circulation librarian, beckoned him over. "This just came in recently, and I thought of you. I know you like wolves, and research them and all. And this is kind of along those lines." She held out a book entitled *Werewolves: The Dark Cousins of Wolves*. The author was Jokob Stavlowsky. "It's pretty lurid," she said. "Kind of like that murder. The Leesons. Do you think werewolves could have done that?"

"I don't believe in werewolves, Alice. But thanks, I'll give it a look."

"Wait a minute, honey, and I'll check it out for you."

He brought the book home, tucked himself into the sofa, and began to flip pages. Some of the material was similar to what Sachi had sent him, and that on Dmitri's website. The night he emailed Dmitri seemed so far away, almost as if it occurred in another realm. He couldn't remember exactly what he'd told Dmitri in his hasty message. He'd been desperately drunk. And later, had he actually called him back and said yes, he wanted to be a wolf? Entered into some sort of weird pact? He'd been drinking far too much lately. Blacking out.

A knock on the door interrupted him. It was Monica Sands holding a digital recorder and a notebook. Monica always had a pert look about her. Pert and alert. Her light brown hair let the breeze tease it. Levi was instantly wary.

"Got a minute?"

"A minute. That's it."

"Are you involved in the investigation of the Leesons' murder?"

"Very peripherally. I offered some observations, but that's about it."

"What observations?"

"You know I'm not allowed to comment on an ongoing investigation."

"Do you think wolves killed the Leesons?"

"No."

"Why not?"

"Again, I don't want to comment on an ongoing investigation."

"Were you deputized?"

"No."

"Are you a suspect?"

"You'd have to ask Juicy."

"Anything else you want to add?"

"No. Is that all?"

She stared at him a long moment, then tucked her recorder into her bag.

"Call me if you think of anything."

"I will."

He shut the door, stood for a minute shaking his head, then went back to his reading.

Levi read how werewolves had been mentioned in the *Epic of Gilgamesh*, how werewolves there "became" wolves when humans put on wolf skins and masks. In Greek culture the origin came from the fable of Lycaon and his followers, where humans actually shape-shifted into wolves. However, werewolves, known by the Greeks as vrykolakas, were more broadly recognized. The Greeks traditionally believed that a person could become a vrykolakas after death due to a sacrilegious way of life, an excommunication, a burial in unconsecrated ground, or eating the meat of a sheep wounded by a wolf or a werewolf. Some believed that a werewolf itself could become a powerful vampire after being killed, and would retain the wolf-like fangs, hairy palms, and glowing eyes it formerly possessed.

In Europe during the Middle Ages, hundreds if not thousands of people were persecuted for being werewolves, an off-shoot of witch hunts fueled by Christian churches. Later on, the condition was considered to have psychological causation. Contemporary psychology rarely dealt with the topic, but considered it treatable. There were interviews with several men in mental hospitals, in the States and Europe, who claimed they were werewolves.

There were numerous photos and drawings, and they blurred as he flipped the pages, but one caught his eye. It was a scene of a murder in Poland by three self-described werewolves. Two bodies lay on the floor of a torn-up room. The bodies were severely injured, damaged, and superficially at least, the wounds bore an uncanny resemblance to those of the Leesons.

Levi got up, stretched, and walked into the kitchen to make another pot of tea. The weather had turned nasty, and rain blurred the kitchen window. Sachi would be arriving in Missoula in two days, and he hoped a freak storm wouldn't delay her. He felt her absence as a physical ache, one he needed to assuage. Her quick liquid voice, her smell, her kiss all haunted him. In his mind's eye he saw her standing, her lithe figure bent to the doorframe of her office. He wanted more of her than a voice on the phone, a trail of letters in an email. Much more.

He was walking back into his study with a cup of tea when he noticed that one door of the hutch braced against the hallway wall was slightly ajar. The hutch was filled with specimens from wolves—fur, bones, skulls, teeth, as well as some arrowheads, feathers, and other miscellany.

As Levi clicked the door shut, he noticed a disturbance to the dust under a wolf skull. It appeared the skull had been picked up, then set back in a slightly different place. He opened the door and lifted out the skull. It belonged to a mature male timber wolf from near Banff, British Columbia that had been hit by a car. As Levi turned the skull over, he noticed what looked like traces of dried blood lodged where two of the canine teeth entered the skull, and felt a chill seize him.

He carried the skull out into the light of the living room for a better view. It had been wiped clean with a rag, which had also removed the faint layer of dust that covered the other specimens in the hutch. Levi set the skull on a side-table and walked outside. He looked under the metal milk can for his spare key. It was there, but not exactly where he kept it, two o'clock to a pebble he'd placed there. Had Callahan broken in and taken the wolf skull. For the murder? Was the blood on the teeth Leeson's or his wife's?

If Callahan was trying to frame him, he'd have to do a better job. Levi took the skull. And then, as he stood holding the skull, a very different, very disturbing thought entered his mind. What if it hadn't been Callahan? What if it had been him? He'd been drinking heavily, forgetting hours of his life. And after the wolves hung on the rail, Mirr's death, he hated no one more than Callahan and Leeson. He shook his head to clear it. No matter, he thought, I've got to get rid of this blood. He ran a sink full of hot soapy water, immersed the skull in it, and left it there.

Later that night he awoke from a dream that refused to fade easily. He was standing in a high-ceilinged room, wall-papered with roses to the oak wainscoting. Bodies, most of them nude, torn and violated, lay strewn as if scattered by a giant hand. And gorging themselves were wolves, among them the woman bowhunter, Althea, her lips and cheeks dripping with blood. They looked up at him beseechingly, as if innocent of anything but their base instinctual desires, as if they were just sating a hunger. But Levi was acutely aware that he was not innocent, and had partaken of the feeding as well. The taste in his mouth was divine.

Thirty four

Levi parked and waited for Sachi in the baggage claim. She'd texted from Seattle that the flight was on time, that she was "excited—kiss, kiss, kiss" to see him. And he in turn was ecstatic, his heart racing.

And then, there she was, pensive, lovely, scanning the room, smiling as her eyes settled on him. She walked over and gave him a hug, then a kiss on the lips, a long one.

"Hi! It is so glad to see you!" She laughed, breaking their embrace.

"Yes! You are sight for my sore eyes." Levi also laughed.

"You have sore eyes?" She punched him playfully in the shoulder. "My eyes are sore. I barely slept."

"Long flight," Levi commented.

"I had so much work to do. I stopped in London for two days, then flew to Vancouver, then Seattle, then here."

"Ah, you should have said. I could've driven up to Vancouver."

"No, it's OK. I got a lot of work accomplished in the airports. I always work well in airports." She looked suddenly tired.

"We'll get something decent to eat after we get your bag."

"You have decent food here, in Montana?" she asked playfully. "You eat cows here, and potatoes, and what else?"

"We eat frogs. And bats. And if you're good, I'll introduce you to grasshoppers."

"I LOVE grasshoppers!" This kidder was a side of Sachi he hadn't seen before.

They walked together to baggage claim, their hands finding each other's. A few minutes later, she scooped up her blue bag from the conveyor belt.

"You travel so light." He almost added "for a woman."

"I travel a lot, so I'm good at it. I wash my clothes in the shower."

"You can do that at my house, too," he said, guiding her out of the baggage claim, "or you can use a washing machine. Your choice."

She linked her arm through his as they walked across the parking lot.

"Mountains, like the Peloponnese. So green. It's lovely here."

"This is a great time of year to visit. The hills dry out later in the summer, and there are often fires."

"Just like Greece."

Levi thought she looked happy. Tired, but happy, and that made him happy as well. It was like sunlight breaking through the clouds that had engulfed him for the past weeks. He had so much he needed to tell her, but was terrified as to where to begin.

Levi took them to The Shack for lunch.

"A famous Missoula meat and potato joint," he told her.

"I always eat the local favorites," she told him, dipping a French fry into a small blue bowl of mayonnaise stirred with Sriracha. "Yum." She licked some mayo off the corner of her mouth. "No grasshoppers?"

"Not yet. We save them for dessert."

They caught up. She was working on an ambitious report for the Department of Native Ecology that examined the complex ecological relationships between urban areas and wilderness. Sachi spoke of it passionately, gesticulating, as if conducting an invisible orchestra.

"Ever since Aristotle placed humanity on top of the natural hierarchy, we have been handed an excuse to use nature and her resources as we will. Christianity did no better, nor did most of the other major religions. Oh, they might preach kindness towards animals, or vegetarianism, but visit their cities. See how they treat nature.

"Capitalism has been a disaster, at least in its current

incarnations. Take what you want, carte blanche, and pay nothing. In fact, as happens in your country, get the tax-paying citizens to pay the costs."

Levi could see the advocate in her, her love of telling the stories she cared about. "We have what's called the Bureau of Land Management, which is federal land, owned by all of us, yet ranchers are allowed to graze and overgraze livestock with no consequence and minimal cost. And the Forest Service builds roads, paid for by taxes, so that timber companies can go in and log."

Sachi continued, "Or fisheries, or mines. The list goes on and on. So, there is an economic ecology at play as well. I am not a computer scientist, but we have the talent now to model extremely complex algorithms, that allow us to measure the exact costs of these abuses. In the long run, then, is wilderness more valuable as wilderness, or as exploited resources?"

"And the economics can now reflect money spent on outdoor pursuits, giving wilderness an actual economic worth. Gear, gas, travel funds, meals, hotels, and hobbies like photography, fishing," she added.

Sachi seemed to breathe, and eat, in the spaces between her words. "I don't necessarily like the commoditization of wilderness, but it is a necessary step politically. If we can say Zagoria, for example, brings in seventeen million Euros a year in outdoor recreationist money, that can provide a valid argument for keeping it wild."

Levi just watched her, nodding occasionally, drinking her in.

He took several detours on the way down to Hamilton, showing her a hidden waterfall, and a natural salt lick favored by mountain goats, where they were lucky to spot two female goats, her first.

During the drive, Levi's tongue loosened, and he told her some of what had happened since they'd last talked seriously. He left out the suspicion that he, under some spell or blackout, had committed the murders. And he left out the details of the Leeson murder. But he told her enough that it felt like a confession. As difficult as his depictions were, and horrific, he felt unburdened for the first time in months.

He pulled off the highway and drove west up a gravel road that led to Leeson's place. The crime scene was deserted, curtailed with yellow tape. The massive gate was shut. Sprinklers were shooting water over a rectangle of obscenely green lawn, the spray dissipating in late spring sunlight. The copper roof of Leeson's house burned in the sunlight. Levi cut the ignition.

"This is where it happened."

A crow lifted from the fence, cawing, and flew off.

After a moment of silence, Levi described the murder scene in detail, and the recurring image of the wolf tracks transforming into human tracks and entering the spring. He told her about his dreams, what he was learning about werewolves, about the traces of blood on his wolf skull. He told her he'd washed it off, as if to deny or remove a certain reality from existence. It was probably a foolish mistake, he told her, tampering with evidence, but the blood under the teeth told him that his skull had most likely been used in the Leeson massacre. And then he was finished, and again felt emptied, and that silence absorbed itself in the landscape.

"Jesus, Levi. You're scaring me."

They sat in the car for several minutes without speaking.

"So what do you think happened, Levi?"

"I've been thinking about this constantly, from every angle, and I can only think of two plausible scenarios. The first is that wolves actually did kill the Leesons for revenge. Not just any wolves, but those I saw in my dream. Mirr, the woman bow-hunter, and Lycaon."

"You were in that dream as well."

"I know." Levi sat without moving. A meadowlark sang out, the pastoral scene belying Levi's state.

Sachi interrupted the silence and asked what the second scenario was.

"The second possibility, and to me the more likely one, is that someone made it look like a wolf kill."

"I sense there is more to it than that."

"The second option is complex. It could be someone revenging the wolf killings, such as me for instance, as Juicy seems to think. It could be someone making it *look* like revenge for the wolves.

Someone who had something against Leeson, and possibly his wife, and was waiting for the right opportunity." He didn't mention Callahan by name.

"But you don't believe that, do you?"

"I don't know. And there is also the possibility that werewolves or shape-shifters committed the crime. Their motive would also be vengeance, I would think. As I've been reading, they often use wolf parts, legs with paws to leave prints, hair, wolf masks, skulls to simulate bites. That's the only way I can explain the fresh blood stains on the skull in my hallway case. Someone took it and used it in the crime."

They were silent, and despite the warmth of sun, and the beautiful, bucolic scene outside the truck, a chill passed over them. Sachi shivered as goose bumps rose on her naked arm resting on the console.

"You don't suspect me, do you?"

"God no, but what are you involved in?" And then, in a declaration of solidarity, "What are we involved in?"

And once again Levi was forced to admit that he had no idea. He started the car and pulled a U-turn, angling back to the highway, Goat Creek canyon and the Bitterroot Range receding behind them.

"I wish I could just drive away from it all," he finally said. "Turn a corner onto a new stretch of asphalt and enter another life."

And then Sachi laughed, a robust, beautiful and honest laugh, and covered Levi's hand with her own, thin, strong, and tan. "It will be OK. You will see. We will figure this out together."

Levi wanted to believe her, but there was still something he hadn't told her.

Thirty five

THAT EVENING, AFTER A meal of elk steaks, kale salad, and cabernet, they lay on the worn Gabbeh rug in the living room, sated, talking softly. Levi got up, turned down two lamps, and turned on the stereo, choosing a selection of Chopin Nocturnes. When he rejoined her, she was pulling her top over her head.

"I thought I'd get more comfortable," she said.

He leaned over and kissed her. He could taste the meal in her mouth, and he felt her response to the pressure of his lips and tongue.

Breaking off, he said, "I'll join you,"

They slowly undressed, exploring each other's bodies like visitors to a new land, lingering and quickening as they traveled each other. Levi smelled the ocean on her neck, her salt and lust as he moved lower. And then they joined, rising together to a place they both desperately wanted, a place of clarity and exploding sun.

Music floated from hidden speakers as they held each other after, neither wanting to release the other, to step back into the life they'd momentarily escaped.

"Come," Levi said softly, "I need to show you one more thing."

He got up and dressed, watching Sachi, who was shyer than he expected, do the same. In jeans and T-shirts they crossed the yard, over to a small garden plot, where behind a six-foot deer fence Levi had planted several varieties of lettuce, kale, chard, beans, peas, broccoli, tomatoes. The newly emergent vegetables were neat and prim in their exact rows, bursts of verdant green in the rich black river till.

Levi grabbed a shovel from where it rested against the fence, and walked between two rows of lettuce to an untended area of the garden. Several worn wooden boxes, containing a variety of pottery, rested side-by-side, weeds sprouting around them. He lifted them aside. Sachi could see the soil underneath had been disturbed. Levi drove the shovel into the earth and threw it to the side. After a few minutes, he bent over and pulled a black plastic garbage bag out of the hole. Sweat had beaded on his forehead, though it was cool.

Carrying the bag, Levi retraced his steps out of the garden, and dropped the bag on the backyard grass. "This is the only thing I haven't told you."

Sachi bent closer as he opened the bag. He pulled out the clothes one by one and laid them on the grass. A plaid flannel shirt, a plain gray sweater, a pair of black jeans, socks, a black T-shirt, and a cap reading "Bitterroot Anglers." A salty, intoxicating scent rose from them.

Sachi gasped. "Are these yours?"

"Yes. I found them in my bedroom the day after the murder, in this bag, in the corner by that lamp table."

"They're covered in blood."

"Leeson's."

"How do you know?"

"I just do."

"Did you do it?" This time it was a real question.

"I woke from a dream the night they were murdered. A violent dream. I don't remember the details, but it involved running with several wolves, possibly killing an animal or animals. I found the bag hidden behind a small table. I remember I woke with a terrible headache, and when I got up to get water I tripped, and the table tipped over."

"Did you do this horrible thing, Levi? I have to know."

"I don't think so. I hope not. That's the best I can do right now." He struggled to keep control, then lost it, sobbing. "I was so angry after those pelts were hung downtown. So angry. God, this is so fucked up."

Sachi hugged him, hard. He was shaking.

"Come on, Levi. Get control." She held him tighter. "Do the police know about these?"

"No. I took them out and buried them where you saw. I wanted to show you before I did anything."

She let him go. "This doesn't look good, Levi. The skull, the clothes. Your trances or dreams, your states of disorientation."

He looked at her imploringly. "What should I do?"

"I think we should burn these."

Levi knew she was right. They needed to erase this reality. He split two logs into kindling, while Sachi went into the house and found some newspaper. As they crumpled the paper and tossed it into the backyard fire pit, Levi noticed the headline of a story he hadn't read. "*Leeson's Murder: What's the Motive?*" It was a question that Levi thought about constantly.

They stood holding hands, watching fire curl and consume the newspaper, kindling, larger splits, and finally the clothing that Levi had placed carefully on top. Dark smoke billowed from the fire, carrying the clothing, and the blood on it, into the air where it gradually disappeared. It felt ritualistic to Levi, and he had a clear memory of sitting on that beach in Greece so long ago. As the flames died, the embers glowed amber and evening descended. Several thrushes began to call out into the darkness.

He squeezed Sachi's hand, and they went inside. "I need you, Sachi." He led her into his bedroom.

They climbed into Levi's bed, where they made love again, slowly, achingly, before drifting into deep sleep.

They woke to sun blanketing the bed, and pounding on the front door. The sharp buzz of the little-used doorbell, then more loud knocking. Levi swung himself out of bed, flashing Sachi a weak smile. She grimaced and pulled a pillow over her head. He pulled on a pair of jeans.

Juicy stood solidly in the doorway, his battered cowboy hat riding back on his head. To his left stood Taylor, and behind them two deputies. Levi vaguely recognized one of them. Fear coursed him. But this was not unexpected.

He forced his voice to be steady. "Gentlemen."

"Levi, I've got a warrant here to search your place." He held out a piece of paper. "You can read it if you want."

"We'll be quick," said Taylor.

Levi waved the paper away and opened the door. "I have a guest."

"Tell her to get dressed," Juicy said, brushing past Levi. The others entered the house and set to work, methodical and hasty. Levi walked into the bedroom and shook Sachi.

She groaned. "I heard voices."

"We've got company. Get dressed."

She pulled on the clothes she'd arrived in, jeans and a sweater. She ran her hands through her hair. "I'm a mess. I need to brush my hair."

"Later."

She looked at him and seemed to decide he was serious.

"Let's take a walk," he said.

As they entered the living room, Juicy asked Sachi who she was.

"You don't have to say anything," Levi told her.

She ignored him. "I'm a biologist visiting from Greece. I'm working with Levi on several projects."

"OK if we go for a walk?"

"Be back in a half hour at the latest. We may have questions."

"Let's go," Levi said, opening the front door and letting Sachi exit first.

"You didn't tell me I was coming to visit a criminal," Sachi said, taking Levi's hand.

"I didn't know I was a criminal," Levi said, giving a surprised laugh. "This is all new territory for me." He pulled her to him for a quick kiss. "Do I look like a criminal?"

"Oh, yes, certainly." She wrinkled her nose at him. "But I am worried for you," her tone suddenly serious.

"I am, too." Levi began to realize how naïve he'd been. He should have gone to Juicy immediately. It was too late now.

In nearly every yard lilacs were blooming, and the morning air was sharp, penetrated by the mating calls of numerous birds. They walked silently to the corner.

"Will they arrest you?" Sachi asked hesitantly.

"No. They have nothing on me. They're just being thorough. Chasing down all the leads." Even as he spoke, he doubted himself.

"I just can't believe you murdered anyone. Even as a wolf. Wolves don't kill for vengeance, only food and territory."

"We know that, but I'm afraid they don't." Levi remained silent for a moment. "I doubt by now they think actual wolves did this. I'm guessing they think someone tried to make it look like wolves."

"To send a message?"

"I don't know. As I said, it may have been opportunistic. Someone knew that Leeson was at least partly responsible for the wolves on the railing, and made it look like revenge. Which would point directly at me."

"Who would do that?"

Callahan. But he didn't say it out loud.

Thirty six

THEY WALKED DOWNTOWN AND had a cup of coffee and a danish at the *Clean Bean* coffee shop. Levi told Sachi about Callahan, and his suspicion.

"Callahan could have gotten into Leeson's with no problem. He could have stolen my clothes, and the wolf skull. I don't know his motive, but maybe Leeson was trying to screw him. It could have been anything, hell, I don't know. Maybe it was about some land dispute."

"Will the police question him?"

"If they find evidence tying him to the murders, they will."

"In Greece we would think of how to do that."

"What?"

"Give them evidence."

"Let's think about that, shall we?" He smiled ruefully.

When they returned, the four police were sitting in the living room talking.

"Levi, we need access to your email," Juicy told him.

"My email?"

"It's on the warrant. Who's your provider?"

"Gmail."

"Could you please log in?" asked one of the deputies, holding a thumb drive.

"Look, guys, that's private."

"This is a murder investigation, Levi," Juicy said coldly. "It's not private any longer."

Levi sighed, sat down at the computer, and logged into his Gmail account.

"I'd like to shower and change. Is that OK?" asked Sachi.

"Ask him," Levi said pointing at Taylor, currently the only cop in the room.

Taylor hesitated like he wanted to say something else, then said, "It's fine. We're finished with the bedroom and bath."

Levi gave him a nasty look, which he ignored.

As Sachi left, headed for the bedroom, Taylor gave Levi a look.

"Don't say it, Taylor. You've got a job to do. I understand. I don't like it, but I understand." He almost mentioned the other night.

Taylor grunted, and Levi handed him the thumb drive with his inbox on it, then sank into the couch.

He looked around the room, invaded now, as if it were no longer his, and came to rest on a photograph of a large male wolf. It stared unabashedly at the camera. It registered no fear, no curiosity, no animosity. Its stare transcended anything human.

The photograph had been given to him by the renowned wolf photographer Andrian Leutroch, with whom Levi had spent a number of months in Mongolia, tracking and counting wolves. This was a majestic wolf they'd discovered trotting along the cobble of a dry river channel. The wolf had been quite close, but didn't spook. It had stopped and stared at them for almost a minute, while Andrian clicked a number of photographs. Levi had always thought there was an otherworldly quality to this wolf. But now he was thinking all wolves had this quality, as if they were connected to some primal, mystical world humans had fallen out of.

"Levi." Juicy stood above him, shaking him from his thoughts.

"What?"

"We're taking some things with us to study further. This skull," lifting a plastic bag containing the skull. Levi was initially glad he'd soaked it in soapy water, but his knowledge of forensics was limited. It was possible there were still bloodstains on the roots of the teeth. And it was obvious the skull had been handled lately, and he'd wiped the shelf with Pledge, ignoring the other two shelves. Dumb move.

"And this." He held the folder of papers and articles that Sachi had sent him. Levi didn't think he'd kept the note that she'd sent as accompaniment, but he wasn't sure. He wasn't sure of much these days.

"And these we found in the fire pit." He held up another baggie containing some blackened buttons and a zipper. "Looks like somebody burned some clothes recently. Wonder why?"

"Maybe they no longer fit," Levi said belligerently.

"Maybe. And this." He held up another baggie containing a single key that looked like it fit a front door, and a small piece of paper under it.

Juicy rolled his chaw from one cheek to the other.

"What is it?"

"What's on that little scrap of paper is the password to Leeson's alarm system. And I'm betting that key fits the front lock."

"That's insane! I never saw that before. Where did you find it?"

"In your bedroom under the lamp."

"Under the lamp!?" Levi couldn't believe it. The only time he'd lifted the lamp was when he put it on the bedside table years ago.

Levi stood as the sheriff did.

"Don't plan any extensive travels," Juicy said.

Levi followed them outside.

One of the deputies got into a squad car and slammed the door.

"Have a good day, Levi," Juicy said, walking over to his Jeep Cherokee.

"You too, Juicy." Then under his breath, "Have a fucking *great* day."

Later that day, Levi was returning from the garden with a handful of greens when he noticed a thin, bright flash on the backdoor lock. He stooped and studied the lock carefully, noticing a series of tiny scratches made by a tool. And he suddenly realized that someone had jimmied the lock and broken into his house, stealing the wolf skull and his clothes, and leaving Leeson's combo and key. Levi practically went down on his knees with relief and thanks. This was definitive proof that in some spell or black-out or altered reality, he had not turned into a werewolf and killed the Leesons. There was no doubt that this was Callahan's work.

Levi took several pictures of the scratches and sent them off to Juicy, with the note *Found these on my backdoor lock—someone broke into my place.*

A few minutes later Juicy shot back, *How do I know you didn't just do this?*

And Levi thought, yeah, how do you know?

Thirty Seven

The tea kettle rattled. Levi swung, grabbed a pot holder, lifted the kettle off the stove, and poured water carefully into two mugs. He lifted his mug and sloshed tea, he was shaking so badly. He'd barely slept, thinking about Callahan, how he could force a confession out of him.

"Hey, sleepyhead!" he yelled down the hall. "Wake up. Tea time."

A few minutes later, Sachi emerged from the hallway wearing one of Levi's flannel robes. Her hair was tousled, eyes half-shut. She yawned loudly.

"Let's not think about that... stuff, today. Let's just..." She kissed him.

"OK. I'll try, but..."

She kissed him again, harder. "Shhhh. It will all be OK. You'll see."

He turned the burner up, the boiling water rattling the kettle, then turned it off, feeling the release of tension, the softening of the boil.

"I want to eat you for breakfast. With jam," she said.

He was staring into her eyes and suddenly felt oddly calm. "I'm not sure I'd taste very good. Even with jam." He forced a smile. "You know what I like about you, Sachi?"

"What?" Smiling.

"That you don't have to stand on your tiptoes to kiss me."

"Hmmm. You want another, don't you?"

"Yes."

Softer this time.

"I thought tea-time was in the afternoon. It's a British thing, isn't it?"

"Bitterroot Valley tea time is at," he glanced at the microwave clock, "7:13 a.m. And we are as exact as the Brits. 7:13 or no tea."

She punched him lightly in the chest. "Glad to see you people have some class."

"Oh, we have class alright. We're all class." He was smiling now.

She took the mug he handed her. "Hot."

"It's white tea from Sri Lanka. You like?"

Sachi nodded, combing her hair back with her fingers.

"Sleep well?"

"Very." She walked into the living room. Levi watched as she sat on the worn leather couch, setting her cup on the maple slab-wood table. She lifted the cover of a white coffee-table book and flipped the first few pages.

Levi knew the book well. *Wolves in Photography, Art and Mythology*, by Josiah Wojeiski. He walked in and sat lightly next to her. She turned to him and smiled, then kissed his lips, running her tongue around them. "The tea tastes good on you."

"Better than jam?"

"I don't know. I haven't tried jam yet." She turned back to the book, flipping through more pages, stopping at a riveting photograph of a massive male wolf looking up from a freshly killed elk.

"Yellowstone Park," Levi said.

"What is it about wolves, Levi? Let's discuss this."

"OK."

"Let's look. And talk." She pointed at the wolf, its eyes filled with what? Curiosity? Appraisal? "What do you think?"

"It's a large male. Elk kill. Photographed in Yellowstone Park two years after their re-introduction. They were reintroduced to Yellowstone because the elk had no predators, and were seriously overpopulating, doing extreme damage to a number of plant species and riparian zones. The wolves were brought in to thin the elk. This wolf knows a human is pointing something at it. It's aware, but not scared. Curious, maybe. Cautious."

"A camera, not a gun."

"Wolves live safely in the Park. That's why this one is not scared."

"They can't be hunted."

"Not in the Park. But the Yellowstone wolves occasionally roam outside the Park, where they are definitely hunted. But you're right. I think most of them know the boundaries. He knows he won't be shot at here. What about his eyes? What's in them?"

"Curiosity, maybe. Defiance. Indifference. Certainly not fear."

"I don't think I've ever seen fear in a wolf's eyes," Levi said.

Sachi turned a few more pages, stopping at a brilliant photograph of a white wolf cresting a ridge, surveying what lay beyond, filling the camera frame and the page.

She gave a tiny gasp. "It's beautiful!"

"Well, you ask 'why wolves?' and that's a partial answer. They are beautiful. Also majestic, noble, aloof, mysterious. Magical, maybe. And like everything in nature, they belong. They don't think, 'Why am I here? What is the purpose of life?' They live with a certainty we seldom, if ever, know."

"They are wild," Sachi said. "Not inhuman, but unhuman. But I think all people, despite their humanity, have a taste of this feeling in their soul. That of the animal. Some fear it and suppress it; some let it out to play; and some, like the followers of Lycaon, let it take control."

"I agree," said Levi.

Sachi flipped a few more pages, stopping at a two-page photograph. The reproduction depicted a photo that was raw, aged, worn around the edges. In it a Nunamiut man in a heavy fur anorak, knelt, holding the head of a dead wolf. The man's face bronze crinkled with a wide smile. He had no teeth.

Sachi picked up her tea, sipped, then asked, "What do you think of this one?"

"It's nature. Kill and be killed. Wolves are predators, but so are we. And native tribes have ancient relationships with wolves. They hunt them for fur, totems, sometimes meat."

"This doesn't bother you?"

"No."

"How about when a wolf is killed for killing livestock? Is that alright?"

"If it's legitimate, I'm OK with it. How about you?"

"I have to be. Greece is a county with many agriculture, farmers. When wolves become a problem and kill sheep, or cows, the government will send a hunter to kill the wolves. The farmers know this, so they tolerate wolves."

"Knowing the problem animals will be taken out."

"Yes."

"I wish it were more like that here. Here it's irrational. A crazed distortion. A hatred."

"I think it is probably fear."

"You are very wise, Sachi." Levi bent towards her and kissed her. Their tongues played with each other.

"One more." She indicated the book.

"Random."

She made a production of closing her eyes and turning a chunk of pages, letting the book fall open.

"Wow," said Levi.

The right-hand page was a reprint of a woodblock by Gustave Dore, depicting a dark wolf towering over Little Red Riding Hood.

"The remarkable thing is the girl shows no fear," Sachi noted.

"It's from a fairy tale," said Levi.

"How's that?"

"Like a myth, sort of. The story is about a girl who goes to visit her grandmother, but the wolf eats the grandmother, then climbs in bed and pretends to be her. Then the wolf either eats, or depending on the version, tries to eat, Little Red Riding Hood."

"But this meeting is in the woods. And it's sexual. Look at the girl's eyes."

"She's barely pubescent. It's strange." Levi blew across his mug, then sipped, set it down. "Here in America, a womanizer, a Romeo, is called a wolf. This plays on the belief that male wolves are sexually sneaky. Trying to get into a girl's pants."

"But this girl looks unafraid. Like she knows what he wants."

"Maybe she does. You know this painter? Dore?"

"His name only. That he was French."

"Knowing about him would help. It's a mysterious piece. And I agree. She doesn't look afraid."

"Like she's the wolf's equal."

"Hmmm."

"They don't make books like this about other animals, do they?"

Levi laughed. "Yeah, I haven't seen too many *Chipmunks in Art and Mythology* books."

"I think wolves frighten us and attract us simultaneously. Some people, you for instance, want to be close to them, don't you? You want to know them, communicate with them. Close the gap between human and animal."

"Yes, to an extent. I used to think, if given a choice, I would become a wolf. Now I'm not so sure. It would require the wolf's consciousness to usurp my own."

"You are afraid of that?"

"Yes. I think I am."

Thirty Eight

The following morning, after a breakfast of huckleberry scones, "yummy" by Sachi's standards, they sat on the porch swing and rocked slowly, talking over the events of the past few days. Levi was amazed at how much compassion Sachi showed him. He hadn't taken her for the compassionate sort at first, but now realized that compassion was what fueled her in her work. Compassion for wilderness, nature, animals, wolves, even certain people. He felt privileged to be included.

Sachi volunteered to do the dishes, and Levi scanned *The Ravalli Republic*. An article on the Leeson killing by Monica Sands caught his eye.

"Huh," he said out loud. "They have a person of interest."

Sachi was singing softly and didn't hear him.

Sachi had work to do, so Levi plugged her into his wifi network, kissed her goodbye, then walked down to the library. He had a few books that needed returning, including the werewolf book, which had been interesting, but other than the graphic depicting a werewolf slaughter of two women, which had a similarity to the carnage at the Leeson's, had not been that insightful. That graphic, however, was eerily similar to the details—the biting, sporadic wolf tracks, the slashing—of the Leeson murder. If he could find out who had checked the book out previously, and when, it might shed more insight.

The Hamilton Public Library was on State Street between Third and Fourth Streets, a seven-block walk. The day was heating up already, and Levi's quick clip was drawing sweat. He waved to Mrs.

Riordan, who was tending to her hostas. Catherine Riordan had headed up the Missoula Children's Theater in Missoula before retiring to Hamilton. Her husband had died years before, and she never remarried. Catherine, along with a Missoula author named Clyde Justin Thomas, and Levi, had written, directed, and produced an alternate version of Little Red Riding Hood, in which the wolf helps Little Red Riding Hood thwart a kidnapping.

The Library was a Carnegie Library, and built in the style over a hundred years ago—red brick, iron railings, high ceilings. Nearly impossible to heat in the winter, but today windows were open wide, and the morning breeze danced through the lofty rooms. Levi dropped the books in the book drop by the circulation desk, then walked over and poked his head into the office of the head of circulation, Amy Cedar, an old friend of Taki's. Levi hadn't seen her in nearly two years.

Amy looked up from her computer, a petite, pretty woman wearing olive glasses. "Well, hi there, Levi. Long time."

"Yeah. It has been. Too long. You know Taki left?"

"I did. She's in Hawaii now, caring for her mom. I'm not sure what's going on with her and Art. She wouldn't tell me much."

"Nor me, but I surmise they've split up."

"Too bad. I thought they'd both found what they were looking for."

"Art thought so as well. As did I. Guess you never know what's inside someone's head, do you?"

"Nor what's in their heart. Anything I can help you with?"

"Nothing really, just popped in to get a book and thought I'd say hi."

Amy was a skier, and her office walls were adorned with photos of skiers doing crazy, precarious things. One of a skier outrunning an avalanche caught Levi's eye.

"That guy survive?"

"Don't know. Makes for a good photo, though." She moved a pile of books to the side. "I heard about the wolves killed and hung at the pub. Ignorance is alive down in the Valley for sure."

Levi was glad she didn't mention the Leeson murder. Yet. "That's what libraries are for. To combat ignorance, right?"

"I guess. Want to sit for a few minutes? I've got a meeting at 10:30, but I have a few minutes before that to catch up."

"Sure." Levi sat in the chair next to her desk. "Hey, I do have something maybe you could help me with. I read a book last summer. I think it had the word *fire* in the title, but can't remember for sure. And I can't remember the author's name either."

"Well, you are getting old, aren't you?" Amy chuckled. "But don't worry. It's a common enough problem. I can look up your patron record and find out." Amy hit a few keys, typed in Levi's name, and pulled up a list of books he'd checked out, turning the monitor so it partially faced him.

"How far back does this go?"

"All the way to the beginning of time." She chuckled again.

"There, that's it. *Young Men and Fire* by Norman MacLean."

"He wrote *A River Ran through It*, but I'm not familiar with this one."

"It's about a group of college kids who died fighting a fire over on the Missouri. Very tragic," Levi said. "Mind if I scroll through this list?"

"Be my guest. Just scroll down. If there's more than one page, just click to advance it."

"Thanks." Levi began scrolling. "Whoa, I'd forgotten about a lot of these."

"Hey, Levi, I've got to hit the bathroom before my meeting. I'll say goodbye now. Just leave everything open when you leave."

"Sure. Great seeing you!" Levi couldn't believe his stroke of luck.

After Amy left the room, he chose a title option, and typed in the title of the werewolf book. It was relatively new, so he didn't expect much, but a second later a short list popped up. His name was at the top, and the book had already been checked in. Below him there was only one other name. Michael Callahan had checked it out last November. Callahan.

"That's it," Levi said to himself, navigating back to his list of titles. "That is fucking it."

Part Four

Thirty nine

Sachi stayed another three days. Levi forced himself to put the Leeson murder aside, feeling his time with Sachi was sacred. During that time, they lay low, getting to know each other, taking walks, making love, cooking simple meals. One exception was a drive into Missoula where they saw a movie and visited Broadway Market, a small southern European delicatessen. Sachi picked up ingredients for moussaka, loukoumades, and Greek salad, as well as a variety of olives, all the while chatting with and charming the owner, Alfredo Cippolato, in a hybrid of Italian and Greek.

On the day before Sachi returned to Greece, they floated a stretch of the Bitterroot River with Art, who had gone into a depressed hibernation since Taki left. Levi's purpose for the float was to introduce Sachi to Art, and give her a taste of floating a wild Montana river. He also hoped to cheer Art up. And he was right on all counts. Sachi was charming and interesting enough to bring Art out of his shell, and Art loved the Bitterroot, loved sharing stories and observations. They cooked burgers on a sandbar, and ate watching a pileated woodpecker turn a dead cottonwood into sawdust. Later in the afternoon, Art showed Sachi how to throw a decent fly, and told her where to put it. Her reward was her first-ever cutthroat trout.

After the shuttle back to Art's truck, Levi pulled him aside to thank him, and Art actually jokingly said, "Can I hook up with another of your old girlfriends?"

"Wish I could arrange that, buddy, but she may never be back. You'll have to go to Greece."

"I've always wanted to go to Greece," Art said, smiling.

The late afternoon breeze carried the scent of new alfalfa and cottonwood blooms.

"Hey Art, I need to talk with you about something. Something important. And it has to be soon."

"Stop by on your way back from the airport tomorrow. I'll be around tying flies and sipping cerveza."

"Thanks, man. I should be back around three or so. I'll see you then."

Levi was just setting the table for dinner when there was a solid knock on the door. Opening it, he saw Juicy and Taylor standing like there was no humor in the world.

"May we come in?"

Levi saw immediately it was not a question and moved aside. After they'd entered, he closed the door. Taylor was staring at the floor. He looked exhausted, and there were lines on his face where none had existed before.

Juicy spoke first. "Levi, you're under arrest for the murder of Ted and Brittany Leeson. Whatever you say can, and will, be held against you."

"What!?" He stared. "This is a huge mistake, Juicy. C'mon. You know me."

"Sorry, but the evidence just keeps adding up."

"Fuck, I can't believe this."

"You're going to need to come with us."

"Can I call Art? He'll need to take Sachi to Missoula for her plane."

"Five minutes."

Levi walked into the bedroom.

"What's going on? Who's at the door?" Sachi asked.

"I'm being arrested for murder. The Leeson thing." His voice was dead.

"That's ludicrous!"

"I'm going to call Art. He'll drive you into Missoula tomorrow so you can catch your plane. Stay here tonight. Maybe this is a mistake, and I'll be back later."

"Jesus!" Sachi flung herself at him and began crying.

"Don't, honey. It's OK. I'll be fine. I'll call you as soon as this straightens out."

"I can't believe this."

"I will miss you so much, Sachi." He hugged her hard. "So much." He let her go. "I have to call Art." He kissed her hard. Then he called Art and filled him in. "Sachi will call you. She'll need a ride to the airport. Be there for her, OK?"

"Of course, man, of course. You take care. This will be over soon."

"I hope so."

A few minutes later, Levi joined the others on the porch.

"Let's go." Juicy and Taylor walked to the squad car.

"Aren't you going to cuff me?"

"You want us to, we can. Now get in."

He waved bravely to Sachi and smiled, but there was no joy under it. He felt disbelief, and under that, absolute rage.

Sachi blew him a kiss through the squad car window. He could see tears glistening on her cheeks. Her face was panicky.

"Call Art," he yelled at her. "His number is on the counter."

He felt like such a shit, putting her through this. As they drove away, several neighbors hovered, watching the scene. He was too angry to be embarrassed. And then suddenly he was in a different world, the squad car smelling of stale sausage, onions, sweat and leather, his rage turning to ice.

Five minutes later, Juicy pulled the wheel hard, and the squad car swerved into the police station's parking lot.

"Out," Juicy said, opening the door.

"This is a huge mistake, Juicy."

"So you said."

They guided him through the station, the chaotic mess of desks, computers, cubicles, piles of paper, and into an interrogation room.

Taylor read him his rights again, told him he had the right to a phone call after they'd reviewed the evidence.

"What evidence? It's all circumstantial. It's all bullshit." He felt suddenly drained.

"This isn't bullshit, Levi," Juicy said brusquely. "Two people were murdered in a very bizarre fashion, under my watch." He motioned Levi to sit in a hard plastic chair.

Levi turned to Taylor. "You going to good cop-bad cop me?"

Taylor ignored him. His eyes were bloodshot.

"So, before we begin, do you have any questions?" Juicy started.

"I have a ton of questions. You can't do this."

"We can and we will. You'll get your chance to talk with a lawyer. Your own, or we can provide one."

"Can I go home tonight?"

Taylor snorted. "Are you crazy? Don't you realize what's happening here? You are going to jail for murder. We're going to review the evidence, Levi, just to let you know how strong the case is. Then we're going to lock you up. Since this is Tuesday, we can get you into court tomorrow morning for the arraignment. Then the judge will set your bail. Since it's a double homicide, it will be at least half a mil. You can get your friend Art to start a Kickstarter fund, but my guess is that you're locked up for a good long spell." Taylor wiped his mouth with the back of his hand.

Levi said nothing. He was gripping the table so hard his knuckles went milky. He forced himself to relax, and folded his hands in front of him on the table.

"OK," he said. "Let me have it."

Juicy started, "As I said, we're charging you with the double homicide of Ted Leeson and his wife Brittany Leeson." He reached down and lifted an Albertson's shopping bag onto the table. "First, we have motive. We know that you were researching the wolf pack behind Leeson's place up Goat Canyon. We know you are a wolf biologist, and wolf fanatic, who has argued publicly in favor of wolf reintroduction and preservation. In short, you care deeply about wolves."

Taylor shifted his gaze to Juicy, who continued the monologue.

"We also know that *you* suspect Leeson, and probably Callahan, killed three of the wolves in your pack. It's our thinking that you took it upon yourself to commit retribution." Juicy spit some chaw into a mason jar. "Got anything to say?"

"Yes. Have you looked into any enemies Leeson might have? You don't get to be as large as Leeson without hurting someone. The motive could be financial, personal, could be a family thing, or maybe he boffed someone's wife. Have you driven down any of those roads?"

"Of course we have," said Taylor. "We're not stupid. You seem determined to pin us as hick cops. If we were that stupid, we'd have had arrested you immediately. We've had the feds involved. Even a private guy good with banks. And we've turned up squat. Nada. Sure, Leeson has enemies. And maybe he or Brittany had affairs, but there's nothing there."

"Can I continue?" Juicy asked Levi.

"You're going to anyway."

"Second, we have what we call supplemental evidence toward motive. An email to someone called Dmitri in which you state that you want to become a wolf. Additionally, there is a collection of materials on werewolves, which indicates you were interested in them and their tactics. One of which was to kill animals and people in the fashion of wolves. Which is what happened to the Leesons. Got anything you want to say?"

Levi looked around the room. The fluorescent light stripped any nuance from the small, rectangular cubicle. Ultra-shiny beige walls, the camera in the corner of the low ceiling, plastic and metal chairs, the wire mesh embedded in the glass of the door, even the metal table were fraudulent, at odds with the world of nature. Levi felt trapped. He shook his head.

"Third," Juicy said thickly. "We found Brittany's blood on the wolf skull we took from your house. When teeth were extracted, blood was found in several of the teeth cavities. Your attempt to wash it failed, and dusting the shelf was a foolish move. It only drew attention to it. We also found the wolf paw responsible for the tracks. Your friend Steve McCandless verified it was one you'd received from a Nunamiut elder you were working with in Alaska. As you know it had rather distinct markings. Steve said you were very fond of it."

Levi was stunned. He kept it on a bookshelf in his study. He hadn't even noticed it was missing. He wondered what else the intruder, the murderer, took.

"Then we found charred fabric, buttons, and a zipper in your fire pit, indicating that you burned some clothes. Probably those you were wearing when you committed the murders. And finally, we have Jacob Blackburn's, Leeson's ranch foreman, sworn statement that he saw your truck parked off to the side of the gate around seven pm, Tuesday, May eighteenth, when he drove into town to burn off a little steam. He said that Leeson had made reference to a meeting he'd scheduled with you. He was apparently considering giving you access to the canyon wolf pack through his property. Anything to say?"

"I've got nothing else to say to you."

Juicy leaned across the table, getting his face up in Levi's.

"You come across as an affable guy, a bit cool, as scientists tend to be. But I think you're as cold-blooded as the wolves you love so much. I intend to nail you on this one, Levi Brunner." He stood up. "Let's go get you locked up."

"You might think about confessing, Levi. It would go better for you if you cooperated." Taylor stood as well.

Levi stood, and they each took one of his arms and led him out of the interrogation room, down a narrow hallway, through a cage-like security gate, and into a cell. Here they turned their backs on him and slammed the door shut.

Forty

LEVI GLANCED AROUND. ON one side of the cell was a small table with a folded newspaper and two plastic chairs, a mute TV that flickered erratically, and in the corner a toilet with no lid. The setting sun speared a small window with wired glass on the back wall, filling the room with ruby light. There were two bunks, and on the bottom one sat a tow-headed kid with half his teeth missing, a serpent tattoo winding up his neck and onto his left cheek.

"Whattaya in fer?" the kid asked, looking up from a car magazine.

"Nothing. I guess I get the top bunk."

"You ain't in here fer nothing. They don't put people in jail fer nothing. You better be nice to me. Whatcha in fer?" The kid shifted a toothpick from one side on his mouth to the other. Levi saw his lower gum was oozing blood.

"I'm accused of a double homicide."

The kid's face livened. "Murder, huh? Two of 'em. Didja do it?"

"No."

He leaned forward. "Wasn't that couple got killed up in the mountains, was it? I heard wolves done it."

"Maybe they did, but I sure didn't."

"Wrong guy, huh?"

"So I guess I take the top bunk."

"You got the top bunk, but don't step on my bunk getting up there. Use a chair." The kid pointed to one of the plastic chairs. "Don't know how to fix a TV, do ya?"

"Nope."

"I wished I was a wolf. I'd slash the shit out of a bunch a fuckers. Tear 'em apart with my teeth. That would feel *goooood*. Real good. Just slashing 'em up. Damn." The kid was grinning insanely.

Levi took off his shirt.

"Hot in here, ain't it. Always like that. Don't matter what season it is."

"You live here long?" Levi asked.

"Been six, seven months. I'll be getting out soon, though. Get back to selling sweet stuff." The kid laughed. "Fuckin' cops ruin all my fun." He laughed again, a hollow, cheerless laugh.

Levi pulled a chair up to the bed and climbed up onto the top bunk. The kid got up and put the chair back under the table.

"Just don't step on my bunk when ya get down, ya hear?"

The kid rambled on as the light faded, and the TV continued to flicker. At some point Levi fell asleep, waking later from a vivid dream. He lay on a cot in a tiny rustic log cabin. The front door was open, and he could see a heavy scattering of stars across the black expanse of sky. As silently as shadows, two wolves entered the room. One was Mirr, who stopped just across the threshold and stared at him. The other, a larger female of striking ash color, walked silently across the floor to where he lay. Although her face was inches from his, he felt no fear. She stood silent and still, her golden eyes frozen on him. And Levi felt himself falling into them, and falling and falling, and then he woke again to another Montana daybreak, in a jail cell.

After a tepid shower and breakfast, Levi was led over to the courthouse for arraignment. The courthouse seats contained a smattering of people. Scanning the crowd, he saw Monica Sands sitting with her laptop. She gave him a weak smile.

Levi waited forty-some minutes for his name to be called, then approached the bench where a man, late-fifties with sandy hair, sat in judge's robes meting out the law.

"Levi Brunner, you are accused of the double homicide of two Bitterroot citizens, Ted and Brittany Leeson. How do you plead?"

"Not guilty."

"Noted. Bail is set at five hundred thousand dollars. The date of your trial will be determined, and you will be notified." He banged the gavel. "Next."

Levi managed to get through the next two days without a fight, which was not easy. His cellmate, Jesse, seemed to have it in for him, accusing him of stepping on his bunk and stealing his radio. He freaked and went into a rampage when Levi turned off the flickering TV.

Levi spent as much time as he could in the prison library perusing the tattered paperbacks and out-of-date textbooks, strangely finding a copy of E. O. Wilson's *Sociobiology,* into which he dove and wished to remain. The disbelief was beginning to fade, and the depressing state of his condition becoming more apparent.

Later the first day, Art visited him, handing him the newspaper, pointing with his thumb to a front-page story above the fold. "You're infamous, dude."

Levi scanned it. The first sentence read, "Levi Brunner, a wolf researcher providing information regarding the horrific murder of two of the Valley's finest citizens, Ted and Brittany Leeson, has gone from assisting the investigation to being its prime suspect. He is currently being held in the Ravalli County jail in Hamilton."

"Fuck this." Levi threw the paper down.

"Here's your mail."

"Just put it in the house, Art. You know where the spare is. My roommate will steal it here. Did Sachi get off OK?"

"Yeah. I ran her up early, and left her with plenty of time to catch her flight to Seattle, then on to London. She talked a lot on the way up. She's really shook up. And she is really something. You have extraordinary taste in women, my man."

"Lots of good it does me."

"Oh, well," Art said, "at least you have someone." He looked depressed and awkward. "If it's any consolation, I've got two lawyer recommendations, both from my brother Alec, the lawyer. Both in Missoula. Alec said he'd take the case in a pinch, but this sort of thing isn't his forte. He's a corporate guy."

"No dice, Art. I need someone local, someone from the Valley, not some out-of-town big shot who will be held against me in trial. How about Sam Doke? He's had some high-profile Valley cases. And he's been sympathetic to environmental causes in the past."

"I'll call him." Art spun an ashtray on the counter behind the thick wall of glass. "How you doing in this shithole?"

"Terrible. I hate it. It gives me a taste of what zoo animals must endure."

"Hmmm. I asked about your bail. Five hundred grand. Whew. That's mammoth bread. I've already started talking to people. I can do a second mortgage on the house. We'll come up with it somehow."

"Don't mortgage your house, Art."

"It's not a problem."

"Thanks for the thought, but don't do it. I think it's hopeless." Levi's face hardened in anger.

"Who do you figure did it?" Art.

"Someone who would benefit from framing me. Someone who wants to shut me down."

"I don't know, Levi. I hear you. I really do. I just can't think of anyone that cares enough about you or wolves to slaughter the Leesons. I mean I hated those fuckers worse than just about anyone, but I couldn't even imagine doing that. Cutting them up like that. It was inhuman."

"I think this is personal, Art. Someone who hates me so badly, they did something monstrous to frame me."

"I can't think of anyone like that."

"I can," Levi said icily.

"Who?"

Levi didn't answer right away. When he spoke, his voice was neutral. "Thanks for coming, Art. Call Doke. I'll see you later."

That afternoon Sam Doke stopped by. The police let him and Levi use a small interrogation room for their meeting. In his first gesture of decency, Doke had the police take Levi's cuffs off.

"Can they hear us?" Levi asked, after shaking Doke's hand and sitting down across the small table from him.

Doke was tall, over six-three, and had the build of a cowboy, narrow hips and wide shoulders. He'd been a bronc rider for several years before breaking a pelvis and deciding on a safer career. He came out of solid Bitterroot ranching stock, his grandfather homesteading here in the late 1890s. Levi knew him casually through environmental functions and fundraisers.

"Against the law. It could get your case thrown out." Doke opened his briefcase and pulled out some papers, along with a notepad and pen.

"I've already read a lot about this case. Papers, TV, and Internet have been full of it. It's brutal, and intriguing. No one I've talked to can quite figure it out."

He looked into his briefcase again, shuttling some papers, pulling another few out, pointing at them.

"The police aren't saying much, but I suspect they're rushing this a bit. It's the type of crime that destabilizes a community. You can't leave it hanging open too long. They need to close it, even if it means pushing a bit too hard. There might be a technicality we can capitalize on."

Doke sat back, flipping the notebook open. "Now why don't you tell me your side of what happened?"

"I didn't do it."

"OK. Where were you that night?"

"I was home."

"Did you have any visitors? Telephone anyone? Send any emails? Anything that can substantiate that?"

"Not that I can remember. I checked my email, texts, phone. It's a blank."

"The police have a witness, won't say who yet, who puts you at the scene."

"It's Jacob Blackburn, Leeson's foreman. He says he saw my truck there as he was leaving for town. He told the police that Ted Leeson told him he had a meeting with me. He's lying, but hell if I know why. Unless he did it."

"You ever meet him?"

"Nope."

"You call him? Have words?"

"I wouldn't know the guy from Adam. I think I saw him in a bar once, but could be mistaken."

"Why would he lie? Think about it, Levi. This is a critical question."

"I don't know." Levi let out a long sigh. "Someone is trying to frame me."

"OK. Tell me about any evidence the police have. We'll need to counter it."

"They claim I have motive. I was researching the pack that was shot up and hung like meat downtown. That pack lived in Goat Canyon, where Leeson's Ranch is located. What else? I've been outspoken about wolf reintroduction, the place of wolves in the ecosystem. I care passionately about wolves."

"So do a lot of people. That seems rather weak."

Levi shrugged. "I piss a lot of the local ranchers off."

"Motive for a frame."

"I guess."

"Have you had any encounters with Ted Leeson and his wife Brittany before?"

"When I first headed into the canyon, I talked with Brittany over the phone about granting me access."

"What did she say?"

"That she hoped every wolf on earth would be eliminated."

"But you said you were studying the pack up above Leeson's place, in Goat Creek Canyon. If they didn't give you access, how did you get in?"

"Climbed around it."

"You climbed those cliffs?" Doke seemed surprised.

"Yeah. Lots of people can substantiate I'm a good climber."

"No shit." Doke shook his head. "I did some climbing, too, but I'd never climb anything like that. Especially alone." He was silent for a moment.

"Did you suspect the Leesons in the slaughter and public display of the three wolves that were shot."

"I suspected Ted Leeson and Callahan."

"Mike Callahan?"

"Yeah. And then I substantiated it. I climbed in and documented a snowmobile track from his place to where the wolves were shot. They had a den."

"Did you get photos?"

"I did."

"OK, so we know a snowmobile left Leeson's and took someone up to where the wolves were shot. How do you know who was on it?"

"I'm guessing Leeson and Callahan. Seeing as the snowmobile left from Leeson's place, they are the likeliest suspects. They've been meeting with a small group and discussing how to eradicate wolves. You can prove that pretty easily. Leeson threw a bunch of money into it, and Callahan runs it."

Doke flipped the page of his notebook. "And you have photos of the snowmobile tracks, the wolf den site?"

"I do."

"I'll need those."

"They're on my phone, which is in custody."

"OK, we move on. You have motive, but I think it's fairly weak. It would take someone pretty unstable to kill two defenseless humans as retribution for the death of three wolves. And you've never struck me as the least bit unstable. You're a biologist, right?"

"Yeah. I've got a bachelor's in wildlife bio from UM, and a PhD from the University of Minnesota."

"Got all the papers. OK, let's talk about evidence. What did they tell you they have?"

Levi recited the list for Doke.

"It's all circumstantial except for the eyewitness, and the blood on the wolf skull, and the paw, which exactly matches the prints found at the murder scene. How do you explain that?"

"Someone broke into my place. They scratched the metal around the lock, gouged the wood. I didn't notice it right away."

"You have photos?"

"Again, on my phone. The skull was in a cabinet in the hallway. I noticed it had been moved slightly, and when I took it out, I saw dried blood on several of the teeth. I washed it off."

"That wasn't a wise decision."

"Hindsight and all. The paw was stolen from my place and left outside Leeson's. I didn't even notice it was missing."

"And how do you explain the burned clothes?"

"I found a grocery bag hidden behind a table in the corner of my study. In it were my clothes covered in blood. I burned them in my fire-pit. I have a witness, a woman who stayed with me a few days."

"Why didn't you turn them in to the police? Them and the skull?"

"They incriminated me."

"They might have. Could have been beef blood on the clothes." Doke pulled out his phone and glanced at it.

"Like I said, I wasn't thinking straight. It's been a pretty fucked-up time for me."

"Is it possible someone could have seen this alleged break-in?"

"It's possible. The back yard can be seen from both of the neighbors' back yards. One of them, Myrtle, is elderly and home a lot. No one lives in front of me, though. It's woods from my place down to the river."

"Did you notice anything that might have been dropped?"

"I didn't really look."

"OK, we'll get an investigator to look at this. I use Ed Garnow."

"Don't know him."

"He's top notch." Doke turned another notebook page. "OK, you said someone was trying to frame you for this. Who?"

"I have some ideas, but that's all they are."

"Shoot."

"Mike Callahan. He's hated me for years."

"Why would he kill the Leesons?"

"I have no idea. The only other motive I can think of is that he's trying to frame me and get me put away for life so I'd be out of his hair."

"You really believe he hates you enough to murder a man he

hung out with, and that man's wife, to frame you? It doesn't make sense to me."

"It's all I've got at the moment."

"Did you mention Callahan to them? Have they looked into him?"

"I mentioned him, and they didn't say."

"OK, let me take this back to the office and think about it. I'll get Garnow looking into witnesses who might have seen someone messing around in your back yard. When would that have been?"

"Before the murder, probably shortly before, since there was the risk of me noticing the missing skull and paw. Then after the murder to return the clothes and skull."

"So we have a window of about four or five days. The murder happened the night of May 18, so we'll look at May 16 through May 20."

Doke began scooping papers back into his briefcase.

"There's a couple of other things?"

"Oh?"

"They have an email I sent to someone saying I wanted to be a wolf, and there's a pile of papers, articles and such, about a wolf-worshipping cult. The cultists might be considered werewolves."

"Werewolves!? We're not going there, Levi. Let's keep this rational." Doke put on his jacket and hefted his briefcase. "You going to be able to make bail?"

"Five hundred thousand dollars? Are you kidding me?"

"You could use a bondsman. I have a recommendation."

"That would still be fifty thousand. I can't raise that kind of money. At least anytime soon."

"Yeah. You like novels? Action stuff, crime?"

"I don't read much, except technical papers, scientific books."

"I'll bring some page-turners by. They help the time pass. We'll get a trial date set soon, and get this ball rolling. Keep the faith, and I'll be in touch soon."

They shook hands.

"Thanks," Levi said.

Doke opened the door and yelled for the guard.

Forty one

BACK IN HIS CELL, Levi walked over to the window and stared out. The parking lot below was blurred by grimy, scratched glass and embedded wire mesh. But it was still a window. There was a hint of evening light, a slight purple hush on the Sapphire range across the Valley. Levi pictured elk drifting into high meadows to feed on sweet grass, and his heart broke. The tumult of emotions, guilt, anger, and sorrow he'd successfully held in since the wolves were killed broke free. He began sobbing uncontrollably, his body shaking as grief used him as its conduit. A keening wail joined the tears that ran freely down his cheeks, dripping off his chin onto the floor. He couldn't stop it, and Jesse, wisely, said nothing.

The next morning, after a breakfast of tepid oatmeal and bruised bananas, Art came to visit again. He talked with Levi through the scratchy speaker in the thick glass wall.

"I took out a second mortgage, Levi. But it's not enough. I only got $125,000 and the bondsman, Kerlew, wants two hundred grand. Says you're a flight risk. I tried a different bondsman, but got the same story. What with all the press generated, it's a high-stakes game."

"Thanks, Art. I'm eternally grateful, I am, but take the money back. I'll be OK. It's all a mistake. They'll clear it up."

"Man, I can't believe this. You are the *last* person I ever thought I'd see in here."

"I'm the last person I ever thought I'd see in here, either." Levi forced a laugh. "Look, I met with Sam Doke. He, or an investigator working for him, might contact you. Or if you can think of anything useful, give him a call. He's a good man, I trust him."

"I will." Art seemed like he was struggling with something, and muttered a few words Levi didn't catch.

"What did you say?"

Art looked him directly in the eyes. They'd been friends a long time, and Levi couldn't remember Art hedging like this.

"C'mon Art. What? Say it!"

"Sorry, but I have to ask. Did you do this, Levi?"

The words hung in the air like heavy smoke.

Levi let out a long breath. "Of course not, Art. Someone's trying to frame me."

"Callahan." Art practically spit the word. "Maybe I should go pay him a visit."

"So we can be cellmates? Stay away from him." Levi changed the subject. "What's going on with Leeson's place? They sell it yet?"

"It's in probate. They cut most of the staff, and I suspect the family'll sell it to some other rich asshole as fast as they can. I did hear, however, that the probate judge is an uncle, and he can wrap this whole thing up ASAP. The family wants no reminders."

Levi laughed hollowly, but absolutely nothing in the world was funny.

Late afternoon of the fourth day, a guard came by and ordered Levi to come with him. As they walked down the hall, he said, "You're free to go, Brunner."

Levi was stunned. "What!?"

"Somebody made your bail. You're a free man until they lock you up again."

The unreality of this, and the last three days, hit him. He started laughing.

"What's so funny, Brunner?"

"All of it."

Levi followed the guard to a locker room, where he retrieved his clothes, wallet, and cell phone.

"Get changed, Brunner. We want our duds back."

After he'd changed, the guard led Levi into the front waiting room. "You're on your own."

Levi looked around, but there was no one waiting for him. He walked across the room, past empty wooden chairs with their cigarette-burned arms. He pushed open the heavy door and broke into the warm early June sunlight.

Standing on the cement steps of the police station, he took a deep breath, then another. The air was intoxicating. His eyes came to rest on a black Jeep Cherokee parked across the street. The woman in the driver's seat, sporting a pair of over-sized sunglasses, looked familiar, more familiar as she got out and walked across the street to meet him. It was Althea, the bow-hunter he'd met in Goat Canyon, what seemed like years ago.

"Hi," she said, slipping off the sunglasses. Standing less than a foot from him, she pulled his gaze into hers. A breeze caught a wisp of her hair and lifted it toward the sky. Levi was filled with its vastness.

"What the hell!?" he managed. "What the utter hell?"

"Come on." She took his arm firmly and led him towards the Jeep. "We've got work to do."

Forty two

"WHO ARE YOU? I mean really?" Levi asked, as Althea twisted the Jeep sharply into traffic.

"Who do you think I am?" She flashed a teasing smile.

"I have no idea." They were silent for a few minutes, and Levi watched the maple trees on the parkway stream by. "Did you bail me out?"

"Someone had to."

"Well, thank you."

"You're welcome. How was it in there?"

"Hellish."

"Many of our friends are caged. All over the world." She had a trace accent that Levi recognized now from Sachi and the women by the spring.

"You're Greek?"

"I have been. I was born a long time ago, Levi, and have lived many places since then."

"That's cryptic."

She laughed. It was a rich, warm laugh. "You look like you haven't slept in a while."

"I couldn't sleep much in there. My cellmate was a tweaker prone to night-long rants."

"Close your eyes and rest a bit. We'll be at our destination soon."

Levi had no more closed his eyes than the Jeep came to a sharp stop.

"We're here," she said.

They were parked in front of a small log cabin set in a mix of meadow, wild rose, and ponderosa pine. A beat-up Ford 150 pickup was parked off to the side. Three whitetail deer browsed on the right side of the cabin. The cabin looked ancient, but the white caulking between the logs was new, and shone brightly in the sun.

"Where's here?"

"Command center." Althea got out of the car. "You coming?"

A porch swing and several chairs occupied the porch, as well as a large crow perched on a trapeze. The crow was not leashed.

"Caw, caw," it said as Levi and Althea walked up to the door. Althea cawed back, and the crow allowed her to stroke its head.

"This is my friend Karnesis," she told Levi, opening the door.

"We're home!" she yelled as they entered the house. "I've brought the prisoner."

A voice answered from the kitchen, and a second later Cali came running out with a shout of joy, grabbing Levi in a bear-hug.

"Cali! What the hell are you doing here?"

"Althea's my friend," she said, letting go of Levi. "I came to help her. You're just in time for lunch." She disappeared back into the kitchen.

"What the...?" Levi shook his head. It was too much to grasp.

"Have a seat." Althea pointed to a chair pulled up to a maple table that had seen better days. In fact, the entire place and its contents had seen better days. It seemed to be a collage from thrift stores. Althea pulled out a chair and sat across from him.

Levi scanned walls filled with photographs and drawings of wolves. One photograph jumped out at him. It was a large white female wolf. It was Mirr.

At that moment of recognition, Cali walked out of the kitchen with a platter of sandwiches.

"That's Mirr, isn't it?" Levi said pointing.

Cali set the tray on the table, then set three stone cups of cold water next to it. She gave Althea a look.

Althea held up her hand. "Wait a moment." She took a bite of the sandwich, chewed for a minute, then answered. "I'm sure you've figured some of this out already, Levi, but here goes. The spring you discovered up Goat Canyon is a portal. This world, and by that, I mean the world of space and time, are connected in part by subterranean waterways. "Cali and I are Greek, as were the other two women you met, Arianna and Kayla. We are a little... group." She paused as if expecting Levi to say more, but he was silent, listening.

"Cali and her two friends are Pegaiai." Althea said this matter-of-factly.

"Are what?" Levi asked, then remembered Sachi telling him the same thing.

"A Pegaiai is a water nymph associated with springs, as were her companions. We were in the canyon last autumn because of Mirr. She is my lover."

Levi had taken a bite of food, but seemed unable to swallow. Finally, he spoke.

"You said *is*. Mirr is dead. That's what this whole Leeson thing is about."

"She isn't dead, she's a spirit. We oscillate between the spirit world and that of matter. That is why my real name is irrelevant." Althea tossed a strand of hair back.

"So you, as we call it, shape-shift? You take the shape of animals?"

"Yes, we can do that. Mirr..." She took a long drink of water. "Mirr is also very old, and has been many forms. But in essence, we are both huntresses, both wolves."

"Are you seeking vengeance?"

"We want to understand exactly what happened. We think you can help us. You see, when Cali took you down into the spring, it was a test. You survived, which proved you were also one of us, one of the ancient ones, but you've forgotten."

"Cali recognized this in me?"

"She thought she did. She took a gamble."

"And if she'd been wrong, I would have...?"

"Died."

Levi shook his head. "Jesus."

"Wouldn't have helped you." She shrugged. "Many old spirits lose their memory of the old ways. Cali was thinking the visit to Greece, the ocean night, would rekindle your memories. But it didn't.

Not fully, anyway."

"What about the temple of Lycaon? It wasn't an accident you took me there, was it?" Levi asked Cali.

"No. Nothing is really an accident."

"So you killed the Leesons? As retribution for what they did to Mirr?"

"No. It's more complicated than that. I would have shot him in both eyes and his mouth with arrows, along with Callahan. That way they could not see or speak in the spirit world. It was the two of them that killed Mirr, her mate, and her pup." She hesitated, then took another bite of sandwich. "Someone else killed the Leesons."

"Not Callahan?" Levi asked, more confused.

"That's where we need your help."

"How do you know I'm not guilty?" Levi asked.

"Oh, Levi, I know what's in your heart. I know you far better than you think. You are a lover of wolves. You are a wolf assuming, in this life, the form of a human. And before that? Maybe something else."

Levi was stunned to silence. He thought of all the dreams he'd had. It was all making some kind of terrible sense. "You've been leading me along this whole time."

"You are like the horse we lead to the water of insight. We hope that you drink." Althea laughed.

"You expect me to believe you have magical powers?"

"You can believe whatever you want," she said. "No one's forcing you to believe anything."

"But belief does provide a foundation for action," said Cali, who'd reentered the room with a sandwich for Levi, "and we need to act."

"There is also another complication." Althea paused. "Lycaon is here. He followed us. Lycaon is a black wolf, not just in color, but in heart and spirit as well. He wreaks havoc wherever he travels."

"I don't believe wolves are good or bad. Wild animals operate outside of human morals."

"For the most part I agree with you, Levi, but you forget that Lycaon was human once, and that he was turned into a wolf by Zeus because he killed and cooked a child, then tempted Zeus with the child's meat."

"Why did he follow you here?"

"Lycaon is also in love with Mirr." Althea paused again, her voice becoming hushed. "He came for revenge."

"Then Lycaon killed the Leesons."

"No. I don't think so. But maybe."

Levi threw up his hands in despair. "This is crazy."

Cali, who'd been largely silent, spoke up. "You don't realize the power of the spring in the canyon. It is a portal to heaven and hell. It is perhaps an accident that someone like Leeson bought access and shut it off, but it is also a good thing. These sites, what few of them remain, are sacred, and the more hidden they are, the better."

Althea added, "You say it is accident that someone naïve and greedy like Leeson bought the land at the canyon mouth, and closed access. But maybe it is not an accident. We do not know who Leeson and his wife are. That is one thing we are here to find out." Her voice sent a chill through Levi.

"Leeson was a rich asshole, nothing more," Levi said coldly. "But he didn't deserve to die like he did."

"Maybe," Althea said. "And maybe not."

"What do you know about Jacob Blackburn?" Cali asked him.

"Nothing. Never met him socially. I'm not even sure I'd recognize him. I just know he was Leeson's foreman. And he is testifying that he saw my truck parked at Leeson's the night of the murder. He's lying for some reason."

"He's disappeared."

"Disappeared? I don't understand."

"We believe he is Lycaon, that he came through the spring into the canyon. We discovered Leeson had another foreman, Hank Walkins, who disappeared when Blackburn showed up. We believe Jacob killed Hank. He either ensnared the Leesons, or they were colluding. We need to find out, and we need to find him. And somehow I think that Callahan has these answers."

"Don't tell me that Callahan came through the spring as well?"

"No, he came from California, which is worse."

Forty three

BY THE END OF the afternoon, Levi was willing to believe anything.

Both Cali and Althea communicated with animals. It was common for birds to land on them, which was intriguing enough, even more so that a Steller's jay groomed Althea's hair. Levi watched as Althea shot arrows with a long bow into a tripod target, splitting the previous arrow down the center every time.

"Want to try?" she asked Levi.

Levi could barely pull the bow-string back, and the arrow flopped uselessly in the direction of the target.

She put the bow aside. "Sit with me," she told him.

He sat across from her on the grass.

"Give me your hands."

He reached out his hands, and she took them and held them. Then she began crying softly. Her eyes were fully open, and again he was lost in them, falling or rising he knew not. And then, miraculously, he saw Mirr. She was standing in front of him. They were in the canyon, just above the den site, in a rock-strewn meadow. The sun was strong, but she cast no shadow.

And then he heard her voice in his mind. "Levi. You must help me return."

"How?" he heard himself ask.

"You will know. It will be revealed when you need to know."

"Did Leeson kill you?"

He heard only the wind blowing hard across a field of grass. Then, "Take care of Althea."

"Are you in love with Althea or Lycaon?"

"I love them both."

"But they are bitter enemies."

"I love them both, but I fear for Althea. She is vulnerable in love."

Levi woke, sitting on the porch with a crow staring at him. Everywhere he looked, he saw Mirr.

Forty four

THAT EVENING THEY DROVE to his house, where he took a shower and got into some new clothes. Althea was very interested in seeing the tampered back door lock, the location of the wolf jaw and paw, and where the bag was left. She walked about the house sniffing like a feral animal, putting her nose to things and inhaling sharply.

"Smell anything?" Levi asked.

"I create a scent map over time. I smell the police. I don't recognize them, but can smell their gun oil. Then your girlfriend, Sachi." She gave him a smile, and he knew she smelled their sex.

"Before that, someone else, no gun, then you alone, for a while, then that someone else again. He was here twice when you weren't."

"The person who broke in. What else?"

Althea smiled. "I think that's enough for now."

Levi grilled venison steaks out back, watching the ponderosas across the road turn darker as the sky burned brilliant orange. Cali produced two bottles of red wine with Greek labels. Remembering what happened last time he drank wine with Cali, he was temperate. But after a glass, he began to relax.

After dinner he lit a fire and they sat around it, the two women telling unbelievable stories. Levi no longer doubted them, as fantastical as they sounded. The evening was a feast of surreality, perception accentuated to unimaginable heights. Levi felt as if the very air was his skin. It was a night of no moon. Stars appeared out of darkness in the dome of sky. An owl hooted in the forest across the street, and then they heard a wolf howl, far away, across the river in the foothills of the Bitterroots.

Levi had never heard a howl that chilling. The howl seemed to pull everything warm and human into it like a black hole. It sent shivers through him, and in the flickering firelight he saw goosebumps on Althea's arms.

"Lycaon," Althea said. "He's close."

"You said he took the form of Jacob Blackburn."

"He's now a wolf."

Forty five

THE NEXT MORNING, AFTER coffee and oatmeal, Levi called Sachi. She had just returned from work, and was dashing out to meet someone for dinner.

"Should I be jealous?"

She ignored him. "Are you still in prison? That was horrible, what they did to you. They have no right."

"I'm home. Someone bailed me out."

"Who? Art?"

"No. Althea. Artemis. I'm not sure. And Cali, the woman who took me through the spring to the beach below the temple."

Silence froze time, then, "This is all too strange, Levi. Are you OK? You're not imagining this, are you?" Concern in her voice.

"No. The women are going to help me." He didn't go into detail.

"Look, I've got to run. I worry about you, Levi. I'll call later, OK?"

"When this is all cleared up, I need to see you again. Hell, I need to now."

Momentary silence. "I would like that very much. Maybe I'll come visit again. I have a conference in Berkley in August."

"It's a date, Sachi." And then before he could think it and reflect, "I love you."

He heard a sharp intake of breath, then Sachi said, "I also love you. You take care, Levi."

"Goodbye."

"Goodbye."

Levi found the two women sitting at the picnic table in the back yard, and he was momentarily filled with disbelief at how normal they looked. Two women, dressed in contemporary western-style clothes, talking. And yet they were mythological beings who traveled across space and time. Levi laughed, shook his head, and walked toward them.

Althea spoke. "We need to pay Callahan a visit."

"What makes you think he'll see us? His place is a fortress. He's a paranoid man fearful of attacks by the deep state."

"The what?" asked Cali.

"Never mind. The point is, no one can get near him unless he wills it."

"He lives alone?"

"Yes. His wife left him years ago, and he never remarried."

"Girlfriend?"

"Nope. He's a recluse." Levi was thinking he wanted to talk to Callahan as well. Before he killed him.

"Where does he live?"

"Over by Skalkaho. Across the Valley. He's got a spread of around five thousand acres."

"Two thousand hectares," Cali said. "That's a mammoth amount of land. I can think of only a few people in Greece who have that much land."

"It's really not much for the West. Many ranches are much larger."

"I think you should try the direct approach," Althea said calmly. "Call him."

"OK, I'll call him. But I want you to come with me. I'll need witnesses if he trips up and says something incriminating."

"We won't go with you, Levi, but we'll be there."

The phone call came to nothing. As soon as Levi identified himself, Callahan hung up.

"What's plan B?" he asked Althea.

"Where does he hang out?"

"Mostly at The Antler Bar in Darby. But I'd get in a fight if I went in there. That's where the right-wing wackos drink and share conspiracy theories."

"I'll go," said Cali. And that settled it.

Since Taylor had the best intel on Callahan, Levi called him, but didn't expect much, considering how he'd behaved the last few times Levi had seen him. But at least Taylor didn't hang up immediately, rather hounded him about who this Althea was who had bailed him.

"She's a friend."

"Another one of your Greek women friends? What's the matter? The local women aren't interesting enough?"

Levi ignored him. "What's the best night to connect with Callahan at the Antler Bar?"

To Levi's surprise, Taylor was cordial.

"He doesn't hang there anymore. Had a falling out with a couple of Birchers there."

"Where does he drink?"

"That new place just south of Hamilton, just past the bridge. The Flintlock."

"That new log building?"

"That's the one."

"Seems a bit fancy for Callahan's taste."

"Callahan's a rich man, Levi. You know that. And he has rich friends, though two of them just died. But don't get near him. If I hear of anything happening between you and Callahan, you'll be back in prison, pronto."

Levi said nothing.

"I still think you did this, Levi. And you're going down for it. This making bail thing is just a bump in the road."

"We'll see. So what's the best night to find him there?"

"I told you I don't want you hassling Callahan, Levi. I shouldn't have told you what bar he frequents."

"I didn't kill the Leesons, and I'm not going to kill Callahan, though I'm mightily convinced that some people shouldn't have been born."

"Bye, Levi."

Levi told Althea and Cali where to find Callahan. It was Tuesday, but Cali decided to stop in and see if she got lucky.

"What's he look like?"

Levi pulled up the *Ravalli Republic* on his computer and did a quick search. There were over twenty results. He limited it to graphic content and came up with four photographs, all within the last two years.

Callahan had to be around fifty. He wore his sandy hair short under a bruised white Stetson. In all four photos he wore a cowboy shirt with pearl buttons and black jeans. His egg-shaped face wore a permanent scowl, and it seemed he never tanned, rather was burnt rusty red.

"What a catch," said Cali, laughing.

"He'll be suspicious, Cali. Why would someone like you be interested in an old cowboy?"

"You just told us he has money. Two thousand hectares of land. Maybe I'm just looking for a husband to shelter me from the storm."

"Be careful, Cali."

"I can handle Callahan."

Forty six

The few, subtle touches Cali made, a bit of mascara, hint of pink lipstick, shampoo that caused her hair to shine in a dark room—made her irresistible.

"Every guy in the place will be trying to get in your knickers."

"I only have eyes for one."

Althea and Levi stood outside and watched Cali drive off in the truck. Luminous cumulus clouds luffed in an immense sky transitioning into evening. It was just after nine o'clock.

"You think she'll be OK?"

"She's a big girl. Besides, it's a reconnaissance trip. If he's there, she'll meet him and promise to be back tomorrow night. If it works out, he'll take her to his place tomorrow night, and we'll be waiting."

"I told you he lives in a fortress. He's probably got state-of-the-art security. Cameras, alarms, the whole bit. How do we get in?"

Althea smiled.

"You worry too much." She caught his eyes and tipped him off-balance.

"How do you do that?"

Althea just smiled. "I need to get back to our place for a bit. Why don't you come by tomorrow mid-afternoon or so, and we'll see what's what."

Levi tried calling Sachi again, but there was no answer. He left a message, then sent her a long email detailing what had happened thus far. Then he went for a walk through the mixed cottonwood and ponderosa forest across the road from his house. He'd traveled the game trail so often it was second nature, and he wasn't paying attention. He almost stepped in a leg snap-trap for a wolf, set in the middle of the trail, superficially covered with cottonwood leaves. He snapped it shut with a cottonwood branch, then pulled the stake from the ground and carried the trap to the Bitterroot River, where he threw it out as far as he could. Nice try, Callahan.

The next afternoon Levi followed the poorly detailed map Althea had drawn him. Althea and Cali were living near Woodside, an area Levi never frequented. With some trouble through a maze of curvy gravel roads, many of them private, Levi found her place. He pulled up next to the Ford truck and Jeep. As he got out, the crow on the porch leapt up and down on its perch, cawing.

Althea opened the door and let Levi in. She looked distraught.
"Where's Cali? How did it go?"
"She's sleeping. Not great."
"What happened?"
"Callahan attacked her."
"What!?"
"I guess she came on sexy. They sat, talked, had a few drinks. Callahan had already had a few drinks, so a few more. Then Cali broke it off, attempted to leave, saying she'd be back tonight. He insisted on walking her to her car, then threw her against the car and tried to kiss her. She turned her head away, and he grabbed her breasts and pushed his knee between her legs."
"Jesus! It didn't happen, right?" Levi burned with anger.
"She managed to push him back far enough to reach into her purse, pull out some mace, and spray him. Then she got into her car and drove away. He was running after her, clawing his face. She didn't expect that. She's pretty shaken up."
"The bastard!" Levi hissed.
"I want to go tonight to his house, and be there when he gets back from the bar," Althea said.
"How do we get in? Have you thought that out?"
"Yes. It is no problem. We'll be there waiting for him."

"OK, I'll trust you on this."

"Good." She took his hand, and he felt suddenly calm.

"I'm making tea. I'll get you a cup." She squeezed his hand and got up, walking into the kitchen. Levi scanned the wolves, photographed and drawn, tacked to the walls. When he came to the place where Mirr's photograph had hung, there was an empty rectangle. Levi heard stirring in one of the bedrooms, and a minute later the door opened, Cali poking her head out.

"Hi, Levi. I thought I heard voices. How are you?"

"How are you? Althea told me what happened."

"I was careless. It's my fault. It was not a big deal."

"It most certainly is not your fault," said Althea, as she entered the room carrying two mugs of tea. "Sit. I'll get you a cup."

Cali sat across from Levi. She smiled weakly.

"Did Althea tell you we are going to his house tonight?"

"She did. One thing is certain, you can't go back to that bar and hustle him."

Cali laughed. "That would actually be funny. To show up and act like nothing happened. Start hustling him again."

"Does he have a criminal record?" Althea asked.

"Not that I'm aware of," answered Levi.

"So, plan C. It is lucky we are flexible women."

"Yeah, plan C."

Althea came back with another mug of tea and set it in front of Cali.

"How are you feeling?"

"Fine, now, just fine." She smiled, her eyes as infinite as the Aegean Sea.

Forty Seven

THEY SPENT THE AFTERNOON using Google Earth to map it out. They were able to study his house, which lay at the end of a long, serpentine driveway, and the surrounding yard, two corrals, barn, and several outbuildings. The south end of Callahan's land was bordered by national forest.

It was just after eleven when they turned off the eastside highway onto a gravel road that bisected the national forest land, and a half-mile later pulled the truck onto a set of tire-tracks hunters used in the fall. It climbed several hundred yards into the forest of mixed Douglas fir and ponderosa pine.

They wore dark clothes, headlamps, and carbon-rubber-soled trail shoes, virtually silent. Black bandanas hung around their necks, and could be slid up to cover their faces. The sky did not entirely cooperate, however, awash with stars, the moon over half full and waxing.

Tension was palpable in the cab, and they didn't speak on the drive in, nor after heading up the ravine on foot. The house was approximately a mile in, and roughly a quarter of that was national forest. After ten minutes of climbing they came to a nine-foot barbed wire fence with prison wire across the top two feet.

Levi pulled a pair of wire-cutters from his daypack and snipped the lowest three strands, stepping through, holding the top wire up for the two women.

"I hope that didn't trigger an alarm," whispered Althea.

"We'll find out," Levi whispered back.

Althea took the lead. They followed the ridge-top for another five minutes through scattered trees, headlamps off. Coming into a slight clearing, they could see the house several hundred yards below them, mercury-vapor lights painting the yard with harsh white light. A truck was parked next to the house, and in the front driveway was an old Pontiac GTO. It looked like Callahan was home, and optimally tucked into bed with a few drinks fuzzing him up. Levi checked his watch. It was nearing midnight.

"We're going to split up now," Althea whispered.

It was a point Levi had argued against. None of them were armed, except for Cali's mace, and Levi thought there was power in numbers. But he had lost the argument two-to-one. Levi was to enter the back door, making noise as he went to attract Callahan, while the women entered the front. They would take him once he returned back inside.

"He'll have a gun," Levi said.

"So?" Althea had said, as Cali had looked nonplussed. "It will be his problem, then."

Levi descended through a clump of lodgepole pine. The going was thick, and he stopped every time he stepped on a dry stick, letting the crack reverberate in his ears and die out silently. A cow lowed several times, and off to his right a barn owl gave a long, harsh scream. Moments later, its shadow crossed the ground in front of Levi, and he looked up. He followed it with his eyes as it flew on, then he continued descending.

Levi had to scale three fences to get to the yard immediately behind the house. The light was unkind, giving him no shelter. He ran across the last thirty feet or so, ducking onto the back porch. It was a large space, sheltered by mature lilacs. A pile of tack, a number of boxes, garden tools, a couple of ladders, and assorted bric-a-brac clumped to his left. There was a small, square wooden table and single chair to his right. On the table was an ashtray full of cigarette butts. The back door, faint yellow, wore a heavy piece of cloth covering the window. Levi glanced at his watch, which he'd synchronized with Althea. He had two minutes before he'd start making noise, trying to break it down. He'd already planned to kick it in, aiming for the area just above the knob. He thought it would collapse easily.

Levi had been scoping for cameras. He glanced around again, but didn't see any. Maybe all the burglar alarm stuff Taylor had told him about was bull. Callahan pictured himself a self-reliant man. He wasn't likely to rely on others to protect him. Levi remembered him saying a number of times that he'd never call 911.

Just then, Levi saw the cloth over the door window tremble, then still. He was riveted on it when he felt the gun press into his side just below his ribs. Callahan had moved silently out of the shadows of the piled junk.

"Hi, Levi. Welcome to my spread. Your first time here, I believe." He pushed the pistol deeper. "Don't do anything stupid now, or you're just an intruder I shot on the back porch in self-defense. Cops will probably figure you're here doing recon to murder me, now that you got Leeson." He spat. "Stupid bastards."

Levi worried now for the women. He wouldn't be able to signal his break-in, and they wouldn't know Callahan had a gun to him.

"Now turn that knob and walk inside. We'll go through the kitchen and into the living room. Get ourselves comfy." Callahan's voice was cold and harsh. Levi didn't doubt for one minute that Callahan would kill him. Turning quickly wasn't an option. Callahan had the gun jammed in too tight. He decided to wait and see how this played out. He opened the door, and then the gun was off him, and Levi knew Callahan had it leveled at his mid-back.

"Walk slow, now. This here is an 1881 Colt .45 Peacemaker, and believe me it will give you peace. Break your spine clear in half." He cleared his throat. "Hold it there."

Callahan opened a drawer and shuffled the contents around. "OK, move."

There was no sign of the women as Levi walked into the living room. The room itself was a tribute to the old West and Manifest Destiny. Western art, some of it looking like authentic Russells and Winchesters, hung everywhere. Motifs of cowboys, trappers, the noble savage. A large, worn, brown leather couch and matching loveseat filled much of the room. There were two other chairs, bookshelf, a large TV.

"Put the backpack down."

Levi slid the backpack from his shoulders and set it on the floor.

"Sit there. In the rocker." The rocking chair was ancient, built of hard, heavy wood. As Levi sat down, it hardly budged.

"Here." Callahan tossed Levi a roll of duct tape. "Now bind your legs to the legs of the chair. Careful now."

Levi did as he was told, tearing the tape with his teeth, wrapping it tight around his calves, but not too tight. If the opportunity arose, he wanted some wiggle room.

"OK, now wrap your right arm to the arm of the chair." Again, Levi obeyed.

Callahan got up and took the tape from Levi, binding his left arm to the chair, a much tighter wrap. He checked the other wraps and grunted. "They'll do."

Callahan picked up the backpack and walked over to the other chair, a straight-legged wooden chair with a woven back. Turning it, he set the backpack down next to him and sat, straddling the chair about six feet from Levi. He held the gun steady.

The Colt looked ancient, and more deadly because of it. Callahan held it casually, but with control. "Now, wolfman, we're going to have us a conversation. First off, why are you here?"

Levi said the first thing that came to mind. "You were right. It was a recon. You were next."

Callahan laughed harshly. "Bullshit. You no more killed Leeson than I did." Levi thought he saw him soften. "You know he was my friend?" Callahan stood up and walked over to a small table, taking a photograph and showing it to Levi.

"See this? Me on the right, Leeson on the left. Saigon, 1969. We enlisted together, were grunts together. Saved each other's lives more times than I care to think. We grew up together near Sacramento, went to school together. Best pals. There's no way I'd kill that man." Callahan paused, staring hard at Levi. "There's no way you would either. You may hate, but you're no killer."

He paused for a long moment. "No, I figure we got one thing in common. We both want to find out who did this and why. You, so you don't go to prison for something you didn't do, and me so I can kill the bastard who did it."

Levi was shocked, but didn't show it. He had never doubted that Callahan had murdered the Leesons.

"Now tell me, wolfman, what do you think? About who did this?"

Levi hesitated. "Until a few seconds ago, I was dead certain you did."

Callahan nodded. He seemed to be thinking. Then finally he let out a long sigh and said, "Well, I didn't. Leeson came here because I was here. I found him the land. I was his best man when he married that woman, Brittany. I didn't approve of it, but you can't tell a man who to marry. I thought she was a money-grubber."

He wiped his forehead, and Levi could see now that he was tired. Probably had more than a few drinks in him. The initial adrenaline flushing his system was receding.

"So we're back to square one. Except what the hell am I going to do with you?"

"Call the sheriff. Tell him I was snooping around."

"Can't do that, wolfman. They'll just lock you up again, and the wrong guy will get strung for this."

"I can't imagine that would give you much pause, Callahan."

He laughed again. "There's a lot you don't know about me, wolfman. And some of it's even true." He laughed again as if at his own joke. "I adhere to a code of honor. I'm an honorable man. If a man commits a crime, he pays. He doesn't send someone else to the chair in his place."

It was the first time Levi had heard the phrase. "The chair." It sent a shiver through him. For the first time since he'd been arrested, he was aware he could get the death penalty. Frontier justice, twenty-first century style. And then suddenly, he wasn't sure if he believed Callahan. He remembered what the man had done to Cali. Not something an honorable man would do.

Just then there was a commotion in the yard.

"You wait here now," Callahan said, getting up and over to a monitor. He stared at the screen for a minute.

"No camera in the back. That surprised me."

"Haven't gotten around to it. This security crap is new. Since Leeson ate it." He walked to the window, drew the heavy curtain back slowly and stared outside, then let the curtain fall back.

"Don't get any dumb ideas. That chair weighs over a hundred pounds. You won't get far."

He opened the front door and walked out into the night, leaving the door ajar. A few seconds later, Levi thought he saw a flash of movement, but when he blinked it was gone. He shook his head. The adrenaline was leaving his system as well. A few seconds later, Callahan walked back into the house.

"Damn coyotes. They can go the way of wolves for all I care." He walked over and settled himself into his chair.

"Let me ask you something," said Levi. "Why did you check out that book on werewolves?"

Callahan stared at him with mild shock. "How did you know that?"

"I asked a librarian who checked it out."

"That's confidential. Private. They shouldn't have done that." He hesitated for a moment. "But it don't matter. I'll tell you. Truth is, I'm fascinated by wolves. I hate 'em to death, and would eradicate every last one, but they fascinate me. I saw that werewolf book in the new releases section and checked it out. I only had it for a coupla days. What do you care?"

"No reason, really. Just thought it was odd."

"Don't matter. None of it does." He raised the gun again, pointing it directly at Levi's face.

Levi sensed something behind him, then saw Mirr, only feet away, step silently past him, crouching, ready to spring at Callahan.

Callahan gasped. "Impossible! I killed you. And damn it, I'll do it again."

He raised the Colt, but before he could squeeze off a shot, Mirr was on him. He tried to twist sideways, but Mirr smothered him, biting him furiously on his face and neck. Callahan was shrieking, but the sounds gurgled through the blood pouring from his mouth. Sounds Levi had never imagined possible. A shot rang out, the bullet shattering the glass door of a hutch. Callahan whimpered faintly, his right arm spasming. Then everything stopped. Mirr dropped silently to the floor and glanced Levi, her almond eyes shining, lit by a light both ancient and alien. Then she loped out the front door and slipped into the night.

Levi choked on his bile. Callahan's face, throat, and neck looked like oxygenated hamburger glistening in the yellow lamp-light. Blood pulsed from his torn carotid like a fountain slowly dying. His eyes were wild with fear, but he was no longer fearful, no longer among the living.

Forty eight

LEVI WOKE IN CRISP sheets, the ceiling above him dusty blue. A faint breeze, carrying the scent of lilac and cottonwood, blew through the screen covering an open window, flicking the white cotton curtain open. Sun washed the far wall, part of the floor, the bottom of the bed. He flexed his hands, stretched, raised his head, and then he remembered. But what he remembered was impossible. He lay his head back down and was out.

He woke again to Cali's voice. "Levi," then a little louder, "Levi."

He opened his eyes. Cali was standing on the side holding a glass, which she set on a small table next to the bed. "I brought you a glass of water. You should drink some."

"Where am I?"

"At our place. You've been asleep since we left Callahan's."

"I remember. I remember Mirr."

"Shh. Just drink. We'll talk later."

Levi woke to sunlight on the far side of the room. He got up, took a shower, dressed and walked into the kitchen, smelling coffee and grilled cheese.

"Hey, sleepyhead," Althea said. "Coffee? Sandwich?"

"All." Levi stood there staring at the women, first Althea, then Cali. They seemed calm, content.

"Did I really see what I think I saw?"

"What do you think you saw?"

"Mirr killing Callahan." His voice wavered.

Althea handed him a cup of coffee. "Cream?"

Levi nodded. "You're not answering."

She handed him a small pitcher of cream. "You saw what happened," she said matter-of-factly.

"How?"

"We brought her into this life to do what she needed."

"Not for herself. For her cub," Cali said.

"She's back in the spirit world," said Althea.

"How is that possible?"

Althea shrugged.

"How is it done?"

"One being has to open to the spirit, and then surrender to its form."

"Shape-shifting," Levi said.

"If that's what you want to call it."

"Which of you did it? Allowed Mirr to change you?"

Cali nodded toward Althea.

"I heard you howl in the canyon that night." He thought of the tracks as well, that changed from wolf to human at the water's edge.

Althea nodded. "I have a relationship with Mirr. I know her, and she knows me. We would do anything for each other, even die."

"But as you say, death isn't final, it's just a transition to another form."

Althea smiled.

"Is it risky? Shape-shifting?"

Mirth drained from her smile. "Everything's risky," she said. "Being here is risky."

No one said anything, then Cali broke the silence. "We cleaned everything up."

"Any evidence we were there," Althea added. "You don't have to worry."

"How did I get back here? I don't remember anything."

"You were sleeping."

"And?"

"We put you in the truck and drove here."

"You carried me to the truck?" Levi shook his head in disbelief.

"She carried you," Cali said.

"You're not that heavy," Althea said. "Not like an elk."

Levi shook his head. His new normal. "Callahan didn't kill the Leesons," he said.

"So you said. You were quite talkative on the way back here."

"I can't believe any of this."

"You don't have to. You're free to believe anything you want. As we all are. Toasted cheese? I make them with a lot of onion." Althea smiled, and suddenly the mood shifted, tension draining from the room.

"Fine."

"After this, I need to take you home. The police will suspect you. We were here all night. The three of us. We have timed selfies, you made a phone call to Sachi from our phone around midnight. It's all taken care of."

"We played around. Had three-way sex," Cali said, laughing.

"Was it good?" Levi asked, finally smiling.

"It was for us," said Cali, still laughing.

Forty nine

A CRUISER WAS PARKED at the curb in front of Levi's house when Althea pulled into the drive behind Levi's truck. He got out, leaned in and kissed her cheek, then straightened. The grass needed mowing, and the lilacs were fecund with blooms, swarming with bees.

Taylor and Juicy were exiting the cruiser. "Wolfman," Juicy said. "Mind if we have a word?"

"That the gal who bailed you out?" asked Taylor.

"Yes, and yes. She's a friend."

"Must be a hell of a friend to put up five hundred grand to jump you. Seeing as you're guilty as sin," said Taylor with a smirk.

"Want to talk out here, or come in?"

"Let's go inside," Juicy said, nodding at Myrtle, the older woman next door who was staring at them.

Taylor shot her a look. The woman turned her head away, but didn't move from the fence.

"Neighbors must be curious," Taylor said.

"They're good people. They haven't judged me yet. Unlike you."

Levi opened the door and led the two policemen in. He waved to the kitchen table. "Have a seat."

Juicy and Taylor sat down. Taylor immediately began playing with a salt shaker. He looked nervous.

"Want something to drink? I've got water and beer. Otherwise I have to make something."

"Water's fine," Juicy said.

Levi went to the sink, filled two glasses, and set them on the table. "So?"

Juicy spoke first. "So you heard Callahan died last night." It wasn't a question.

"Callahan!? No, I hadn't heard. What happened?"

Juicy scratched his nose. "So where were you last night?"

"With Althea and Cali. They're friends of mine from Greece. Biologists."

"You sure have a lot of friends from Greece," Taylor said sarcastically.

"I guess. I was over there working for a while. I didn't plan it this way."

"So why would a woman you've only known for a few months, from another country, bail you out?"

"First of all, I've known her for longer than I can remember. Second, we've been romantically involved. And third, she's filthy rich."

Juicy cleared his throat. "It seems that Mike Callahan was killed by a wolf."

"By a wolf! That's bullshit. It's probably the same person who killed the Leesons. They made it look that way."

"Afraid it isn't. It's a much different murder scene than at Leesons. His throat was torn out. He was holding a firearm, his old Colt. One round discharged, but looks like he hit the hutch, not the wolf."

Levi said nothing.

"We have footage," said Taylor.

"Footage?"

"Callahan had a video surveillance camera in front. It filmed a wolf, a white wolf, running across the lawn and onto the porch. It entered the house somehow and attacked him."

"Unprovoked? Just went into the house and attacked him? Bullshit."

Taylor smiled weakly.

"We already determined that the prints, there were several in blood as it left, were not the same as your paw," Juicy said.

"Which you claim was stolen," added Taylor.

"I don't believe this," said Levi. He was using this phrase far too much lately.

"You don't have to believe it. We brought up Steve McCandless. He looked at the scene, the tape. He couldn't believe it either, but he couldn't deny it. And in the end…"

"He verified our theory," finished Taylor.

"So where does that leave me?"

"I assume you have proof you were with the two women last night?"

"Well, I didn't save the condoms."

Juicy grunted a laugh.

"Some selfies. I called Sachi in Greece from their phone at some point. That can probably be tracked."

"Sachi? She the gal who was here when we arrested you? You called her while you were cavorting with these other two? What kind of asshole are you?" Taylor had a strange, twisted smile on his face.

"You wouldn't understand. We're all friends. We're pagans."

"Pagans, huh," Juicy laughed wryly. "I guess there's other words for it."

"Is that all? I have to return some calls and mow the lawn."

"Don't go anywhere, Levi."

Juicy and Taylor got up, Juicy heavily, and started for the door. Juicy turned back and gave Levi a harsh glare.

"I know you hated him, Levi, but Callahan was my friend. I'm going to find out who's behind this."

Levi started the mower and began hacking through the heavy grass. Mowing always took his mind off other things, and he had many things to take his mind off. Juicy's comment made it clear that he was suspect for Callahan's death as well as the Leesons'. He had to clear himself of all of it. He just didn't know how.

His cell was ringing as he entered the house. It was Sam Doke.

"Levi, we should meet. Soon."

They met at Moe's Place, an old bar near the railroad that had a calculated run-down feel. The new owner, a guy from Oregon, had bought it for a song. He'd redone the infrastructure, painted it, and replaced the bar with gorgeous fir, but left much of the original furniture, the photographs of old patrons on the wall, the jukebox of fifties C&W. "Nouveau funky," the new owner called it, and it had become the darling of young professionals who wanted to slum without really slumming. And Moe's had an obscene selection of beer.

Doke was sitting nursing something out of a viola-shaped green bottle, ignoring the empty glass in front of him. Levi walked over and sat down. Doke pointed to another bottle. "I took the liberty of ordering you one."

"Thanks." Levi picked it up and took a sip.

"You a beer freak?"

"I like a beer every now and then."

"I'm a freak," said Doke. "This new brewery in Butte, *Glacier Lust*, makes an incredible wheat beer." He held up the bottle as if to prove his point. "I even go on brewery tours. Just did one in Portland. Five fucking days. They have a ton of breweries in Portland. I drank a lot of beer."

"Hope it didn't affect your judgment." Levi laughed. "What's on your mind?"

"Oh, several things. Cops talk to you yet about Callahan?"

"Yeah."

"You have an alibi?"

"I was with a couple of women all night."

Doke chuckled. "That's what happens when you get old. You need at least two." He set his bottle down. "One of them the woman who paid your bail?"

"Yeah."

"What's her name?"

"Althea."

"Althea what?"

Levi hesitated.

"To be honest, I don't know her last name."

Doke's chuckle became a laugh.

"You don't know the last name of the woman who paid your bail and who you spent last night with? That beats all." He sat musing for a minute. "Leeson's foreman, Jacob Blackburn, has dropped out of sight. The cops suspect that you eliminated a witness."

Levi thought of Lycaon running wild out there, a wildcard.

"Got anything to say about that?"

"Maybe he didn't want to lie in court."

"Hmmm." Doke took a solid hit of beer, swishing it around in his mouth. "We maybe caught a break in the case."

"Oh?"

"Your neighbor, an older woman named Myrtle Burnett? You know her?"

"Of course. She's the only Myrtle I know. She's been my neighbor ever since I moved into that house."

"When was that again?"

"1989."

"That was another era. Anyway, she saw a guy go into your backyard shortly after the murder. Late afternoon. She said your truck was gone."

"Did she get a description?"

"Oh yeah. She said it was the cop with Juicy when they first came to your place. She identified the car he drove as a Ford Explorer."

"A cop? Taylor Dikestay?"

"Taylor Dikestay owns a Ford Explorer."

"That doesn't make sense. Maybe he was prowling around, looking for evidence."

"Can't do that without a warrant. Anything he found would be inadmissible. Plus, he was dressed in nondescript clothes, jeans and a light tan wool coat, not a uniform."

"Maybe it was recon." Levi turned the bottle in his hand. The label featured a rendering of a mountain crevasse that yawned into blackness.

"Maybe not. Maybe he was the guy who stole your skull and paw."

"No way, not Taylor. I can't bel—" He stopped himself. He wasn't going to utter that phrase again. What if it had been Taylor all along? He remembered him with an anxious smile at their last visit, when he spotted Myrtle. Maybe what happened to Callahan had put a scare in him.

"We think he was dicking Leeson's wife Brittany. We're pursuing a few leads that could verify it."

"Whoa, that adds a wrinkle. Have you told Juicy yet?"

"No. I will, but I want to wait until we know something more substantial about Taylor and his relationship to Brittany. Don't get your hopes up yet, though. Still a lot of threads out there that need to be tied together. It would help substantially if we could find Jacob Blackburn."

Levi wanted to tell Doke that Jacob was now a wolf named Lycaon, but didn't think it would go over well. "Anything else?"

"All for now. Keep in touch."

Doke drained the bottle. "Stay and nurse it. It's on me." He threw a twenty on the table and walked out the door.

That evening Levi was wading through email when his cell rang. It was Steve McCandless.

"Levi! It's been awhile."

Levi sat back. He hadn't talked to Steve once during this entire affair. The police had indicated that Steve was helping them build a case against him. Levi and Steve had been friends for a long while, and it hurt him that Steve would turn against him.

"Steve. I hear you've been busy assisting the forces of justice."

"And you've been busy pretending to be a wolf and murdering people." There was a brief hesitation. "I'm joking Levi, joking."

Levi held his breath then let it out slowly. "I'm not laughing."

"Yeah, I suppose not."

More silence.

"Hey, what do you make of this Callahan thing?" Steve asked.

"It's bizarre. I saw the footage of the wolf approaching Callahan's house."

"I didn't see the wolf from your pack that was killed, but I heard it looked like her."

"Yeah, it looked like her, but it wasn't." He'd almost called her Mirr, but that would have opened the door on subjects he did not want to discuss with Steve. "My wolf had a scar across her muzzle," he lied. "This one didn't."

"Think it could have killed Callahan?"

"I didn't initially, but now I do. I think the wolf entered the house through an open door, encountered Callahan in a closed room, and attacked him out of fear. Like a dog attack sparked by fear. Callahan had a gun. One shot was fired. That's the only scenario that makes sense to me." Levi walked over to the back door and looked out across the back yard, dusted by moonlight. "You looked at the wounds. What do you think?"

"The wounds were made by a large canid, there's no doubt about that. And given the video, and the timing, it's the most logical scenario. I heard of a similar situation in Romania. A middle-aged couple were home when a wolf entered the house. Discovering them, it ran for the door, which had blown shut. The man went to hit it with a ski pole, and it attacked. It didn't kill him, but wounded him quite badly. His wife witnessed the entire thing."

"What I don't understand, though, is why did it just go for Callahan's throat? There were no wounds on the arms, legs, or torso. You would think Callahan would try to fight it off."

"I think it surprised him. Juicy told me he had a look of shock on his face. It's unusual, but his throat presented the best target."

"I guess. Anyway, wolves are getting a bad rep in this neck of the woods. First the Leesons, now this."

"I saw photos of the Leeson murder. That wasn't a wolf. It was someone trying to make it look like a wolf."

"I know, Steve," Levi said sarcastically. "They used my paw and skull in the process."

"Sorry. I knew that. Do the police have any real leads yet?"

"Nope. I'm out on bail, but still the prime suspect."

How's all of it going?"

"It's starting to sort itself out. There should be some developments over the next week or so. Least that's what my lawyer told me."

"You go with Justin Murphy?"

"No, a local guy named Sam Doke."

"Well, have him call me if he wants more input into the biological aspect."

Levi didn't answer right away, then said, "Taylor made it sound like you were incriminating me."

"That's totally untrue Levi. I testified to the origin of the paw. I did tell them, after reviewing the photographs, that wolves did not kill the Leesons. But that's certainly not telling them *you* did. I even told them that someone was trying to frame you, but they didn't seem interested in that scenario. To tell you the truth, that cop Taylor pissed me off. He seemed to have his mind made up."

"Yeah, I think you're right on with that one, Steve."

"I have to admit it's pretty weird that…" He didn't finish.

"That what, Steve?"

"Well, don't get pissed, but it's pretty weird that the two people responsible for killing those wolves that were hung up are now dead."

"Justice works in mysterious ways, Steve. What can I say?"

"Well if you need support, of any kind, don't hesitate to call."

"OK, Steve. Thanks."

As soon as he cut the cell, his landline rang. He ducked back inside and answered. Sachi's voice flowed into his head. "I tried your cell, but it was busy."

"Yeah, I was talking to Steve McCandless. The wolf biologist from the University."

"Are you still out of jail?"

"Yeah, Althea has made sure of that."

"How is it all going?"

"Very strange, but I think the situation is coming to a head."

"Did you find out who murdered the Leesons?"

"Not quite, but we're close."

"Oh?"

"Lycaon is here."

"Jesus, Levi, be careful. I'm not sure how much of this I believe, but you are no match for these powers."

"Of course, I'll be careful. I'm a biologist, not a gunslinger. I feel good about what we've learned. And I think it's almost over."

They were quiet for a long moment.

"I miss you so damn much," Levi said.

"I miss you, too. So much. When this is over, I'll come visit."

"That would be very nice," he whispered.

They talked awhile about a mammoth project Sachi had been chosen to spearhead. The mission was to identify all wild lands in Greece that needed protection. Public and private both. It was the first comprehensive project of its kind in Greece, and used the Roadless Area and Evaluation studies, completed in the 60s and 70s in the U.S., as their model.

"You are OK?"

"Yes, I'm OK. Just tired."

"You'll come vacation with me when it's over?"

"Most definitely."

"Love you."

He felt like he was on an emotional see-saw.

"I Love you, too. Truly."

"Don't let those wild Greek women tempt you."

"I won't. I promise."

Sachi made a kissing sound, then the line went dead, and Levi was left with joy that deflated slowly, but deflated nonetheless.

He poured a healthy two shots of bourbon into a mug and walked back out into the moonlit yard. Bats were flitting in and out of Myrtle's garage light, and he heard a barred owl in the woods. He wondered how all the pieces in play would manifest. He took a sip and swished it around in his mouth, relishing the sweet, harsh taste. He needed to get out of here for a few days. He needed to get into the mountains.

Fifty

Morning dawned as if it were eternal late spring. For the first time in a long while, Levi felt excited, anticipatory. He'd decided on several possible locations for a getaway, and called an old friend, Danny Mouch, who was a caretaker for the Macleans east-side ranch. There was a canyon off their place, on national forest land, that interested him. He'd seen it from the air—steep cliffs, narrow for the first mile, then opening into lush meadows. They would be full of wildflowers and wildlife. Access was through the Maclean spread.

"No problem," said Danny. "Stop by, and I'll unlock a couple gates for you."

Levi packed quickly, taking trail-mix, a couple apples, ample tea. He also included an eight-piece spinning rod, reel, and a box of spinners. The freshet that ran through Bear Draw was loaded with native Westslope cutthroat trout, and there was no better way to supplement trail-mix. He added a small plastic bottle of olive oil and some Cajun spiced salt.

He drove to Althea's place and pulled his truck alongside her Ford. It was still cool, and smoke drifted from the chimney. The crow, Karnesis, cawed at him and bowed his head. Levi had learned when he did this he wanted his head scratched, so Levi obliged. The crow seemed to purr.

Levi knocked at the door.

"Come in," Cali answered.

He opened the door and was instantly hit with the smell of bacon.

"Have you eaten?" Althea asked.

"I had half a stale bagel," he said, laughing.

"Well, sit down. As you can see, we have plenty."

Levi sat across from Althea and pulled his chair in. "You eat like this every morning?"

"Sure. Why not? And we knew you were coming by."

"You knew? How?"

"She can feel things," Cali said, bringing Levi a plate and silverware wrapped in a cloth napkin.

The table was elegantly laid out: Sliced melon, oranges, mango; scrambled eggs, bacon, croissants, coffee, and cream. Levi took the plate and helped himself, heaping the food high.

"I thought you ladies ate yoghurt and honey."

Cali laughed. "We eat anything!"

"And everything," added Althea.

Levi told them he was disappearing into the mountains for a few days.

"Does the sheriff know?" Althea asked with a twinkle in her eyes.

"Hell, no. I just need to get away from the murders, my arrest, all of it."

Just then his phone rang. He glanced at the number. "I've got to take this," he said, getting up and walking out onto the porch.

"Doke. What's up?"

"We've had a major breakthrough. My investigator got into Taylor's laptop and downloaded over a hundred emails to and from Brittany."

"Holy shit! I had no idea."

"Why would you? The emails make it pretty clear that Leeson knew about the affair, and he and Brittany were trying to work it out. The emails get very heated on Taylor's end, then stop about a week before the murder."

"I am in awe here, Doke." He cupped his face and let out a long breath. "This isn't legal, is it?"

"Damn right it's not, it's illegal as hell, and the emails are inadmissible as evidence in court. But I think they'll have a profound effect on Juicy and Taylor. I chose a most salacious selection. Taylor is quite the creative writer. He's a downright poet at times. 'Breasts as soft as fruit-tipped snow.' That sort of thing."

"God, Doke."

"I didn't say it was good poetry. But the last ten or so emails are full of threats, some of them violent, some threats to commit suicide."

"Taylor threatened to kill himself over this?"

"He was in way over his head, Levi."

"Wow. I've heard a lot of crazy things lately, but this is right up there."

"Anyway, I've arranged a meeting with Juicy and Taylor at two this afternoon, to discuss some 'evidence' I've found. I'm going to tell them we got the emails from the Internet provider, total bullshit, but we'll see what happens. I'm fairly certain that Juicy knows nothing about Taylor and Brittany. If Taylor admits he was having an affair, it will make him the prime suspect, particularly with the content of the emails I'll show them. Add that to him being identified by Myrtle, God I love that name, and the case against Taylor congeals further. It's my hope that this gambit causes Juicy to shift his focus away from you and onto Taylor. Which is where it should be."

"What if Taylor denies everything?"

"Then we watch him and see what happens. He'll know we're onto him, and the odds are that he'll do something stupid."

"He may be a hard nut to crack."

"Even so, all we have to do is introduce some slight doubt into Juicy's mind. That's all. Reasonable doubt, my man. Keep the faith."

"OK, but I'm heading into the woods for three or four days. I won't have a phone."

"Call me when you get out. More research?"

"No, a clarity of mind trip."

"Go clearcut your mind, Levi. We'll take care of the heavy lifting."

Levi slid the phone into his pocket and walked back into the room.

"Your food's getting cold," Cali said.

Levi began wolfing it down, telling the women what was going on with Doke and Taylor.

"It sounds like a breakthrough," said Althea, sounding pleased. "I knew there would be one."

"What else do you know?" asked Levi, teasing.

"Not much," she responded, giving him a seductive smile. "I talked with a real estate agent."

"A real estate agent? Are you moving here? Buying this place?"

"Not even close. I'm interested in the Leeson place."

"The Leeson place!?"

"The family wants to shed it quickly. It's going on the market in a few days for three million and some change." She caught his gaze, dizzying him.

"I don't understand."

"Access to the spring, Levi. The wolf pack. Mirr's pack."

"They'll be gone."

"No, they won't. I want to buy it for your organization, WolfRecovery. I want Sachi to be a partner. We need to preserve that canyon, Levi, and this is the perfect way to do it."

Levi was stunned. "But what if I'm convicted, have to spend the rest of my life in prison?"

"You won't."

"Where will you get the money?"

"You ask too many silly questions."

Fifty One

LEVI DROVE TO DANNY Mouch's place, still disoriented from the conversation with Althea, the look she'd given him. He knew he hadn't witnessed even a tiny fraction of her power.

Danny lived in a small cabin built in 1886 by the original homesteader, Garth MacLean, one of thousands of westward settlers who wittingly or not destroyed the Indians, the wolves, and the wilderness. Window-boxes stuffed with marigolds, impatiens, geraniums, and lobelia hung outside every window. Danny sat in a canvas chair smoking a thin cigar, leafing through a magazine. He got up and walked over as Levi got out of his truck, giving him a hug.

"Sorry for all the shit you're going through, Levi. Everybody knows you're a stand-up guy. This is all bullshit."

"Thanks, Danny. Say, can I ask you something? You know Taylor Dikestay. What do you think of him?"

"Candidly?"

"Yeah."

"He was a friend till he became a cop."

"How did that change things?"

"The power went to his head. He started rubbing shoulders with people that, well, that I wouldn't give the time of day to. He severed contact with a lot of his old friends. Unless he needed something from them. Then he was all back in the game. But the minute he had what he needed, be it information or a loan, he dropped them again." A flicker of discomfort shadowed Danny's face. "I probably shouldn't say anything, but there's talk that he and Leeson's wife were tossing and turning a bit."

"Interesting."

"Want some coffee?"

"No, I need to get up the canyon ASAP. Why don't you come out with a bottle? I won't be up far. Just where the cliffs end and the meadow begins."

"That sounds fantastic. I'll bring a sleeping bag. It will be good to visit. Been awhile." Then he added, "There's a nice herd of elk up there. You bring a camera?"

"I don't go to the bathroom without a camera. You know that."

Danny chuckled, his round, ruddy face reflecting morning sun. "You best leave your truck here. Throw your shit in mine, and I'll take you up to the canyon mouth."

They drove, bantered a bit, Danny not prying, radio tuned to a country station out of Lolo, playing soft. The road, a track really, wound through meadows and cottonwoods. Danny got out to open a couple of gates, then they were weaving through a herd of black angus cattle, the bulls off to the side, cows clogging the road. Danny had to ease along, bumping a few, their complaints rending the morning air.

Once out of the cows, Danny pointed to a birdhouse on the split-rail fence, new pine, glistening in the morning sun. "I'm building houses for bluebirds, trying to increase the population. We had some kind of die-off a few years ago."

Over the next hundred yards or so, Levi saw a series of pine boxes, small hole, flap roof. A couple looked inhabited, and several bluebirds perched on the fence, taking off and skipping ahead as the truck approached.

Danny stopped in front of an old log bridge and cut the ignition. The bridge, the left side caved in, stretched twenty feet across a slough that once was a channel of the Bitterroot River.

Levi stepped down from the truck as a meadowlark's call sliced the air. Across the slough, a sagebrush field stretched for a quarter mile or so. Levi could see the cliff mouth of the canyon, the lush green bordering the creek that flowed from it. He took a deep breath and let it out slowly.

Danny lifted Levi's pack out of the truck bed. "God, this thing's light."

"Around eighteen."

"You into that ultralight backpacking thing?"

"I could bore you for hours with material science, dude."

"Expensive, yeah?"

"Yeah. Pretty pricey."

"Well, take care. I'll see you soon."

"Don't forget the bottle."

"Hell, I'd forget my sleeping bag before I forgot that."

Levi swung the pack onto his shoulders, shook Danny's hand, thanked him, crossed the bridge on the safe side, and began weaving through the sage toward the canyon. He was thinking he had a thing for relatively inaccessible canyons, and was also thinking this probably revealed a personality trait, but at this moment he couldn't care less. He felt the breeze kick, carrying the scent of sage and rabbitbrush. Beyond him the Sapphire Mountains, a far smoother, smaller sister range to the Bitterroots, stretched dark with fir into the perfect blue sky. The backpack felt like a welcome friend, and he began to walk faster, stretching out. Three or four days alone in the mountains. What a gift.

Levi reached the canyon mouth and made his way up the creek bed, small cutthroat trout scurrying into deeper water. Lichen painted the cliffs, which quickly cut off the sun. Water ouzels bobbed in the creek, and warblers of all kinds flitted from willow to cottonwood.

He rested on a sunny, grassy promontory that knobbed into the creek. Shedding the pack, he dipped a cup into the cold water and drank heartily. No liquor could beat icy pure water. As he rested awhile, his mind wandered, but his awareness returned to the sound of water, the sparkling sun, the water striders, and small trout. For a few lost minutes that became all there was, and Levi was lost in it.

The narrowness of the canyon forced him into the creek on more than one occasion, the icy water numbing his feet. Once a great blue heron looked up, meeting his gaze with one as ancient as the first beings who roamed the earth. Levi met its eyes and suddenly understood nothing. Tears flooded his eyes, and he gave silent thanks for all he revered yet would never know.

By mid-afternoon he'd cleared the narrow canyon and broken into the meadows, which merged to sageland as they climbed the hillsides. Here the canyon was wide and the sky vast. The meadows were full of paintbrush, larkspur, and lupine, and the dizzying scent of nectar filled his nostrils. The air was wild with the humming of bees.

Levi found a campsite farther up, where the grass stroked a gravel beach, the creek deepening on the far side against a cottonwood snag. He set up his tent, fluffed his bag, then sat, made tea, ate an apple and some trail mix. He was in awe that most people didn't know how simple life could be, and how cluttered they made it.

He stripped and waded into the water up to his waist, the cold taking his breath away. When he ducked his head under, electricity bit into him and his ears roared. He straightened swiftly, shook himself like a bear, and waded back to shore. Even stubbing his toe, the brutal, quick pain, brought more life into him. He was bursting with it.

He spread some torn grass on the gravel and lay down, letting the sunlight return warmth to his body.

Later in the day, he walked to the top of the ridge above his camp and sat watching shadows change shape over the land, the dimming light alter color and texture in anticipation of night. A small herd of elk, cows and calves, descended a side canyon and entered the meadow, grazing. As dusk closed in, coyotes began yipping, and a short-eared owl, probably a male, gave a series of hoots. Levi felt emptied and simultaneously sated. Night quickened, and eventually he made his way back to his tent, which glowed faintly below him in the starlight.

Waking to strong sun warming the tent, he saw his breath in clouds. Levi guessed it was barely above freezing. Early June, like autumn, was Levi's favorite weather. Hot days, cold nights.

He lay in his sleeping bag and listened to the voices in the creek, the language he understood without understanding. He picked up the book by the Greek poet Cavafy that Sachi had sent him. Levi had never read poetry before, but the poet's words, so grounded in the small details of life, took him places he'd never been. But mostly, he thought about Sachi. She came to him often these days, like a ghost out of air.

He rose slowly, did some yoga, naked, in sun and chill, then dressed, made tea, and ate some trail mix sitting on a chunk of weathered rock. He watched three young bull elk amble over the ridge he'd climbed the night before, descend to the creek less than seventy yards upstream, drink heartily, then wander off into the day. He wondered what it would be like to live that rootless, sleeping somewhere different every night, somewhere unplanned, with only vague, instinctive urges governing his movement.

Once while in college, he'd traveled to Canyonlands and southern Utah with a friend during spring break. They had no plans other than to camp, hike, and travel leisurely through terrain that was so different from wintery Montana. The stark red, orange, sulfur, and ochre rock was seductive. They found over time that the rhythm their lives took became who they were, and they ultimately decided not to return for the beginning of Spring quarter. It ended only when he called home and was shamed by his father for wasting his life. It was one of the only times in his life he had "wasted his life." Out in nature, in the field, he was constantly doing research, taking photographs, notes, making observations. Everything was put to use. He realized that his father had won out. He looked around and swore he'd waste at least a couple of days here.

Mid-morning, he put the spinning rod together, tied on a small Mepps spinner, and began walking the creek upstream. His casts into the riffles took small trout, six, seven inches, but in the pools, there were always a few over ten, and once a behemoth of fourteen, with slashes of red under its throat, thick-spotted and golden on its dorsal. He kept six for dinner, sliding them onto a willow stick, and immersing in the pool just below his tent, the stick weighted down with a rock.

Danny showed up as Levi was cleaning up from dinner.

"Wasn't sure if I should bring dinner or not, then I remember you'd packed a rod. How was fishing?"

"Tremendous. You could catch them all day. I've got two left if you want them."

"Don't mind if I do. I love trout, but don't fish. Art gives me some from time to time."

Levi handed him a plate with two fried trout on it, and watched as Danny expertly stripped the spine out. He ate quickly, talking as he went, licking his fingers when he was through.

"I bet Art would appreciate that. How's he doing, by the way? I know Taki left."

"It was rough, but the soul heals, as you well know."

"Amen to that," Danny said.

Levi remembered Danny's major heartbreak, the one that had sent him west from Iowa, into the Valley, and ultimately into this life of a hermit on the MacLean's spread. Love was powerful medicine. Or in some cases, toxin.

"I'll make some tea."

Later they gathered dry sage and willow, and Levi built a fire. As the flames caught and flared, Danny broke out a bottle of Dickle.

"You got me into this, you know," he said, waving the bottle.

Levi laughed. "What bourbon, or Dickle?"

"Dickle. I never doubted my love of bourbon." He poured a healthy couple of inches into a plastic cup and passed it to Levi, then did the same for himself.

"Skol," he said, raising the cup, which Levi met.

"Skol."

"Did you know Dickle acquired its Montana fame due to Richard Brautigan? It was his poison of choice," Danny said.

"I did know that. Art told me once. He's a huge Brautigan fan. I never caught on to his work myself."

"You're not much of a reader of creative literature, as I recall."

"Afraid not," said Levi. "If it isn't stuffed with data, it doesn't do much for me."

"Then what's with the poetry?" Danny pointed to the book Sachi had gifted Levi.

"A woman friend gave me that."

"Cavafy. He's renowned for his love poems, you know."

"I can tell. They're quite moving."

"Stuffed with a different kind of data," said Danny, smiling.

As night descended and the whiskey disappeared, Levi told Danny much of what had happened, leaving out anything too weird. Danny reciprocated by detailing the on-again, off-again relationship he was involved in with a woman named Margaret Whipple. Margaret was thirty-four, had a five-year old boy, and was an on-again-off-again alcoholic and drug addict. It was Danny's fate in life to fall for flawed women, to try to save them, and usually fail.

Somewhere along the line they both began howling, then laughing hysterically. As the night deepened, Danny passed out on his sleeping bag, snoring like a bear. Levi was staring at the sky just over the ridge-top when he noticed movement. Riveted, he watched a large human figure appear and stand tall, silhouetted against the lighter sky. The figure stood motionless for some time, then, with a lift of its chin, let out a howl so intense that electricity radiated through Levi's body. His every atom desired to merge with the creature's presence, surrender to it.

Levi started to stand but tottered, the whiskey knocking him back. The creature howled again, then was gone, and Levi sat for a long time staring at the empty ridge, before crawling into his tent and passing out.

Levi was up early. The sun had yet to crest the Sapphires, and the meadow glimmered with dew in the half-light. As he walked to the creek for tea water, Levi's nylon pants and gym shoes became soaked with it. The memory of the creature from last night faded in the new day, but Levi could not entirely forget it. Lycaon.

It was chilly, but he resisted the desire to build a fire, instead boiling water on the single-burner stove, pouring it over dried Darjeeling tea. Sometime during the night Danny had climbed into his sleeping bag, and was just now stirring and stretching.

"Damn," he said sitting up. He picked up the nearly empty whiskey bottle and sloshed what little remained. "Did we drink all of this?"

"You drank most of it, my friend."

"Feels like it. My head is stuffed with smog and pain."

Danny had packed in eggs, and he whipped up a cowboy omelet, chopping onion, green pepper, tomato, cheddar cheese, and cold bacon. He took six eggs, beat them in a bowl, then poured them into a greased frying pan, where they spread thin and began to bubble. When they were firm enough, he added the ingredients, then folded the egg over and hollered at Levi, who was futzing around in his tent.

They ate sitting on rocks, watching a hawk glide low over the meadow, listening to the warblers and the emerging whistles of marmots. Then the sun broke the peaks and flooded the meadow with golden light, igniting the dew into diamonds.

"Wow," Danny said. "Just frickin' wow."

Lounging around, they talked most of the morning, then did a short hike around noon, eating apples on a giant boulder up-valley. Levi thought of the time he'd climbed a boulder and met Althea. Or should he just call her Artemis?

Back in camp, Danny gathered up his gear. "Fences to mend. It's never-ending."

Levi watched him hike downstream toward the cliffs, getting smaller and smaller, until he disappeared.

Levi stayed another night, leaving around midday. Danny wasn't in, but had left a note pinned to the front door.

"Out fencing south pasture. Fun times. Keep in touch. And good luck with all the bullshit."

As he started his truck, Levi imagined the original MacLeans living year-round in this tiny cabin that was no more than 500 square feet. Danny had rebuilt the outhouse and painted it barn red, a stark contrast to the dark ancient logs of the cabin. A large Honda generator stood in a hutch next to the cabin. It took a certain kind of person to live back here, where contact with people happened only when someone dropped by.

Fifty Two

It was around three when Levi got back to his house in Hamilton. He set his pack on the living room floor, then took some elk salami out of the fridge, wrapped it in a leaf of butter lettuce, and ate it. Then another. And another.

Sitting at the kitchen table, he opened his laptop and turned it on. Seventy-eight new emails. He started scanning them, then gave up, clicking the computer off.

There was a blank message on his land line. He heard someone breathing, then the click as they hung up. There were two messages on his cell. The first was from Taylor.

"Hey, man, we need to talk. Give me a call."

Levi dialed. The phone rang several times, then transferred to voicemail. He left a message saying he'd been out, but was back.

The next message was from the Sheriff. "Wolfman, Juicy. Give me a call as soon as you get this."

He dialed the second number, and Juicy immediately picked up.

"Sheriff's office. Sheriff Jones speaking."

"Juicy."

"Levi. Where have you been?"

"Out camping. Clearing my head."

"Clearing your head, eh? Wish I could clear mine. Where were you?"

"Up a small draw out of MacLean's eastside spread. Danny Mouch gave me access."

"Danny Mouch. Now there's a boy who lives off the grid. Spend any time with him?"

"We got drunk one night."

"Danny Mouch," Juicy repeated. "I used to have a thing for his mother. Never went anywhere, but she was a looker."

Levi didn't respond.

"Any wolves up there?"

"Not that I've ever heard about. What's up?"

"You seen Taylor?"

"Taylor? No. Like I said, I was camping for a few days. I just got home." Levi heard Juicy shift in his creaky office chair. "I did leave a message for him to call me, but he didn't pick up. Why?"

"Can you get down here this afternoon?"

Levi glanced at the stove clock. 3:18. "I could be there around four."

"Thanks. It's important. I'll see you then."

Levi pulled his truck into the parking lot of the county sheriff's department, feeling he was getting too damn familiar with this particular area of town. Juicy stood, greeted him, then shuttled him into the multipurpose conference/interrogation room.

"Have a seat."

Levi pulled one of the plastic chairs out and sat. The room looked identical, but there was a different vibe than last time he was here.

"You smell like wood-smoke."

"Haven't had time to shower yet."

"Would Danny Mouch back up your story? About where you were? When?"

"I don't see why he wouldn't."

"Hmmm." Juicy sat heavily. "I may have been barking up the wrong tree here, Levi."

Levi gave him a look.

"I never figured you for this Leeson murder, Levi. My gut didn't anyway. You've always had moral integrity. You never struck me as someone who could do violence to another human."

"It's a little late for that now, isn't it?"

"Your lawyer, Doke, met with me and Taylor a couple days back.

He presented us with some evidence that was pretty incriminating. Some emails."

"I know about them."

"Their contents?"

"Some of it."

"Where did he get them?"

"He told me Taylor's Internet provider handed them over."

"Whatever. They're probably not admissible in court."

"That's what Doke told me."

"He laid them down on the table, just like a winning hand of cards. Taylor went ballistic. Denied everything. Said they were fabricated."

"You believed him?"

"I did at first. Then Doke told us about how your neighbor, Myrtle, would testify that she saw Taylor at your place. Twice. The dates correlated with the theft and return of the jaw and paw. She identified him and his car.

"Taylor said he stopped by to discuss the case with you, but you weren't home. But according to Myrtle, he was there about ten to fifteen minutes." Juicy wiped his mouth. "I never authorized that. That's when I began doubting him."

"So now what?"

"I don't know yet. With the emails inadmissible, the only real evidence we have is Myrtle's account that he stopped by your place. But…"

"But what?"

"I'm dropping the case against you. The emails tell me that Taylor had motive, more than you, and had threatened Brittany. I just need something else to charge him."

"Can I ask you something?"

"Shoot."

"What's your perception of Taylor? You work with him."

Juicy gazed at the ceiling before answering. "Taylor's changed. I think the job infused a darkness into him he couldn't cope with. It happens to cops, and they cope or not. I think Taylor is having a difficult time of it."

"You ever talk to him about it?"

"He never opened up to me that way," Juicy said. "He liked the power he had over people, and he used it to make some poor choices."

"What do you mean?"

"This thing with Brittany. It wasn't the first time."

Fifty Three

THE SKY HAD NEARLY drained its light when there was a knock on the door. Levi put down the book he was reading, *The Yellowstone Wolf*, got up, and answered. It was Taylor holding a taser pointed at his chest. Levi moved to slam the door, but Taylor was faster and had his foot and knee in.

"That's resisting an officer of the law, Levi. Back up."

Taylor shut the door behind them. There was a wild glint in his eyes Levi had never seen. "We're going to have a little talk, then go for a ride." He pushed Levi back with the taser. "Turn around." He had his cuffs out.

Levi knew this was it. Now or never. He feinted to the left and came right. The blast slammed him to the floor. He felt a brief seizure, then his head snapped back as Taylor kicked him. Hard.

"Roll over. Put your arms behind you."

Levi tried to reach out and grab Taylor's leg, but his arm felt like jelly. Then a shot of pain as Taylor's foot smashed into his wrist.

"Don't fuck with me, Levi. Turn over!"

Levi rolled, and Taylor grabbed his throbbing wrist. Levi felt the cuff snap shut, then his other arm pulled back and snapped.

"That's a good boy," Taylor said. "We're going to get along just fine."

Levi tried to talk, but the guttural sounds made no sense. He felt the pinch of the cuffs, notched too tight.

Taylor jerked him to his feet. "Now sit down." He pulled out a chair with his foot and let Levi collapse into it. "I don't think you're dumb, Levi, so stop trying to prove otherwise."

Taylor got himself a glass of water. "Thirsty," he said, taking a long drink. "I haven't been home in a while. I've been driving around thinking about that little trick your lawyer played. Now the ball's in my court."

Levi coughed and shook his head to clear it. "You're digging yourself deeper."

"Oh, you have no idea how deep this hole can go." He stared at Levi and smiled faintly. "Or maybe you do."

"What are you going to do with me?"

"You'll find out."

Neither of them spoke, and the silence was heavy. A dog barked down the block, a hollow sound in the night. Levi's head throbbed.

"Do you know what it's like to really love someone, Levi?"

"Yes, I do."

"Taki, right?"

"Taki. And now Sachi."

"The Greek woman."

"Yes."

"Hmmm."

"It's a tragic thing," Taylor continued, "to love a woman. You want to possess her, but you never can. You want to shape her, own her, but you can't." He spit on the table. The saliva stuck like dry foam to the oak.

Levi said nothing.

"But I suppose you know all that, with all your experience at it."

"I never said I had experience. I consider myself an idiot when it comes to love."

"That's exactly what you are, Levi. An idiot. Why didn't you just rot away in that cell? Why did that fucking woman bail you out? How does she fit into the game? Why didn't you just go away?"

"Stop with the rhetorical shit, Taylor. Do what you have to do."

Taylor slid the chair back abruptly. "Up! Let's go!"

Taylor walked Levi out, letting the door slam behind them. He wrenched the rear door open and pushed Levi into the back seat of the squad car. A heavy metal screen separated front and back. Taylor got in and started the car, gunning it, taking the side streets.

Taylor drove the back roads south of town, intersecting the highway just north of the bridge by Angler's Junction. He drove toward Darby, passed through the small town, exiting the highway at the West Fork Road, driving fast, skidding the car on turns. After a mile or so, he turned onto a logging road that switch-backed steeply uphill. Levi felt the car slide dangerously close to the edge. Then the road leveled out, and after another five minutes or so, Taylor pulled the car over.

He got out and walked around to the rear door, opening it, reaching around and unlocking the handcuffs.

"Get out."

Levi looked around. They were in an abandoned quarry he'd never seen before.

"This way." Taylor pushed Levi to the right, where grass broke erratically through heavy gravel, and the spindly lodgepole beyond glowed like eerie skeletons in the moonlight.

"Now what?"

"We wait."

"For what?"

Taylor didn't answer right away, but a minute later, speaking as if stoned, "He'll come."

"Who?"

"Shut up!" Taylor shouted, and shot into the ground at Levi's feet. The gunshot shattered the night and echoed off the quarry walls, dying slowly into imagined sound.

Then, a moment later, something indescribable. The howl of a wolf. The black wolf. Lycaon.

A few minutes later a man walked out of the trees. He was tall and square-shouldered, and moonlight gave his long black hair a faint aura.

"Well, what do we have here?" he drawled. "Taylor brought a friend."

"I didn't know what else to do," Taylor said. Levi could hear the shiver of fear in his voice.

The man ignored him, talking to Levi. "You're that wolf biologist, aren't you? The one I said visited Leeson when he was murdered. The only person besides Taylor with a motive." His words hung in air.

Levi knew it was the figure on the ridge-top he'd seen recently. The man who'd tipped his head back and howled. "You're Jacob Blackburn."

"Some people call me that."

"What do we do?" asked Taylor nervously.

Still speaking to Levi, Blackburn continued, "I've taken Taylor under my wing, so to speak. Teaching him the ways of the wolf, or as some people call it, the werewolf. And he's done quite well so far. The old man was his first. I had to finish the job, but all in all…" Blackburn spoke slowly, his voice low and dark.

"What old man?"

"Don't tell him!" spat Taylor.

"His first *almost* kill. An old man alone in a large house. On Maplewood Avenue." Jacob Blackburn stopped talking and seemed to tense, as if hearing something no one else could hear.

"But since the Leesons, Taylor's been losing his focus, losing his mind, doing things he shouldn't do. He's unreliable now. Of no use."

Taylor coughed.

Blackburn turned to Taylor. "You really fucked up Leesons, didn't you? Just couldn't pull the trigger, so to speak. Couldn't carve the turkey. We can't let this continue, can we, Taylor? You were such a good disciple, but now the sky's come crashing down."

In far less time than Levi could process, Jacob Blackburn morphed into the black wolf and leapt at Taylor. Simultaneously Taylor screamed, stuck out his arm to block the assault, and fired. It was over in a blur. The black wolf lay quivering in the dirt, its tongue twitching, its golden eyes fading to the color of moonlight. Taylor's face was contorted into a mask of absolute horror.

Levi stepped toward him, and Taylor raised the gun and screamed, "Get the fuck out of here!"

Levi didn't hesitate. He turned and ran out of the quarry as fast as he could. As he ran, he heard Taylor's gasping cries racking the night. He began running down the road. As he rounded the first switchback down, he heard a single gunshot. Levi did not turn back.

Fifty four

Levi flagged an employee driving back to the Job Corps Center on the West Fork Road. The man drove him to the Center, called the sheriff's office, and poured Levi a cup of coffee. Then the man left the room, a lounge area full of couches, a ping-pong table on the far end. Outside the windows night waited. The radiant white wall clock read 11:12.

Juicy and two deputies showed up a half-hour later. Juicy talked briefly with the man who'd picked Levi up, then had Levi show him where his arms had been taped, all the hair torn off. Levi then led them back to the quarry, the two deputies following in another squad car. They didn't speak, and Juicy seemed deep in thought.

As they pulled into the quarry, the car's headlights caught Taylor's body lying in a small, scraped depression in the gravel, the kind a dog scrapes before it lies down. He lay fetal, the gun barrel buried in his mouth, the back of his head gone.

Juicy barked into the radio for an ambulance, giving them the GPS coordinates, then got out.

"Shit," he said. "What a friggin' mess."

Levi walked toward where Blackburn had stood, where the wolf had leaped and fallen. There was no wolf.

"So what happened here, Levi?"

Levi detailed how Taylor had forced him up here with the intention of killing him, taping his arms behind his back, cuffing him to the car. He described another murder Taylor had confessed to, an old man on Maplewood Avenue. He told Juicy that Taylor's mood was erratic, swinging from violent anger to extreme remorse. He had talked about how he was sick with regret.

At some point Taylor had pointed his gun at him and screamed for him to get the hell out of there. Levi told Juicy he was sure Taylor would shoot him in the back, but he'd kept running, even after he'd heard the shot. He'd run all the way down to the West Fork Road where he'd been picked up. Levi did not mention Jacob Blackburn walking out of the woods and turning into a wolf. It would not do much for his credibility with Juicy.

Juicy said nothing. Turning to one of the deputies, he said, "Take him back to his house, and get a lab guy up here. ASAP!"

At some long time after midnight, Levi sat on his back porch nursing a large glass of bourbon, staring into the night and reviewing in his mind what had happened. He remembered how the wolf had seemed to emerge from Blackburn, as if it shed a skin. He saw the wolf recoil from the shot in mid-air, fall, and die, its eyes glazing over. But when Levi had returned with the cops, the body was gone. Had something dragged it off? Had Taylor buried it? But the timing was off. He was positive he'd heard the shot two or three minutes after he'd begun to run, which barely gave Taylor time to scrape his bed, not enough time to bury Blackburn.

The next morning, he drove to Althea and Cali's place loaded with questions.

The cabin was deserted, unlived in, the yard overgrown with grass and weeds. The abandoned Ford truck was parked where it had been, but weeds and vines nearly buried it. Baffled, he looked in the window. Other than a couple of broken chairs and a table layered with dust, the cabin was empty. It looked like no one had lived there in years. As he walked back to his truck, a crow cawed from a fir tree. He wasn't sure, but it looked like Karnesis. But then again, most crows look alike.

Later that day a real estate agent, identifying herself as Kathleen Allen, called Levi, stating she had papers for him to sign. She could run them by if he preferred, but he said no, he'd stop by her office.

A half-hour later he pulled his truck off Highway 93 into the parking lot of Bitterroot Realty, feeling like he was submerged in a dream. He was pretty sure he knew what to expect, what Althea had done for him.

"I'm here to see Kathleen Allen," he told the receptionist.

A few minutes later a tall woman with frosted blond hair, wearing heels and a blue cotton dress entered the reception area.

"Mister Brunner, I'm Kathleen Allen." She offered her hand. It was as cool as the air. "Why don't we go into my office?"

Once settled there, she told him he was the new owner of the Leeson place. "We thought it would take a while to sell, because of that gruesome murder, but a woman bought it for your organization, WolfRecovery. You have some wealthy advocates, Levi."

"What did it sell for?"

"Three million, six hundred and forty thousand dollars."

"What's the acreage?"

"Eighty-three acres. After you get the papers signed, we'll drive up, and I'll show you around. Give you the keys. I take it you haven't seen it yet?"

"Just from the outside," he lied.

"Well, it's a beautiful property. Lovely home. Meadows, a stream running through it, woods, cliffs. The kind of place wealthy Californians are always looking for. It's kind of nice someone local now owns it."

"Yeah, it is."

"Levi Brunner," she said out loud. "Your name seems familiar. Maybe I met you somewhere."

"Quite possible." Levi failed to mention he'd been a favorite target of *The Ravalli Republic* over the past few months or so.

The next forty minutes involved signing numerous pages of documents, Kathleen giving the Cliff's Notes version of what he was signing. Once finished, he followed her Saab, with the bumper sticker "I Drive Highway 93, Pray for Me" on its shiny yellow bumper, up to the Leeson place. While driving, he thought back on when he'd first come there to climb into the canyon. Art driving him up. It seemed eons ago.

Kathleen unlocked the gate, giving Levi the code, then did the same with the front door. The house smelled heavily of disinfectant.

"You'll want to air it out," Kathleen said, opening some windows.

As they walked into the sunken living room area, the bodies of Leeson and Brittany appeared in his mind as ghosts where they'd lain slashed, awash with blood. But the room was spotless, the walls and bamboo floor scrubbed, perhaps many times. The furniture had been hauled off. Levi noticed then what he hadn't the day of the murder, that four sliding glass doors opened onto a shale patio, across which the view embraced the fenced meadows with the glint of stream on the meanders, cliffs erupting, constricting the meadow, somehow intensifying the green of new grass. And beyond, in the distance, peaks scratched sky, the divide between Montana and Idaho, still snowcapped and radiant. It was a truly breathtaking view.

Kathleen gave him keys to the outbuildings and walked him through a perfunctory tour. She was practiced at this and seemed to enjoy lingering over details, such as blinds, hanging copper pots, and Italian marble counters. Levi relaxed and let her talk on.

When she did finally leave, he picked up the envelope addressed to him that lay on the counter.

Levi, I'm sorry I can't be with you on this day, at this moment, in your new home, your new headquarters. I imagine your emotions are mixed, and the scene of the murder lingering. And, since you possess great humility, I imagine that the material excess of the structure irritates or angers you. But this was not a frivolous move on my part, but a truly calculated one. You now have access to the canyon, the spring, and Mirr's pack. Your duty is to protect all of these, and I don't doubt you will. The property is co-owned by WolfRecovery and Eléftheros Erimia, Sachi's organization. She is unaware of this at the time, but I'm certain you will let her know ☺*.*

In addition, I have contracted to have the gate, posts, metal Leeson sign, and the gate itself, removed by SignPro of Missoula. The sale of the posts for timber, and the rest for scrap metal, will pay for the removal. This will happen within the next week or so. I have retained the landscaping service Earth & Wood to care for the grounds for the coming year. You can cancel this if you wish.

I wish you the best in your new home, and thank you for caring so much about things that are wild. They are within all of our psyches. You are a true friend, and I will miss you.

But I will see you again,

Althea

PS I have cancelled security and had all the cameras and alarms removed. I figured you'd prefer to live dangerously

Tears blurred his eyes as he finished reading. He felt a sudden strange fusion of joy and melancholy, but more than that, he was overwhelmed by the immensity of her gesture, and the responsibility laid on his shoulders.

As he left the house, dark bulkheads of cumulus clouds crowded the Bitterroot peaks, and he saw a flash of distant lightning. The wind was kicking up, and the rain would wash the earth clean, as it had done for thousands of years.

Fifty Five

Levi called Sachi that evening, and they talked for several hours, during which time she went from being shocked, to confused, to reluctant, to downright pissed off. Levi was forcing this on her. She had no say. She felt manipulated. These accusations stirred Levi's own doubts. Moving to a remote valley in Montana was not on her agenda, and all her work involved local and national issues in Greece. When Levi finally hung up, they had decided only one thing: she would visit Montana as planned in late July. They would discuss it further then. Levi went to bed distraught, and he imagined that halfway around the world, the woman he was falling deeper in love with shared similar emotions.

The next day he called Joseph Bull Ranger, a Native American wildlife agent he'd worked with over the years. He explained what had happened at Leeson's, a horrific double homicide, and asked if he knew someone who could perform a purification ritual. Bull Ranger knew a Blackfoot shaman who would perform the ritual for $500 plus travel fees.

"I can talk to her if you like."

"Please, and have her call me if she is interested."

The woman, Emily Sukahs, called later that day. She agreed to perform the ritual. She required only that it be done as soon as possible, and that she be unobserved during the cleansing. Levi wired her money for her bus trip down, and she arrived Saturday just after noon at the Hamilton Greyhound station. She was a hunched, stolid woman, wearing a heavy coat and wool hat against the sudden June chill. She was somewhere north of sixty, her braids, silver with strands of black, falling to her waist.

"Are you hungry?" Levi asked her.

She shook her head. "I ate a sandwich on the bus."

She had a small suitcase, and clutched a deerskin bag to her chest. Levi helped her into the car.

She said little on the drive out, and Levi felt awkward sitting in the car with her, watching the wipers swipe across the windshield. The Leeson gate was still imposing its will on all who entered. Levi punched in the door code and let her in. Entering the front hall, she immediately stiffened.

"This is a very bad place," she said haltingly.

"I know."

He began to tell her what had happened, but she shushed him.

"You wait outside. I'll get you when I'm done."

Levi walked around the side of the house and across the back lawn, then climbed a split rail fence. Ahead of him were barbed-wire fences and individualized pastures, stretching away up the canyon. It was the first time he'd been out here, and he felt a sudden exhilaration. Wind came in heavy gusts out of the northeast. There were no longer any sheep. The family must have sold them off after the tragedy. Just barbed-wire fences and empty pastures.

Sheep grazed close to the ground, and the grass was torn down to the roots in places. Piles of shit everywhere. The fences needed to come down, and the pasture returned to what it had been. It would take a few years. Looking back at the house, he could see Emily in the living room, arms stretched over her head, her mouth moving rapidly.

He walked down to the creek, to where the sheep had flattened the vegetation and trampled the banks to mud. Then he turned his face to the sky, let the cold rain strike his skin. For a moment he wasn't sure where or who he was.

He was sitting in his truck listening to NPR when Emily knocked on the window, startling him. Perhaps he'd been dosing.

"It's finished."

She walked with him back into the house, which smelled of sage smoke.

"I had to dismantle the fire alarms," she said. "I'm used to that. We used to use dogs to tell us if there was a fire. Now it's technology."

Levi no longer saw the ghosts of Leeson and his wife Brittany lying on the couches, no longer felt their presence. The room seemed empty and clean, but not cold. An emptiness waiting to be filled with new life.

"See, it's ready for you."

"Thank you so much." Levi felt humbled by this tiny woman.

She turned and shuffled back to the truck, asking only for a piece of pie, before boarding the seven o'clock bus back to Kalispell. Levi drove her to Ma's Diner on 93 and bought her a slice of warm huckleberry pie topped with vanilla ice cream.

The woman ate steadily, pleasurably, saying little. Levi realized she lived in a world he'd never access. She opened up a bit as the pie disappeared, complaining about her kids, and their kids, TV and the Internet, video games, Twitter. Levi sensed that the words all meant the same thing to her. Something that was superficial.

"They think I'm crazy, that the old ways are nuts. But they are the ones who are nuts. The old ways never change. They will be here long after the shiny shit is gone."

Levi drove her back to the bus station and handed her a check. He had given her more than she asked for, but she merely glanced at it and stuffed it into the pocket of her coat.

"You have someone picking you up?" he asked.

"My brother's coming down to shop at Costco in Kalispell. He'll take me back."

"Well, thank you again."

She froze him with her eyes and held him captive. "You have touched the old ways. You have a responsibility. You have work to do."

"I know," Levi said.

She broke eye contact, and the driver helped her on board. Levi walked to his truck. The rain and wind had died as suddenly as they'd arrived, brilliant sun disintegrating what shards of cloud remained.

Fifty six

ART HAD HELPED LEVI marshal a ragtag army of friends and trucks to orchestrate the move from the Hamilton house to Levi's new home. The work began on a Wednesday, after extensive organization and preparation, and was completed late Friday afternoon. Levi hired Bare Bones Barbeque of Stevensville to cater the culminating party and housewarming, and the Bitterroot Public House supplied a variety of kegs. The only thing missing was Sachi, and Levi thought of her constantly throughout the festivities.

Later, as evening descended with a grace found only in the mountains, the *Friskies*, an Americana roots band, plugged in, and people were dancing on the front lawn. Levi was sure this vibe had never existed while the Leesons had owned the place. It would go slowly, but this would become his home and headquarters. He'd already hung several wolf photos on the bare walls.

He was mildly drunk when he turned in. His first night in his new place. An array of tents covered the yards, and a group of ten or twelve people sat around the rear fire-pit talking and drinking. Every now and then there was an eruption of explosive laughter. Levi closed his eyes. For the first time in a long time he was happy, and with it came optimism. He and Sachi would work this out.

The next day Juicy called and asked Levi to stop by.

A few days before, the front page of *The Ravalli Republic* contained an article by Monica detailing the latest developments of the Leeson murder. Levi had skimmed it, noting that his name was barely mentioned. In this age of fickle attention, things flared and faded quickly.

"Wolfman," Juicy said, as Levi knocked on his open office door. Juicy looked relaxed.

"Juicy. What's up?"

"I heard you're all moved in up at Leeson's old place. Must be weird moving in there, after everything that happened."

"It's weird, but it feels right. That's a very special canyon."

Juicy stared at Levi and smiled. "You are one of the luckiest sons-a-bitches I ever met. One day you're in jail for homicide, the next you've inherited the victim's house. Shit, if I didn't know better, I'd think you'd staged this whole thing."

"But you do know better, don't you?"

"Taylor kept a friggin' journal, if you can believe that. Wrote up all this shit about werewolves, how Jacob Blackburn was some werewolf chief from ancient times. Gave me the creeps reading it, I don't mind admitting. He'd gone off the deep end."

"It seems that way."

"He wrote meticulously about the murder, how carefully they planned it. He convinced Blackburn to frame you. You were the only other person with motive."

"Did he say much about Brittany?"

"Oh, yeah. There was a lot of that, too. I'm figuring the guy wasn't sleeping too much by then. We found a pretty decent cache of meth in his house as well. All this right under my watch."

"Sad."

"Hey, I wanted to get your opinion of something. Look at this." Juicy turned his monitor toward Levi, clicking through a few screens to a video. It was the footage from Callahan's surveillance camera the night he'd died. The yard was empty, then Mirr emerged from the darkness, stared at the house, then trotted across the yard. He could see her start up the three cement steps, then the camera lost her. A few minutes later she walked out, looking back over her shoulder, then bounded off and disappeared into the forest across the driveway.

"Look at this," Juicy said again.

The yard was empty for another few minutes, then a black wolf appeared as if out of thin air. It stood still, tilting its head at one point and staring directly at the camera. Levi shivered. Then it followed Mirr's path into the house. A few minutes later it exited, and like Mirr, bounded into the woods across Callahan's driveway.

"You recognize that wolf?" Juicy asked.

"No. It looks superficially like the alpha male of Mirr's old pack, but it's much larger."

"Mirr?"

"That's the name I gave her, the mother wolf who was killed."

"You're one strange human, Levi Brunner."

"I suppose."

"If I didn't know better, I'd say that black wolf looked demonic."

"Yeah, it does," said Levi.

"Why do you think it went into the house?"

"I think it was curious," said Levi. "Wolves are very curious animals."

"Hmmm," Juicy said. "Well, I just wanted you to see it. I got this domestic thing I gotta go sort out." He stood up and stuck out his hand.

"You take care of yourself, Levi. Stay out of trouble."

Levi shook his hand.

"Goodbye, Juicy. I'll see you around. But I hope not too much."

Both men smiled.

Fifty seven

OVER THE NEXT MONTH a number of things happened that affected Levi directly. The Montana legislature passed a bill making it legal for ranchers to kill up to a hundred wolves a year if they were harassing livestock. It was a bill, House Bill 927, that Callahan had supported and pushed for in several Valley meetings, but no one in Levi's circle had thought it had a snowball's chance in hell of making it through the senate. They'd badly misjudged the public's hatred of wolves.

Levi spent a number of days traveling back and forth to Helena, testifying and lobbying. But despite intense pressure from the Sierra Club, Wilderness Watch, and Levi's WolfRecovery, several democratic senators caved, and it squeaked through. Since ranchers were already killing wolves, illegally, it was debatable whether the passage would affect wolf populations, but it would make ranchers more brazen. And it was left deliberately vague what "harassing livestock" actually meant. Ranchers could legitimately argue that the very presence of wolves in the vicinity "harassed" livestock.

Shortly after he moved into Leesons' place, Levi hiked up the canyon and discovered that the Goat Creek pack had returned to their original den site and were thriving. Another female had replaced Mirr, a three-legged older wolf with a beautiful tan coat. Levi set up an observation post behind the set of boulders and watched for the good part of a day, taking copious notes and photographs. Mirr's replacement seemed to be an experienced mother and patiently endured the pups' tail and ear attacks, the endless nursing. The sight of the pack, and especially the pups, made him profoundly happy.

And he couldn't wait to share this sight with Sachi, who had never seen a wolf in the wild, much less an entire pack.

After consulting with a couple ranchers and struggling to remove a short stretch of fence, Levi put an ad on Craigslist advertising free fencing and posts to anyone willing to take it down. He had a number of calls, and people began to show up with appropriate tools to dismantle it. Levi kept one small pasture fenced for the possibility of getting a horse, something his better self had prevented him from doing thus far. But he was feeling a bit frisky these days. One never knew. He wondered vaguely if Sachi liked to ride.

Levi was shocked when he opened the door one early July afternoon to Art and Shayla. They were both beaming, beautiful, tanned and lean, and holding hands.

"Holy shit, guys! Come on in!"

After a quick tour, Shayla told Levi she couldn't believe he lived in a house like this. "It's gorgeous. And I bet your bachelor status has gone way, way up."

"It's a Faustian bargain," he told her, "but having access and the ability to protect this canyon is worth living with gold-plated bathroom faucets."

They spent the afternoon talking and drinking lemonade, during which Levi learned about Shayla's life. She'd come to the Valley from Massachusetts three years back. Through her friendly, outgoing personality, and her waitressing job at the Red Barn, she'd met a large number of Valley residents. Her warm, unassuming nature often turned these acquaintances into dear friends. Art had found himself stopping in more and more on the pretext of having a beer. Then came love, plain and simple.

"When Art started coming in a lot, I wondered what had happened to his girlfriend. I finally asked him, and when he told me, he sounded so vulnerable. My heart just went out to him."

"Aw, shucks," Art joked. "Shayla's into horses. Wants me to take up riding. Can you see me on a horse?"

"Yeah, yeah I can," said Levi.

They took a long walk through the former pastures. Three parties were working on dismantling the longest, south-side fence, and Levi stopped to talk with one of them. When he turned to rejoin Art and Shayla, they were locked in a passionate kiss. They had dinner plans and refused Levi's offer of venison back-strap steaks and turnips, but made plans for the following week. Levi hadn't seen Art so happy in a long, long time.

Levi called Sachi every day. Sometimes he just left messages saying "Hi," and other times they'd talk for hours. His anticipation of her visit in late July intensified to the point there were some days he could think of nothing else. And while he couldn't say she was warming to the idea of moving to the Bitterroot, they were at a place where they could joke about it. He'd emailed her a photo of the unassuming sign in front of the house that read *WolfRecovery and Eléftheros Erimia World Headquarters* with a note that read "Sorry, just had to do it."

She replied, "Whatever floats your raft," noting that her roommate at Berkeley had said that all the time. She followed it with an emoticon of a kiss.

Fifty Eight

LEVI OPENED HIS EYES slowly, afraid of what he'd find.

But she was still there, her face inches from his, her mouth open, breath in and out, slight snores. He watched her sleep, the rising and falling of her breasts.

Outside the tent the world was waking up. Levi heard the early morning symphony of canyon wrens, warblers, robins, black-headed grosbeaks, and towhees. The far-off single yip of a coyote. He slipped out of the sleeping bags, pulled on pants and a sweater, and was out. He slid into his Tevas and walked through the meadow to the stream for tea water, the dew-laden grass soaking his sandals and pants. The sun had yet to break the canyon rim, but when it did there would be an explosion of light. The dew would ignite and disappear within moments.

The water was just beginning to boil when he heard her soft, "Kaliméra." She kissed him gently on the shoulder. "It is so beautiful here. I had no idea."

"So are you, but I had an idea you were." Levi smiled and kissed her. She looked more relaxed than he'd ever seen her. He was always attracted to her intensity, but now equally, he was attracted to her calm.

He poured water into two cups containing tea bags. "Be a minute."

"Three, always at least three." She smiled. "I learned that from a tea master."

"He taught you well."

"But I never drink tea at home. Always coffee. We Greeks have the best coffee. The Turks say they do, but no, it's us. Greeks."

"How about Americans?"

She laughed and wrinkled her nose. "Starbucks, yuck."

"Hah. Never liked it myself. Too bitter. Here." He handed her a cup. "You sleep well?"

"Deliciously."

"Today we'll move up farther. I want to see if the wolves are still where I last saw them."

"This is perfect for them, no?" Stretching her arms in an expansive gesture.

"It's a tad small for their ideal territory, but there's plenty of game. They stayed one year. We'll see if they stay more." But he knew they would because of the spring. This was not your average wolf pack.

She punched him lightly in the shoulder and said, "Maybe you should raise some sheep for them."

"Hey, good idea, but they'd have to beat me to it. I *love* lamb chops."

"I've never seen a wolf in the wild. I've heard them, but never seen one."

"Well, hopefully that will change soon."

He handed her a cup of tea.

"Cheers," he said, touching hers lightly.

"Yiamas."

"Yiamas?"

"To our health."

"I'm so glad you came."

"Do you want to make love?"

"Again?" he said, laughing.

"Again."

When they emerged from the tent for a second time the tea was cold and day had erupted, the meadow frantic with butterflies and bees. Marmot and pika whistled from their rocky havens. Levi had violated his backpacking food policy and brought real food. He stirred four eggs into a bowl, grated in some Greek cheese, Kefalograviera, that Sachi had brought as a gift, sprinkling in oregano and white pepper. He poured a teaspoon of olive oil into an ultralight frying pan, tipping it so it spread, then poured in the eggs.

"You will get me fat," Sachi said.

"Then we'll have to make more love."

After breakfast, they dismantled camp and packed up, Levi carrying the greater load. Sachi didn't play the same card as Althea, who would have carried everything, including Levi. He wondered if he'd ever see her again. He thought maybe, yes.

They walked for an hour, breaking in a clearing for a snack—some trail mix and water—then continued for another hour and a half, winding their way through forest, downfall, and avalanche chutes to the second meadow. Sachi was enthralled by everything. Levi thought she was going to explode with joy when they saw an elk cow licking a tiny calf.

"I've never seen an elk before! Oh my God! Look at the baby! It's so tiny!"

The wildflowers were fading at this elevation, but she wanted to know the name of everything.

"Penstemon."

"Penstemon," she repeated, pointing at the royal blue spikes.

Indian paintbrush, lupine, larkspur, glacier lilies, arrowleaf balsamroot. The real find was when Levi spotted a cluster of bitterroots, the flower the Valley and mountain range were named after, and the state flower of Montana. The bitterroots were ghostly pink in a nest of pine needles and rock. Their roots had provided a precious and delicious gift for Shoshone and Flathead peoples for thousands of years.

It was at the upper terminus of this second meadow where the wolves had denned, where Mirr and her cub were killed. They were still in the area the last time Levi had visited two weeks ago, but wolves could move on a whim, and there was no guarantee they'd be here now. The pups would be large by now, thirty pounds or more, living a life of feasting and playing, and in doing that, acquiring vital life skills.

Levi led Sachi up the south side of the canyon to the cluster of boulders that provided good cover. He realized he was holding his breath. He wanted nothing so much as for Sachi to see a wolf. Peeking out, he saw two cubs mock battling. As he beckoned for Sachi to join him, he watched her freeze, and her face light with joy. Levi heard her whispering something in Greek over and over.

When the wind lifted their way, Levi could hear tiny grunts, growls, and barks. The new alpha female, their stepmother, lay stretched out in a dusty depression. She looked fast asleep, but Levi knew from experience that any sounds of alarm would penetrate instantly, and she'd be up and alert, ready to defend the cubs to her death. They watched the wolves for a long time, the hours stretching into early afternoon. Levi took photos and wrote in his notebook, while Sachi sat absorbed, the look of focused awe never leaving her face.

"This is what it's all about for you, isn't it?" she asked Levi.

"Yes. This is my life. But come, I want to show you one more thing. The spring. We'll camp there tonight."

They left the wolves reluctantly, side-hilling up the canyon wall until they were a good distance above the pack. Levi wanted to disturb them as little as possible, but he also knew they recognized his scent and were not alarmed.

They turned west, and a half-mile or so above the pack, they descended again to the creek, drank, crossed, and continued upstream. They rested where Levi had found the moose kill last fall, the bones still there, scattered, bleached by winter.

He guessed it to be around five when they first spotted sparkling water through the trees. As they broke from the woods onto the gravel beach, Levi stripped without thinking then glanced at Sachi. But she was already naked, and dashed by him into the water.

"Last one in is an avgo."

He ran after her, diving in and surfacing. "What's an avgo?"

"An egg, silly. Isn't that what you Americans say? Last one in is an egg?"

But Levi was laughing too hard to answer.

She splashed him and said, "What?"

As he paddled out, the water chilled, and he felt goosebumps. He could still see bottom, but beyond him a few yards, the depth turned the water black. Memories flooded him, and he was beyond time. He heard Sachi yelling his name, "Levi, Levi, come back," and it was as if he woke from a trance. He turned back, and Sachi swan to meet him. They embraced, and he hugged her hard.

"Don't leave me, Sachi."

She hugged him harder, and he felt himself stiffen.

She smiled. "Come." They swam quickly to the beach.

Levi lay back on the small gravel and sand, and Sachi straddled him. Her lithe, muscular body so beautiful, so strong. He bent up and licked her small breasts, plucking her nipples with his lips. He felt her stiff hair brush against his penis as she teased him, then her wetness that was more than wet. He gasped as they joined. She stilled him, and they held each other with their eyes, entering each other in this way. Then they began to move, and it was the movement of wind or water, natural, often erratic, beyond thought. And when it couldn't continue without breaking, it broke, and she fell on him, and they were both crying.

They came out of it slowly, Sachi sliding off Levi, lying back in the sun next to him. It washed over them, and for a time they napped. Then Levi heard Sachi's voice break through.

"This is where it happened? Where you traveled to Greece with Cali and her friends?"

"Yes. This is where."

"Wow," was all she said, as if the enormity could only be summed up in a word so small.

"It's amazing to think that beings, spirits, pass through this spring. That you did." Then a moment later, "Do you think Lycaon went back through?"

"Yes. I think so. And Althea, and Cali. They went home."

"Home," she repeated. Another short word.

They sat and stared out over the surface. Sunlight danced on riffles the breezes blew. Levi felt both warm and chilled, clear and dizzy. He took Sachi's hand and didn't let go.

Later they set up camp where Cali and her two friends had camped. Levi gathered wood for a fire, and Sachi prepared a feast. They'd packed in broiled chicken and cheese, lettuce and pita, lentils with marjoram. A bottle of crisp white wine from Santorini chilled in the creek. Levi loved the way Sachi unabashedly licked her fingers.

That night Levi taught Sachi how to howl. Initially the wolves below answered them, but soon were bored. Lying together, against a log, staring at the fire, they began talking about the future. It was scary, as if saying the words out loud made them more real. They both had enough life experience to know they wouldn't remain the people they were now, at this time, with each other. They would change, reveal new selves, and how would those selves interact? There was no sure thing.

Sachi told Levi that she was willing to partner with his nonprofit. She could see sending an intern to the Bitterroot. She had one now, a very good one, a student at the University of Munich who was studying global ecology. His name was Stephan Weirgold. He spoke German, English, some Greek.

"Extremely bright and personable. He's interested in thinking beyond national scales. He's drawn to large collaborative efforts. I think he'll be extremely useful."

"Sounds great," Levi said, but wondering where all this was going. What he'd started.

They were drinking from a bottle of limoncello, another luxury Levi had succumbed to. He watched her as they talked and drank. Seriousness and intensity carved her face. He was amazed how quickly Sachi transitioned into the first Sachi he'd met, the consummate, hyper-efficient professional. Skilled at organization, logistics, planning. On this trip she'd relaxed this persona, and he'd seen her sense of wonder, discovery, and joy. Her child-self, perhaps.

"What about you? Can you see yourself moving here?" he asked.

"No. Not like you'd wish, Levi. My home is in Greece. But I have decided, if you'll tolerate it—" she laughed—"that I could work here part-time, a few months a year. I am looking at some grant money for this, and again, collaboration is key. The World Wildlife Foundation needs more research on wolves, and I have contacted them about this. They're interested. So is the International Wolf Center." She hesitated.

"I'm not sure if you realize the consequences of this potential development, Levi. Collaboration means growth. More bureaucracy, more partners. You will not always be able to dictate what happens when. It could drastically change your organization. It will be less, how you say, comfortable for you. Maybe."

"We can change slowly. I'll adapt."

"I don't do slowly, Levi. You should know that by now. I go, how you say it, full tilt, full throttle." She smiled, but it was not to reassure.

He told her, "My interest is only in the wolves. If it's for them, it's good. I can change how this works. I'd welcome it in some ways. I've been making it up as I go."

"I would like to meet other players while I'm here. Your friend Steve McCandless. I would also like to meet with people of Wilderness Watch in Missoula. Can you arrange that?"

"Of course. I know several of them. I can arrange a meeting after we come out."

"Good. I love you."

"I love you, too." He bent over and kissed her softly on the lips. "Good night."

Levi had a difficult time falling asleep. He wondered and worried about what she'd said, and knew it was true. His life would inevitably accelerate if and when this merger happened. What would that do to him? To the nascent "us"? He lay listening to the night, its depth, its complexity. An owl hooted once, and several times he heard the crack of a branch. And then he heard laughter. It was faint, and it blended with the voices of women. Three women. Guardians of the spring. The Pegaiai. And then he slept.

In his dream he was swimming. Sunlight sparked the water, and swimming was effortless. It felt like he was flying. He was buoyant, as if a weightless joy was lifting him heavenward. This feeling went on and on, like the water he swam through, as though it would never end.

Suddenly a cloud drifted across the sun. The water no longer sparked. He was aware of how heavy his arms and legs were becoming. To kick, to pull himself through this water was no longer easy, no longer effortless. The clouds thickened, and the bottom dropped away into darkness. He felt the weight of his body pulled down into that great black depth. He struggled against it, but could barely move his arms and legs. It was if the water had thickened. He gasped for breath but inhaled only water. He was falling more rapidly now, the remnants of light disappearing. Everything went black, and within that black were explosions of light. He felt himself turn rigid and begin sinking faster. Then he heard a voice, a familiar voice.

"Let go, Levi. Just let go."

Levi was dancing for the first time since childhood, his limbs breaking free of their molds and patterns, swinging wildly, then sinuously, curling in, extending, eyes wide to moonlight, tears of absolute joy streaming down his face. There were hundreds of others dancing, waving their arms above them, swaying, bending, crying out in pleasure. They moved to sensuous, hypnotic music, riding its rhythms as a kite rides the wind. There was ecstasy in this meadow. The dancers garbed in chiton, loincloth, peplos, chlamys, some naked, danced through thick moonlit smoke of bonfire and incense. He knew with certainty he was in Arcadia, and it was hundreds, if not thousands, of years from his life in the Bitterroot. Children wound through the dancers wearing garlands of white flowers.

The music slowly faded, and the people evaporated like the smoke. He was suddenly alone in the meadow, moonlight, silence, and stars. The forest beckoned, its deeper silence seducing him. And instantaneously he was a wolf, racing, leaping over deadfall and rocks, weightlessly, the air exploding with scent like wild colors. He heard the tunneling of a vole, the silent wingbeats of an owl, the shriek of its prey, and smelled an eruption of blood as the talons bit.

Emerging from the woods, he saw his tent and trotted over to it. Inside the mesh, bathed in silent moonlight, he saw himself as a human, tangled with Sachi, her mouth open slightly, teeth catching the moon. And he felt a love he'd never imagined, boundless and explosive. As he stared at the two lovers, they aged before his eyes, and he saw them old, wrinkled, gray-haired, still entangled with each other.

Levi woke up, his dreams evaporating before he could fix on

them. He lay a moment before turning on his side and staring at Sachi, as pale as a statue in the moonlight. Watching her breathe. Such a simple thing, breath, but so amazing, thought Levi. We have oceans and rivers within us, springs, portals.

As he watched her, Levi knew he'd never known such a beautiful woman, so fragile yet so strong. He knew then, with certainty, he would love Sachi for the remainder of his life, however long or strange that may be. It would not be easy, it would be difficult, but he felt a strange thrill.

And then Sachi opened her eyes and smiled. Levi kissed her. And the wolf turned and trotted back into the forest.

Acknowledgements

I would like to thank all my early readers for valuable input, editing, and support. They include Frank Haulgren, Daniel Hahn, Sheila Pinnell, Tim Pilgrim, Charles Luckmann, David Taylor, Barry Brown, Miguel Ramos, Gary McKinney, Penny Piper, Bill Borneman, Rick Newby, and Jordan Piper. Sara Stamey and Sherwood Smith have provided extremely insightful editing, and their suggestions considerably strengthened the book. Thanks to Maya Bohnhoff for cover design extraordinaire. Thanks also to L. David Mech and Luigi Boitani for their exceptionally comprehensive book entitled *Wolves*, and to Barry Lopez for his insightful and poetic book *Of Wolves and Men*. Both of these enriched this book. And finally, thanks to my wife Joan for providing loving company and invaluable support.

About the Author

Paul S. Piper is the author of four books of poetry: *Now and Then*, *Winter Apples*, *Dogs and Other Poems*, and *And Light*, as well as several chapbooks. He co-edited three books of essays: *Father Nature*, *X-Stories*, and *A Flutter of Birds Passing through Heaven: a tribute to Robert Sund*; and has a collection of short stories entitled *South Fork & Other Stories*. Mr. Piper lives in Bellingham, WA with his wife, two cats, and a dog.

About Book View Café

Book View Café Publishing Cooperative is an author-owned cooperative of professional writers, publishing in a variety of genres such as fantasy, romance, mystery, and science fiction.

BVC authors include *New York Times* and *USA Today* best-sellers; Nebula, Hugo, and Philip K. Dick Award winners; World Fantasy Award, Campbell Award, and RITA Award nominees; and winners and nominees of many other publishing awards.

Since its debut in 2008, BVC has gained a reputation for producing high-quality e-books, and is now bringing that same quality to its print editions.

Printed in Great Britain
by Amazon